CASHED OUT

Michael H. Rubin

FIERY SEAS PUBLISHING

Visit our website at www.fieryseaspublishing.com

Cashed Out

Copyright © 2017, Michael H. Rubin

Cover Art by Kate Cowan

Editing by Vicki McGough

Interior Design by MLGraphikDesigns

ISBN: 978-1-946143-19-8

Library of Congress Control Number: 2017940781

Printed in the United States of America

First Edition:

10 9 8 7 6 5 4 3 2 1

DEDICATION

To Ayan,
whose love, creativity, and support
make this book (and everything else) possible.

ACKNOWLEDGEMENTS

PROFESSOR MICHAEL ADAMS READ EARLY versions of the manuscript, and his comments and encouragement were invaluable. Attorney Phelan "Chuck" Hurewitz and agent Linda Langton have shepherded this project along. But above all else, I cannot acknowledge enough the contributions of my wife, Ayan. We developed and refined the many characters and plot lines together, and she revised and edited each draft of the manuscript. This book is as much the result of her efforts as my own.

CASHED OUT

Michael H. Rubin

CHAPTER 1

FAILED LAWYER? DAMN RIGHT I'M a failed lawyer. Got a failed marriage, three maxed-out credit cards, and a broken-down office with a mortgage that's underwater.

Until three weeks ago, I had no clients and no money.

Well, no clients except for G.G. Guidry, and he's just been murdered.

And no money, except for the $4,452,737 in cash that G.G. had left with me for safekeeping.

G.G. Guidry hired me on a Sunday morning. Less than a hundred hours later he was dead. His body was found on the industrial plant site of toxic waste processor Camellia Industries, floating in one of the "holding ponds" in a scummy mixture of petroleum waste, drilling fluid, arsenic, lead, barium, chromium, manganese, mercury, and who knows what-all.

The police initially thought that G.G. had been overcome by fumes and had fallen in. But when they pulled his body out, the cause of death was clear. G.G. had been shot three times. Once in the stomach. Once in the chest. And once in the forehead.

He was dead before someone dumped him in all that muck.

CHAPTER 2

THE FIRST SUNDAY IN JUNE

THE KNOCK ON MY OFFICE door startled me. I hadn't had a client – or a visitor – in weeks. And no one ever came by on a Sunday.

There he was, looking just like he appeared on all the TV newscasts. Big cigar. Florid face. Mound of swept-back gray hair. Houndstooth sports coat stretched over a patterned black-and-white silk shirt. The utter confidence of a huckster stuffed in a rotund casing.

"Lawyer Schexnaydre, glad to meet you. G.G. Guidry. Son, this is your lucky day. You're just the man I want to hire, and when you hear what I want, you're gonna thank me."

He pumped my hand and barged right in.

I was more than a little embarrassed that the notoriously successful G.G. Guidry saw how I operated. My office is in my house. An old, run-down house. My conference room used to be a living room. Several windowpanes are cracked. The fireplace hasn't functioned in years. The wallpaper is peeling away at the corners. My conference table is actually two old cypress doors, scratched and faded, set on saw horses and surrounded by six mismatched chairs with torn seats.

Guidry took it all in with a withering glance.

I pulled out my battered faux-leather folio containing an iPad and Bluetooth keyboard and said, in my best professional voice, "So?"

Yeah, that was a little abrupt, I know. I should have engaged in all the perfunctory pleasantries that normally begin a business meeting, but I had dispensed with all that long ago.

Catch Adkinson, my former boss at the biggest law firm in town, had noted as much in my final annual review: "Still has the intellectual ability, but now seems to be lacking the requisite 'people skills.'" Damn right, after what had happened to me there.

"Hell," said G.G. Guidry. "I've got a shit-load of a real estate deal and a bunch of corporate work, and I need you to paper it up."

"Real estate and corporate. Got it," I said, trying not to salivate.

The news had been full of stories about the temporary restraining order that had shut down Camellia Industries. G.G. had been making vast profits there, what with Camellia's "reprocessing" of anything and everything, from asbestos-tainted materials to petrochemical plant waste, oil-sheened swamp sludge still being scraped up years after the Deepwater Horizon oil spill, used drilling mud from oil wells, and spent fracking fluids. G.G. had been a constant presence in the press, excoriating his opponents and promising to get the plant back up, running, and even expanded.

How G.G. had gotten to me, I didn't know and didn't care. I'd show all the other attorneys in town that I was still a lawyer to be reckoned with, not the failure they thought I had become.

"What you've got to understand is this: I own some property out on Bayou Grosse Noir, and I need to assemble some tracts next to it. It's a full quarter section of land, and it's in five parcels, each owned by a different group. One is held by old man Chevallier and the second by the Caitelleau family. You know them?"

"No." He hadn't come to me because of my connections. I'd never been part of the country-club-golf-and-tennis-playing-socially-connected-society-set. My ex-wife wife had – a former cheerleader who turned heads whenever she sashayed by – but I'd been too busy building my law practice, going out of town for weeks at a time to argue cases for Catch Adkinson. And when I finally had time, after I was fired by Catch's law firm, no one wanted me around.

"Well, don't matter." Guidry took the cigar out of his mouth and rolled it between his fingers, looking with obvious disgust at the dusty window blinds in this room and the adjacent kitchen's dirty linoleum floor. "Just do me up the corporate documents. That's the first step."

I didn't care how he felt about my house. I don't like it all that much myself. I had pretty much ceased caring about almost everything, other than trying to figure out a way to stay one step ahead of a bankruptcy filing.

I was already making a mental checklist of items to cover and fees to charge, so I asked, "Do you have purchase agreements on any of these?"

"Hell no, son." Guidry yanked the cigar out of his mouth and leaned forward across the table, its edge making an indentation in his gut. "If I had purchase agreements, would I need corporate work done?" He pointed his cigar at me like a dagger. "You're gonna form me five corporations. You're gonna be the agent for all of them. I got a good right-of-way man who's out there right now arranging to buy up those tracts."

"Five corporations," I said, confirming the scope of the project. "But," I added, "if the owners are all going to sell, do you really need five?" My questioning whether he needed fewer corporations than he had asked for was my way of trying to look like I wasn't as desperate as I really was.

"Goddammit, son. Here I am bringing you the best work that you've probably had in a long while, and you're trying to tell me my business? Look, they sure as hell ain't gonna sell these properties to *me*. So, let them sell to entities they *think* are gonna stop me. You see, son, you're gonna form me corporations that are, let's say, environmental sounding. Understand? Got to have the right label if you're going to have a marketable product."

"No problem," I said. "These will be subsidiaries of Camellia Industries, right?"

"Hell no! Where the fuck did you get *that* stupid idea?"

Now I was completely puzzled. If he wasn't here about Camellia Industries, why was he here at all? And, come to think about it, if it had been about Camellia Industries, why would he have come to me?

No time to ponder that right now. I really needed the money, whatever the job was. "I just thought," I said, trying to sound disinterested, "with the news about Camellia Industries, this was somehow related."

"I ain't hiring you to speculate! This has got nothing to do with Camellia! Nothing! The damn temporary restraining order that those shitty little environmental bastards got ain't gonna amount to a gnat's ass. At the hearing next week, it'll be taken care of. I got the State on my side, after all."

Guidry took a couple more puffs on his cigar. "Just don't you worry none about Camellia Industries. This don't involve that company. At least, as far as you're concerned. Look, there'll be just one shareholder of each corporation…you just gonna sit there listening? Write it down, dammit! I got a lot of ground to cover."

Impatient with the speed of my note-taking, he looked at his watch. "Fuck, I don't have time to mess with this shit."

He got out of his chair and started pacing the room. "You're the lawyer. Do cookie-cutter documents. Don't need to be fancy. Give the corporations any environmental-sounding names you want. Just make sure my name won't appear on any public document. I'll be here at eleven tomorrow morning. Have everything done up by then."

A one-day turnaround. That could be accomplished, but there would need to be a retainer up front. No way I was going to work on a job this size on spec, not even for headline-grabbing Guidry. "Of course," I told him, "there will be filing fees, plus a tax number for each entity, and then there's…"

Guidry cut me off. "Just do the paperwork right, that's all I'm asking." He reached in his pants' pocket, pulled out a roll of bills in a gold money clip, and unfurled three thousand dollars, in hundred dollar bills, placing them on the cypress table. "I know what the going rate is. I know what the big firms in town charge. I told you, you're gonna thank me."

I had thought that money clips and corporate clients paying in cash were relics of the past.

"That's your retainer. Take your initial expenses out of it. I'll treat you right. I'll pay you a grand for each corporation, a grand for each purchase agreement, and four grand for each closing, including reviewing each title abstract. If things go right, you'll have thirty thousand bucks of my money in your pocket before month's end. Understand?"

Guidry was going to be a great client. My career was turning a corner. Opportunities that had been closed to me for years were going to open up. "The corporate papers will definitely be ready by tomorrow. How soon do you want me to head out to start looking at the title papers in the courthouse?"

"What in the hell makes you think I would want you to do any such fucking thing? If you go into that courthouse in St. Bonaventure Parish to search the titles…a tall, lanky city boy down there, who no one knows, trying to pull all them conveyance or mortgage books to figure out who owns what parcels of what dimensions? All you're gonna do is give those ladies in the clerk's office enough to talk about for a week. No, Spider will handle that shit down in St. Bonaventure. All you have to do is review what he brings you."

Someone named Spider?

CHAPTER 3

MONDAY

I HAD THE DOCUMENTS READY AND was sitting on my porch, guzzling my third beer of the morning, when a maroon Mercedes pulled up into my driveway promptly at eleven. Guidry dashed out of his car in a hurry, cigar clenched in his teeth.

A wasp-waisted blonde with big tits and loud red lipstick emerged slowly from the passenger side. She adjusted what little fabric there was in her short skirt. She was decades younger than Guidry.

I held the front door of my house open for them.

Guidry barreled on through, trailing smoke and the blonde. He stalked directly to the conference room. "OK, son, let's not take all day with this."

I brought the files in from my office. "I assume you'll be President of each entity, and this lady will hold the combination office of Secretary-Treasurer?"

"Son, did a leech crawl up your nose and suck out your brains? I told you I don't want my name on anything that has to be recorded. You ought to know that officers got to file those damn annual reports with the Secretary of State. That's why Millie Sue is here. She's gonna be the President, and you'll hold the other offices and do as I say."

Millie Sue was busy examining her nails with their Corvette-red finish. Completing that important task, she turned to look vacantly out the window, chewing on a strand of her blonde hair.

"Let's get on with it." Guidry brusquely snapped his fingers at her. "Millie Sue!"

Millie Sue turned and smiled at Guidry. "Yes, honey?"

"Now you just do as this lawyer says," Guidry said, rubbing his hand affectionately on Millie Sue's bare thigh, just below the hem of her tiny skirt.

What they wanted to do was fine with me as long as I was getting paid. I concentrated on completing the stack of papers. "I'll need," I said to Millie Sue, "your full name."

"Mildred Susanna – that's without an H but with two Ns – Aix. That's A-I-X."

As I pointed out where she had to put her signature on the first set of documents, Guidry's hand was creeping up her skirt.

"G.G.," she giggled, squirming in her seat. "Honey, I can't sign if you keep doing that!"

She playfully pushed him away and wrote slowly, in childlike script, with curlicues circling the capital letters. When she finally came to the last blank of the last document, she excitedly put down the pen, looking around for Guidry. "This is great, G.G., honey. I'm President of five companies! President!"

He was already halfway to the front door. "Let's go, Millie Sue."

Guidry ushered her out. As I followed them onto the porch, Guidry said to me, "Spider will be here tomorrow with the property stuff. Get the rest of the paperwork with the property descriptions done pronto. I'll call you when I'm ready to pick up everything."

****

I was awakened at two in the morning by banging on my front door. Dressed only in a pair of boxers, I peered through the peephole to see Guidry in a tuxedo, tie askew, pounding away with his fist. I turned the lock. He dragged something in, slamming the door behind him.

With some effort, he slung a mammoth leather suitcase, secured with a thick yellow mesh strap, onto my conference table. "You're my lawyer, right?"

"Absolutely."

"And what I tell you, as a client, you can't tell anyone. Right?"

"Right."

"This," Guidry said, stroking the leather suitcase, "is confidential. It's mine. It's my corporation's, and it's mine."

"Corporation? Which one of the five I formed for you?"

"This has nothing to do with those, you idiot. I'm talking about Camellia Industries."

Guidry wasn't making any sense. I had asked him about Camellia Industries when he first came to see me, and he had insisted that nothing I was doing in any way related to Camellia. "Camellia Industries? But I thought…."

"Hell, I'm not paying you to think. I'm paying you to do exactly what I fucking tell you to do." He pointed to the suitcase. "Now look, this here is mine and my corporation's. It's confidential. Highly confidential. I want you to keep it here."

"In this house?"

"Of course in this house. If I wanted to put it somewhere else, it would be there by now. I am a client giving something to my attorney. And you're going to keep this something in your office and give it back to me when I call for it."

Why was Guidry here at this ungodly hour? Why was he asking me to stash a suitcase for him?

Guidry saw my look of puzzlement. His hand clenched into a fist, hitting the suitcase with a solid thump. "You live, breathe, work, and fart in this shitty little building. Just hold onto this until I tell you otherwise. Don't even fucking leave this house until I call you and give you instructions. Until then, keep this goddamned thing safe. Understand?"

I reluctantly agreed.

And that was the last time I saw him alive.

CHAPTER 4

ONCE I HEARD GUIDRY'S CAR take off, my dilemma began. Where was I going to find a safe place to keep this thing? No South Louisiana home has a basement. The water table is too high. And, if you're rich enough to have a swimming pool, you don't dare leave it empty for more than a few days, because it would pop out of the ground. My house is a one-level raised cottage on three-foot-high brick pillars, the underside open and exposed, so there was no place beneath the floor where something could be hidden.

I had no attic, but realized there might be another option. When the house had been remodeled twenty years ago, long before I bought it, part of its high ceiling had been closed off to install ductwork for central air conditioning. Fiberglass insulation had been blown up there. The wooden slats in the hall ceiling concealed the entry. It was so artfully done that you wouldn't notice it if you didn't know where to look.

Balancing on top of a step stool, I pushed out part of the ceiling panel. Pulling myself up into the narrow area around the ductwork, I found a spot that would work and hauled the suitcase up with the twine I had twisted around its handle. I moved the insulation aside until the beams were exposed, jammed the suitcase in, and covered it with insulation.

It took longer than I thought to put everything back in order so that no one looking at the hallway would suspect anything was amiss. I felt curiously relieved, proud of myself even, for finding a hiding place for Guidry's suitcase.

But why had I let his sense of urgency force me to act? Because he paid me in cash? Because he was my only real client? Because having someone as famous as G.G. Guidry hire me stroked my ego, which had been beaten down pretty well over the last few years?

With G.G. as a client, I reassured myself, I had nothing to worry about.

Boy, was I wrong.

CHAPTER 5

TUESDAY

A T SEVEN A.M. I ANSWERED the gentle knock on my front door to find a man on the porch. Now, I'm 6'2, and the guy standing outside was about my height, but he was at least twice my width, and none of it was flab. Light brown hair cut short. A humorless gaze that took in everything.

"And you are?" I asked, suspiciously. Guidry had left only a few hours ago, telling me to keep his suitcase safe, and now a stranger was showing up at my office. Until Guidry hired me, almost no one came to my door except the bill collectors whom I kept dodging.

The man handed me a card. It read: "*Maurice 'Spider' Louiviere,*" with a phone number and email address.

Maurice! No wonder Spider didn't go by his given name.

Spider didn't ask to come in. He didn't say a word. Rather, he went to his car and returned with a big cardboard box containing six huge volumes, each bound at the top. The old wooden planks on my porch barely creaked under his remarkably silent tread as he ascended and placed the box on my mildewed oak swing.

I recognized what was in the box. This was the abstract – copies of all the title papers from the courthouse. These were the documents Guidry had told me that Spider was getting and that I was to review. I'd examine these to trace ownership, making sure that the sellers really owned what Guidry was buying, and to obtain the correct property descriptions.

Spider pulled an envelope out of his back pocket. "Mr. Guidry said to give this to you. If I were you, I'd sure have all the final paperwork ready whenever he calls."

If I was amazed at how silently this big man moved, I was astonished by his voice. It was soft and raspy. Almost a whisper. Flat and unemotional. I had expected a booming voice from someone who looked like he did. Now I understood the nickname. He was as silent as a poisonous spider and probably as deadly.

It's strange how some people have nicknames that follow them through life, while others, through lack of close friends, or perhaps through some psychic parental power that discerned how the newborn's personality would evolve over the years, always go by their given names and no other. Even as children they never seem to acquire diminutives.

Did I get a good nickname? Hell no! My parents had tagged me with "Hypolite Schexnaydre." My folks were fourth generation Louisiana. When they were alive, we used to live downriver in Des Allemands, in the same house where their parents and grandparents had lived among the Cajuns, speaking their own French patois. By the time I came along, it was almost as if the fact that our ancestors had originally come from Germany – and had spelled it "Schexnayder" rather than "Schexnaydre" – had been forgotten.

My parents never thought about leaving Des Allemands, and they never thought that "Hypolite" was an unusual name. To them, it was a good French name of honor. But it wasn't an honor to me. With a name like Hypolite, I had to run faster, work harder, and think quicker than anyone else.

How did I get treated by my classmates when I was young?

What do you think, with a name like Hypolite?

What did I get called while growing up? You name it, I've heard it. "Hippo." Or "Po-Lite." Or "Po-boy." Or "Wheat Schex" or "Corn Schex" or even "Schex, Rattle & Roll." I hated them all, including the one that stuck – "Schex."

Now, Catch – my former boss and mentor at Walker, Thibodeaux, LeBlanc & Adkinson – had a great nickname. D. Bennett "Catch" Adkinson. Little League champ. High school baseball star. Highly touted college third baseman who became a campus hero, which was quite an achievement in a local culture that worships basketball, genuflects to baseball, but downright grovels at the feet of football players.

There was a time when I used to love to watch Catch at work in the courtroom.

When he would demolish an opponent's highly paid expert with a cross-examination as pointed and sharp as a scalpel.

When he would make a truthful witness appear to be deceitful and evasive.

When I thought that winning a case for your client was more satisfying than seeing justice done.

But that was then. When I still admired Catch. When I still could imagine a successful career in my future. When I couldn't imagine what my life would become.

When I never suspected what Catch would do to me.

CHAPTER 6

AFTER SPIDER LEFT, I CARRIED the box inside and put it on my scarred conference table. Only then did I look in the envelope that Spider had given me. Another $4,000 in cash. Guidry knew how to get and keep my attention.

I examined the documents in the box. Spider had done a thorough job on the abstract. Now, there is no single book or piece of paper you can look at to determine who owns a tract of land here in Louisiana. You have to review years of paperwork, some of it stretching back to when Jefferson bought Louisiana from France in 1803, and even before that, back to when Spain and France kept flipping control of Louisiana between themselves.

Two hundred years of paperwork to wade through to figure out the ownership of big tracts of land. Older documents penned in beautiful but difficult-to-decipher handwriting. Documents in French. Documents with names reflecting Louisiana's gumbo heritage, a stew of French and Spanish, with seasonings of German, Irish, Haitian, Italian, Czechoslovakian, settlers, slaves, freemen of color, brothel owners, casket girls, keelboaters, gamblers, privateers, and scoundrels.

I spent the rest of the afternoon working through it all, figuring out the complete chain of title of each of the five tracts, making sure the property descriptions met the legal requirements, and preparing the paperwork that Guidry would need for the purchase agreements.

Everything was ready by early afternoon.

I waited, but I heard nothing from either Guidry or Spider.

Guidry had said I couldn't leave the house. My combination home and office looks like crap. An embarrassment to the Creole Town neighborhood in Baton Rouge where I live.

Now, the block behind mine looks all right. That's where Washington and Durnella Eby live. Washington had been a housepainter all his life and is enjoying a well-deserved retirement in the place he had bought way back in the era when Creole Town was the area where "hard-working colored boys" starting families aspired to buy.

Washington and Durnella Eby, both in their late 80s but still full of vigor, have resided there for more than five decades. They keep a carefully tended vegetable garden in the narrow backyard. Every other spring Washington takes out his ladders, rigs up scaffolding, and carefully checks all the woodwork, sanding it down if needed, touching up where required, and repainting when necessary. It's a remarkable sight. Washington, old as he is, up there at rooftop level, still following his routine.

My weed-laden backyard overlooks Washington and Durnella's vegetable garden. Luther, their rangy Catahoula hound, jumps the fence regularly and has the run of the neighborhood. Washington loves that ugly old dog, with its mottled coat and webbed paws. Luther aggressively guards Washington. If he doesn't know you, he won't even let you near Washington's house.

Luther is pure Catahoula. Marbled eyes. Loyal to a fault. Powerful and strong, a breed created by Louisiana Indians mating red wolves with Spanish war dogs.

When I'm around Washington, Luther tolerates me.

I couldn't leave my crappy house today, not even to go on my usual jog. I run almost a dozen miles daily along the top of the levee's sinuous curves, the wide Mississippi River bronze in the moonlight and a muddy burnt sienna in the sunlight. Until G.G. had shown up, running was the only thing I still felt good about.

But, there was no reason why I couldn't eat well. I ordered a takeout dinner and a six-pack from my favorite dive, George & Beebo's. I made sure to generously tip the delivery girl with some of the cash I had gotten from Guidry.

I sat at my kitchen counter. Over-ate. Finished off the six-pack. Fell asleep before it got dark.

CHAPTER 7

WEDNESDAY

I OVERSLEPT WEDNESDAY MORNING. IN my T-shirt and shorts, I went out to retrieve the morning paper that had been tossed on my unmown lawn. They hadn't yet cut off my subscription, but that was likely to happen any day now.

Above the fold, in the center of the front page, was a picture of a two men clothed from head to foot in white garments with sealed helmets. They were holding a stretcher on which rested a body covered with a sheet.

The story read:

DEATH AT CONTROVERSIAL
INDUSTRIAL PLANT

Gaynell Guidry, Chairman of the Board of Camellia Industries, was found dead yesterday in a holding pond at the plant.

Workers from the Department of Environmental Health have sealed off the site. Carter H. Herrington, IV, Director of the Department, told reporters that his office will be conducting a full investigation.

Camellia Industries, one of the major employers in St. Bonaventure Parish, has been unable to ship product since last week because of a temporary restraining order issued by the St. Bonaventure Parish Court. PLEA, the Parish Local Environmental

Action group composed of those who live near the plant, obtained the shut-down order.

PLEA's attorney, Octavius Radolphus Doucet, issued a press release indicating that his organization would move ahead with the preliminary injunction hearing next week. Doucet told this reporter, "If the plant had been next to a white neighborhood, it would never have been allowed to operate."

Gaynell Guidry left no immediate relatives. The president of Camellia Industries is listed as Taylor Cameron. Attempts to contact Cameron have been unsuccessful.

I stopped reading.

I balled up the newspaper and tossed the crumpled mass onto the porch.

Now, you'd think that I'd be upset about Guidry's death. Well, I was. Upset. Furious. Angry. You name it.

But that wasn't why I stopped reading.

It was the part about Taylor Cameron.

I still hated her.

CHAPTER 8

JUST WHEN THINGS WERE STARTING to look up, Taylor was somehow back in the picture.

I had lost my only client. My chance to restart my career now faded to the point of invisibility.

Taylor always seemed to be associated with things I lost.

Seeing her name in print made the old loathing come back, along with a slew of questions.

How did Taylor get tied up with G.G.?

How did Taylor get to be "president" of Camellia Industries?

Was her route the same as Millie Sue's? Had G.G. put his hand on her thigh and up her skirt, the way he had with Millie Sue? What else had they done?

Was she really back in town?

Why did my life continually intersect with hers?

Why did she seem to be like a vortex, sucking me in and setting me spinning in a new, and always lower, direction?

I couldn't answer any of those questions.

All I had now were the bucks G.G. had given me that I hadn't spent, all those now useless legal documents I had prepared, and his suitcase stashed above my ceiling.

I grabbed the stepstool, pulled my way up into the crawl space, and dug through the insulation until I found it, tossing it through the opening onto the hall floor below and dropping down after it.

The damn thing was sealed up but good.

No matter. G.G. wasn't coming back for it.

I went into the kitchen, got the largest carving knife I could find, and attacked the wide yellow straps. It took some effort to cut through them.

The brass locks on the suitcase itself, however, held firm, bending the knife I was using to pry them open.

In the cabinet under the kitchen sink, behind empty glass jars, old paper bags, half-used scouring pads, and dead roaches, I found a long, heavy screwdriver and a second knife. Even shoving the screwdriver into one of the locks and twisting down as hard as I could, it still wouldn't open. I thrust the second knife into the center of the leather top. The blade was dull, but it penetrated the leather. I sawed away, starting to cut the suitcase open.

But, before I could finish, as if the entire thing had been spring-loaded, green slips of paper started flying out of the suitcase, cascading into the air and fluttering onto the floor.

No, not slips.

Bills. Greenbacks.

Hundreds of dollars.

Thousands of dollars.

Hundreds of thousands of dollars.

My God, I thought, as the cash confettied down around me. It might be millions.

CHAPTER 9

AFTER I HAD BEEN FIRED by Catch, I had gone to work for Old Parish Mortgage. That lasted almost a year. Until the authorities closed it down. Which is when I hung out my shingle. Which is when I found I couldn't get hired by anyone, until G.G. came along.

When I worked at Old Parish, I had handled lots of money, but it was mostly wire and electronic transfers. I had drafted reams of mortgages and promissory notes and became inured to numbers after a while. To get from a hundred thousand to a million dollars, all you do is add a zero at the end. Inserting a number into a computer is easy.

But dealing with cash is far different. Sure, at Old Parish one of my jobs had been to supervise the front teller, but all we handled were small loan payments. Old Parish wasn't a bank and didn't keep a lot of money on hand.

I had never seen so much cash in one place until I pried open G.G.'s suitcase. There were bills of every denomination, except ones, spilling out and littering the hall floor. Now, you might think that counting money is simple, but it's not when you've got reams of loose bills. That's why banks use currency counters. And I didn't have hundreds of greenbacks. I had thousands.

Yet, the suitcase was still half full, so I starting pulling out the loose bills that were jammed inside and found something even more curious – stacks of cash lined the bottom of the large valise. Neatly wrapped groupings of fifties and hundreds. Still machine banded from a currency counter. One hundred bills in each. Fifties in $5,000 packs. Hundreds in $10,000 packs.

I knew from Old Parish that you couldn't trust a currency counter pack from an unknown source, because you can't assume that the packs are properly labeled or that they're not striated – with one dollar bills, or worse yet, with plain green paper – filling out the center of each pack.

There was no alternative but to count it all by hand.

I closed the blinds and got a broom and a dustpan to sweep up the money.

I piled everything – the suitcase, the loose bills, the banded packs – in the conference room. A mess worth a fortune. But how much of a fortune?

I brought out all my pots and pans from the kitchen and spread them around the conference room table. I worked systematically. Loose tens in the casserole dish. Loose fifties in the spaghetti pot. A container for each type of bill. I figured that once I had sorted them, the counting would be easy.

But I quickly found that there were not enough containers. I soon ran out of bowls and dishes and pots and started piling the cash by denomination on different parts of the floor.

It took more than an hour just to get the loose bills sorted.

Once I had all the money separated into different groups, I attacked each pile, making careful notes and keeping a tally of results with an old calculator that printed the results on a paper roll. That took another four hours, plus an additional hour to double check my figures.

Plus, more time to examine each banded pack. To make sure there was no striation. To make sure that the serial numbers weren't identical and weren't consecutive, because if they were, the banded pack wouldn't have come from a bank but was either counterfeit or had come straight from the Treasury.

When I was finally through, my calculations showed $1,652,737 in loose bills and exactly $2.8 million in the packs.

So, G.G. had left $4,452,737 in cash for me to hold for him.

Whose money was it? I sure as hell didn't know, and Guidry couldn't tell me now. One thing I did know, however, was that it wasn't mine.

Well, at least, not yet.

I took several handfuls of loose twenties and fifties and stuffed them in my pocket. No one would miss them.

But where to keep all the rest of the money? I had ripped up the suitcase getting into it.

Big, extra-thick contractor-size black plastic bags that I had bought months ago, for yard work I never got around to, did the trick. I loaded everything into two of them, hauled them back up through the open ceiling panel, and covered them with insulation.

As I was putting the panel back into place, I figured out what to do next.

CHAPTER 10

THAT'S HOW I ENDED UP, late that Wednesday afternoon, sitting in Washington Eby's aluminum bateau floating down Bayou Grosse Noir.

Even though I hadn't been much of a neighbor, Washington had readily agreed to lend me his boat and trailer.

Washington and Durnella were as proud of that flat-bottomed boat as if it had been a yacht. Washington, who knew all about oil paint and Japan drier and how to clean a paintbrush so that it looked like new and would last for years, but who never finished the third grade, and Durnella, who had worked for fifty years as a maid in a starched uniform in the uptown neighborhoods at a time when being a "domestic" was a way out of poverty, kept all their hard-won acquisitions meticulously clean and in repair, in contrast to me, who couldn't keep my life in any kind of order.

I had come up with a scheme to legally get my hands on all of G.G. Guidry's cash.

G.G. had said that the suitcase was his *and* it was his corporation's, but as I thought about it, that didn't really make any sense. It couldn't be both. What shenanigans would involve so much cash?

So, I figured that if I didn't have G.G. as my client, the money was going to be my client. I would create a duty to find out whose cash it was, minus, of course, the amounts – and those could be large amounts – that I would take from time to time to cover my "expenses."

If the money turned out to belong to Camellia Industries, then I would be more than halfway to being the company's lawyer. Or, at least, I'd get a hefty finder's fee. The owners couldn't help but be pleased that I'd return the cash. And if the money was G.G.'s personally, his heirs surely would want to retain me to handle the succession and advise them. After all, hadn't G.G. come to me?

So, the logical place to start was at Camellia Industries down in St. Bonaventure Parish.

I'd put on jeans and a T-shirt, trying to look like a good ol' boy, intending to go first to Camellia Industries and then use Washington's bateau to look at the St. Bonaventure property G.G. had talked about buying. The maps in the abstract had shown them to be near the Camellia Industries plant, and the best way to view the first big tract, which had no road frontage, was from the bayou.

In case anyone asked what I was doing in the bayou, I brought fishing gear. I'd appear to be just another guy trying to catch his limit.

It seemed like a good plan, but it didn't work.

CHAPTER 11

WHEN I DROVE UP TO the Camellia Industries gate, the armed guard wouldn't talk to me. G.G. had been right when he said that people in St. Bonaventure Parish would suspect I wasn't a local, which is why he wanted Spider and not me assembling the abstracts from the St. Bonaventure public records. Despite the jeans and the fishing gear, I still looked out of place.

I hadn't said two sentences when the guard summoned a bear of a man. His jeans were held up by bright red suspenders, taut against his hairy chest. With his wild gaze, wild hair, and even wilder beard, he had the look of someone who had recently emerged from the swamps after successfully wrestling an alligator.

Shotgun in hand, he waved me away, warning in a thick Cajun accent, "Ya' damn well better stop wit da' questions, 'coz no one gonna tell ya' a damn t'ing anyway."

It was tough understanding his accent, but there was no mistaking his meaning. I wasn't going to get to see the plant that way.

So, I drove over to the boat landing, launched the bateau, and slowly motored down the bayou at trolling speed. I headed toward what I figured were the boundaries of the Caitelleau tract. What had seemed so clear from the maps in the abstract, however, turned out to be a convoluted string of entwined marsh waterways.

As the afternoon waned, the mosquitoes came in swarms, dipping almost to the water's surface and then rising again, looking for blood. As each buzzing fog approached, I swatted away, but to no avail. Got bitten more than twenty times. I was stinging and itching as round after round of mosquitoes kept swooping in.

It was time to go. A completely wasted trip.

To get back to the landing, I had to travel back along the bayou by the edge of Camellia Industries. As I passed the plant, I cut off the engine and let the bateau drift. Just one more look.

Nothing had changed since I had boated past the facility an hour earlier.

All I could see over the tall marsh grass was the back end of the plant several hundred yards away. No activity.

Now that the bateau was almost stationary, the mosquitoes pounced again. Had to get moving.

But, just as I reached back to pull on the starter cord, I saw something to the right of one of the huge buildings. Some type of vehicle was lumbering along.

I had a pair of binoculars hidden in the ice chest. I pulled them out, but they were of no great help. From this low angle, everything important was blocked from my view.

I needed a higher perch.

I tried to stand up, but the narrow bateau rocked precariously.

There was a sycamore limb extending out over the bayou that I could just about reach, if only I stretched a bit more. I used it to steady myself as I stood up in the bateau, one hand on the sycamore and the other holding the binoculars.

The vehicle had stopped.

From this angle, I could see a hood, a driver's cab, and a cylindrical container maybe twenty feet high or more. It looked like an oversized garbage truck. There were four men in caps moving around it. They were operating in pairs, two at a time lifting something down over the rear bumper.

Whatever they were moving was heavy and ungainly. Perhaps fifty-five gallon drums, but I couldn't be sure in the dimming light

I felt steady now and, releasing my grasp of the sycamore, held the binoculars with both hands and scanned the area around the truck. I finally spotted, maybe a hundred feet behind it, something I couldn't have seen from my seated position – the roof of a dark car peeking up over the marsh. Standing behind the car's hood was a man. No cap. He seemed to be wearing a suit. I could make out a white shirt and what appeared to be a tie.

I squinted, trying to see what he was doing. The man was holding something.

He was pointing a rifle at me!

Startled, I took one step back, forgetting that I was standing in the bateau.

It shifted under my weight.

I reached backward, grabbing for the sycamore, but as my hand encircled it, the branch moved.

What I felt in my grip was not rough bark, damp with lichens and moss. It was smooth and dry. And pulsing slowly. What I had grabbed was a large snake drooping from the tree.

I panicked and pulled my hand back as fast as I could, which threw me completely off balance and out of the bateau.

The muddy water was chest-deep.

The snake looked at me curiously and then slowly curled all five feet of itself back up onto the branch, where it lay motionless.

I waded back to the bateau and managed to get in. Soaking wet and coated with mud, I started the trolling motor and made my way to the landing, grateful that there hadn't been a gator coasting through the bayou where I had fallen in.

By the time I got the bateau back onto the trailer and got everything hitched up, it was dark. A night sky without stars. The thick Louisiana summer air had become even heavier than before. More dense. A low rumble of thunder came from the far horizon.

I had barely turned out of the landing area when the rain came. Lightning bayoneted the clouds. The wipers, even at their highest speed, did little to clear away the river of thick drops pelting down, distorting everything. For more than forty minutes, I maneuvered, white-knuckled, through the thunderstorm while the trailer holding the bateau lurched and pitched behind my car, threatening to pull me off the narrow, curving road and into the adjacent ditches coursing with water.

It was not until I saw, high above the sugar cane fields, blue-tinged lights floating in the distance that I realized the intensity of the rain had finally diminished and I was at last approaching the St. Bonaventure bridge connecting the west bank of the Mississippi to the east.

I had been concentrating so intently during my drive through the rainstorm that I never noticed the dark car, its headlights off, that had been following me ever since I left the boat landing. I didn't find out about that car until it was too late.

CHAPTER 12

I T WAS PAST NINE WHEN I turned into my driveway. I was halfway up the steps before I realized that someone was sitting on the porch swing in the dark.

"Hypolite!"

I knew that voice.

"SCHEX!"

No avoiding it. I flipped on the porch light.

It was Taylor.

She looked perfect, as always. Hair shimmering and desirable. Lipstick glistening. A model's features and skin. Expensive, high-fashion jeans. A silk blouse that must have set her back a couple of hundred. Four-strand pearl necklace and matching bracelet. Designer shoes with four-inch heels that she could drive through your heart if you crossed her.

"Where is it?"

"Taylor, it's been years. Now you show up?"

"WHERE IS IT? Don't screw around. I'm in no mood. Just tell me where it is and I'll be out of your life again."

I ignored her.

She followed me inside. Uninvited and definitely unwanted.

"Give it to me Schex! It's mine!"

"I'm too tired to argue, Taylor. Stay or leave. I don't care."

I headed for the bathroom, and, closing the door behind me, pulled off my mud-soaked shirt and jeans and turned on the shower.

"Hurry up," Taylor yelled. "G.G. took it. He had no right. It was as much mine as his."

I didn't bother to respond. It was always like this. Taylor whining and grousing.

I was soaping up again when the water turned ice cold. Wiping the suds from my eyes, I saw Taylor standing there, her hand on the hot water tap. "You don't need a shower to tell me where the money is."

I yanked the curtain shut. "How about a little privacy?"

"Dry off and let's talk. Be quick!" Taylor walked out, her stiletto heels clicking on the bathroom tiles.

I emerged, wrapped in a towel, to find Taylor sitting on the edge of my bed, arms crossed.

"How do you think G.G. got to you anyway?"

I really wasn't in the mood for this. I grabbed some clothes and went back into the bathroom, but her voice carried clearly through the door. "G.G. needed someone who would do as he was told, without questions. Someone who would take whatever shit work and money that G.G. can…could offer. Someone whose name would arouse no suspicion if the public records were checked. I'm the reason you got the business at all. Now give me what's mine. G.G. may have been Chairman of the Camellia Industries board, but I'm President, and now I guess I'm everything else as well. Hello in there! ARE YOU LISTENING?"

"I heard." I emerged, barefoot and clothed in old khaki slacks and a worn polo shirt. I needed a beer.

Taylor stalked into the kitchen after me. "I found out what he did. When I got a call from the bank Monday around noon that a check had bounced, well, I knew that couldn't be right. There was supposed to be over $1.6 million in the operating accounts."

I turned away from her, pulled a bottle of Abita from the refrigerator, and, with my back to her, rummaged around the shelves for something to eat. I didn't want Taylor to see my surprise at hearing her talk about $1.6 million. G.G. had left over four million in the suitcase. Why was Taylor mentioning only $1.6 million? Was she really ignorant of how much G.G. had amassed? And if she didn't know about it all, what was its source?

"Schex," she said, settling into one of the scratched metal chairs at the dented kitchen table, "G.G. used to keep all his papers in the study of our house, not at the plant. But the important stuff hasn't been there for more than a week."

I noticed that she had said 'our house,' but I didn't respond. I grabbed the leftover half po-boy from the back of the refrigerator. The bread was hard and stale, the interior soggy, but it was edible, especially with enough beer. I sat at the counter, expressionless, and chewed slowly as she talked.

"After I got that call, I checked the study. The corporate books were still there, but the checkbooks and all the ledgers were gone. That little shit must have removed them sometime over the weekend. Once I found out, I knew what to do. I had signature rights on the accounts. I went downtown to see the branch manager of the bank only to learn that G.G. had cleaned everything out, a little at a time. $5000 in cash here, $2,500 in cash there. Checks to himself. Checks to companies whose names I didn't recognize, but which had to be more of his shell corporations. Checks to that skank, Millie Sue."

I didn't say anything.

"Oh, I see it in your eyes," she said. "You think that by remaining silent you can hide from me? I've read you like a book for years, Schex. You haven't changed. When I mentioned Millie Sue, you didn't ask who she was. So, you know all about her! Figures. You know about G.G. and Millie Sue. You must also know about the money. It's all gone. One-point-six-million-plus-something damn dollars! All the money in the accounts! I *could* have killed him. Hell, I *would* have killed him if he hadn't kicked it anyway. Serves him right."

I concentrated on the po-boy.

"Go ahead. Stuff your face. I know he must have told you something. G.G. might let Millie Sue get her hands on his crotch, but he'd never let her get her paws on his wallet. I suspected something was up the minute he hired Millie Sue as his 'secretary' at the plant. But was I going to say something? No way. Find out what he's up to first, I thought. Watched him like a hawk. Sweet as I could be, I went with him to that stupid fundraiser cotillion the other night like nothing was going on, but there was that bitch at the sign-in table! Millie Sue, at the cotillion, as if she belonged there! And G.G. wasn't acting right from the moment we walked in. I saw the way he looked at her and she looked at him. Right then I knew who he must have brought in on his little scheme."

God, how Taylor could chatter!

"I had it out with G.G. in the parking lot. Ruined my silk ball gown sweating out there in the heat, arguing with him. Well, that's the last thing he'll ruin."

"Why G.G., Taylor? I can see," I said, gesturing at her outfit, "what G.G. saw in you, but what did you ever see in G.G.? Catch, I could almost understand. But G.G.?"

"Just tell me where my $1.6 million is."

I didn't have to tell her squat. Not about 'her' $1.6 million or the rest of the millions I had found in the suitcase. "Taylor, you know better. What G.G. may have told me – and I'm not saying whether he told me anything – was and is privileged."

"Crap! You're loaded with it. Privilege? What's a stupid privilege? The damn corporation was half mine, and now it's all mine. The money's mine too. I've thought about it, and the only person who might know is you, 'cause G.G. wouldn't have told Millie Sue anything. He would have been trying to do something clever with the funds. So, he's got to have put them in some other bank or stuck them away with a broker. And to set up the shell companies to do that, he's got to have someone he could take advantage of, and you certainly fit that bill. Hell, that's why I sent him to you in the first place, thinking he wanted those shell corporations for tax purposes, and I'm all in favor of finding some way around paying taxes. But, oh, you know something all right. You've confirmed it, not asking about Millie Sue and hiding behind words like 'privilege.' Well, fuck you. Fuck G.G. Fuck privilege and all your legal rules. I'll bring you the legal fucking proof you need. I want my money. I deserve it, and I expect you to help me get it."

She stormed out. I heard the front door slam and her car accelerating down the street.

I started on my third beer.

Taylor being involved with G.G. didn't make sense. And it didn't make sense that Taylor was talking about accounts totaling $1.6 million. Why was she concerned about that amount instead of the more than four million G.G. had stuffed in the suitcase?

And why had there been loose bills for more than $1.6 million while the rest had been in banded packs?

What had G.G. been up to anyway?

I couldn't figure any of it out. Maybe it was because I needed some rest. Maybe it was because of the beer. Maybe it was because of those damn mosquito bites that were now itching like crazy. I knew I had some Calamine lotion in the cabinet next to the shower.

I headed through the dark house, not bothering to turn on the lights.

But I never reached the bathroom. As soon as I entered my bedroom, someone grabbed me from behind.

CHAPTER 13

I LET OUT A YELL AND tried to spin around, but the intruder had a grip that would not loosen.

I jammed my elbows into his gut, but it was like punching solid oak. He didn't flinch but merely tightened his hold on me, lifting me off the ground.

I have runner's thighs and calves, however, so I flung my legs up in front of me to get momentum and then snapped them back down, jamming my right heel as hard as I could into his balls.

His grip relaxed momentarily.

I wriggled free and headed for the front door at a dead run, but as I crossed the threshold someone on the porch smashed one of my metal chairs over my head.

As I fell, the man who had attacked me inside slammed down on my back, heavy as a cement armoire. I could smell his fetid breath and felt his thick fingers closing around my throat. I tried to get my hands free to fight him off, but to no avail. He had me pinned.

The man who had wielded the porch chair kicked me in the ribs. Hurt like hell. Knocked the wind out of me.

I tried to catch my breath, but the man on my back tightened his grip on my neck.

I couldn't inhale. It was like drowning without the water. I started to lose consciousness, but suddenly his fingers loosened and he rolled off me, screaming and cursing.

Luther, Washington Eby's Catahoula hound, had sunk his teeth into the man's butt and was drawing blood.

The other man, his face obscured by shadows, silhouetted against the moth-encircled light fixtures on the porch, reached down with a beefy hand and, grabbing the back of my shirt, pulled me up as if I weighed no more than a child.

Then all of us heard a shotgun blast and felt its effects. The pellets swarmed across the porch, shattering one of the light fixtures. The splintered glass, its sharp little shards pelting me, embedded themselves in my skin.

The man holding me let go. The other one, with the bloody butt, was on the lawn, backing away from Luther, who was baring his teeth and snapping at the intruder's calves.

I lurched forward off the porch into the dark and started dashing toward a row of ligustrum, a nine-foot high hedge on the northern property line of my lot. My only thought now was to run as hard and as far as I could. And I can run fast.

Another shotgun blast.

I passed the ligustrum and picked up my pace, sprinting over the lawn and galloping past the sidewalk, across the street into the next yard. The grass was easier on my bare feet than the road, and I figured to continue north and outrun the two guys on my porch.

I was three houses away when I heard a voice calling out, "Neighbor! You can slow down! Ain't no one gonna bother you now."

CHAPTER 14

I WALKED SLOWLY BACK DOWN THE street. Residents in nearby homes peeked out their curtains, but as I passed they shut them quickly, more curious than concerned.

Washington Eby, dressed in pajamas and a bathrobe, was standing on my porch holding a smoking shotgun. Luther was sitting beside him, a scrap of bloody fabric in his mouth.

"Whoever those fellows were are gone now," Washington said as I approached. "One of 'em will need a new pair of trousers after tonight. Luther saw to that. Been hooked by the gills, Neighbor?"

I reached up to touch my cheeks and then examined my fingers. They were covered with blood.

"Neighbor, you ain't even been cut deep enough to ask for more than a thimbleful of sympathy. Scratches, that's all. You'll heal up in a day or two. Just a few red marks is all that'll show. You got some bandages and rubbing alcohol and such? Good. Let's go on inside and I'll get you fixed up."

As we entered the house I asked him how it was he had arrived with his shotgun at this time of night.

"Oh, I got an old man's bladder," he explained. "Can't sleep more than an hour or so at a stretch. Was up and heard noise, so Luther and I came to investigate, thinkin' that it's those gangs. You know, them that come up from New Orleans. We never used to have this kind of trouble. That's why I've started keepin' my shotgun loaded. Here, look up, and let me see what they done to you."

I sat on the edge of my bed while Washington gently removed tiny slivers of glass from my cheeks, ears, and neck. He then wiped down my cuts with rubbing alcohol. Stung like the dickens.

But, when I started to complain, Washington paused. From a throat that had inhaled too many paint fumes and encountered too many unfiltered cigarettes, Washington's slow, contagious laugh emerged. "Look at you. Blood's almost gone, but I've got to rinse you one more time, otherwise you'll just be a red-faced, red-necked lawyer. Don't that beat all. Runnin' more than half fast at that."

"Half fast? I was doing better than a six-minute mile. And in bare feet!"

"Now don't take offense, Neighbor. Half fast's a compliment."

"How's that?

"Look. I was workin' on a turnaround job out at the Exxon refinery when it was still Standard Oil. Biggest refinery in the Northern Hemisphere at that time, just a few miles away. Sixteen-hour shifts we worked. Plant was brought down for repairs, and we had to get it up and operatin' as soon as possible. I was a young'un, on a paint crew workin' near a cat cracker when one of the lines blew. Made a ball of flame that was taller than the state capitol. Singed me good."

Washington laughed again at the thought. "We all took off runnin'. I'll never forget it. Fire behind us. Cat cracker goin' up in flames. Valves burstin'."

"Later that night the fires were still burnin'. Whole plant was lit up. Big clouds of smoke. Plant manager kept us all there. Put all of us who'd been near that cat cracker in a room with the white supervisor. They brought a doctor in, some nurses, and some insurance man. There we are, gettin' looked at, gettin' salves and ointments and what all, and this insurance fella is askin' questions. Never shut up. He turned to Little Charlie, sittin' next to me, and started 'terrogatin' him. Little Charlie, 'bout 6 foot 4, was doin' his best to answer, what with the supervisor there and all. That insurance man talked to us real slow and loud, like we was children who didn't speak no English. Like we couldn't possibly understand him unless he spoke down to us. 'What were you workin' on when it happened? How near the catalytic converter were you? What tools were you holdin'? Were you wearin' work gloves? Were you wearin' steel-toed shoes? Do you understand what I'm askin'?' Never looked up. Just asked questions and wrote down notes in the pad as Little Charlie answered."

"'What did you do when you heard the explosion?' Still writin' in his pad. Little Charlie just stared at him like that was the stupidest question he had ever heard, and it damned near was. But Little Charlie kept being polite; 'Started runnin'.' he said. And that insurance man asked 'How fast did you run?' Little Charlie, now, he had had enough of this white man, so he answered 'Half fast.'"

"That insurance fellow finally stopped writin' on his pad. Said he don't understand what Little Charlie meant. Said he can't figure out why Little Charlie was only goin' half fast if the cat cracker was blowing up behind him. 'What's half fast?'"

"I remember Little Charlie lookin' him right in the eye. 'Well,' Little Charlie says, 'I was passin' some, and some was passin' me.'"

"And that insurance fellow writes that in the pad!"

Washington laughed again. "Mr. Lawyer, you were goin' more than half fast."

He got up to leave. "That's enough for tonight. You get some rest and I'll check in on you in the mornin'."

I tried to thank him, but he brushed it off.

"Weren't nothin'. Want me to call the police?"

I told him not to bother. Sure, my home had been violated. And sure, I wanted to see whoever did it locked up. But, after all, if the police came, what could I tell them? Once they started to ask questions, one thing might lead to another. They might find out that Taylor had been here earlier. They might talk to her. And the way Taylor prattles on, what would she say about the $1.6 million missing from the Camellia Industries accounts?

Couldn't have been a coincidence. While on the bayou this afternoon, I had spotted a man with a rifle at Camellia Industries. Then two men show up here this evening.

No way of knowing if they would come back, but it probably wouldn't be tonight, not with Luther having gotten a taste of one of them and Eby with his shotgun. I figured that I, along with the more than four million dollars hidden in my hallway crawl space, would probably be safe, at least until tomorrow.

CHAPTER 15

THURSDAY

I WAS EXHAUSTED. FROM THE TENSION. From the shock of learning about G.G.'s death. From the astonishment of finding all that cash. From the day in the sun on the bayou in St. Bonaventure Parish. From the drive back in the rain. From Taylor's evening visit and from the attack at my house.

I had collapsed on my bed, motionless for hours, probably snoring loudly, when something dragged me out of the depths of a dead sleep. Something insistent. Something constant.

The phone.

I looked at my clock. Not yet four in the morning.

The phone continued to ring.

I didn't recognize the number, but with G.G. dead, I needed clients again. I had gotten a couple of divorce cases that way in the eight months since I had hung out my shingle. Small, one shot deals. Late night or early morning calls from someone distraught, desperate for a lawyer and willing to pay something.

I reluctantly picked up the receiver.

It was someone desperate all right.

It was Taylor

"Schex, I really need your help." Her voice quivered. It sounded almost sincere.

I had sworn off her years ago. I should have rejected her right then and there, just as she had once rejected me.

But, instead of hanging up, I couldn't resist saying, out of spite, "It's too late for that."

"Really, Schex, no shit. I'm serious. I'm at the…" Her voice cracked. There was a moment of silence, and then she resumed, in a strong, slow tone. "At the St. Bonaventure courthouse. They've got me in the jail here on the third floor and won't let me go."

So that was it. They probably picked her up on a DWI. Drunk, no doubt. "Of course they won't let you go. Not at this hour."

"Don't fuck with me Schex. I've got this one call, and I've called you. You've got to help."

This was vintage Taylor. One minute pleading and almost tearful, the next harsh and demanding. Dammit, I shouldn't have picked up the phone at all, but I had listened too long already. If she was in the courthouse jail, the call was being monitored. She probably told them that I was her lawyer. Now I had to act the part, until I figured out what was going on. After all, the last thing I needed her to do was to start yammering about the money.

"OK, Taylor, just shut up for a minute. Don't say anything more. Just answer yes or no. Have you been there long?"

"I've been here for fucking hour upon hour. Some shitty little sheriff asked me to come with him to answer some questions, and there I went, nice as you please, trying to cooperate, trying to help them find out what happened to G.G., and I followed him all the way out into the middle of goddamn nowhere. Won't even let me go to my car to get my cigarettes."

"Taylor, listen to me. Just answer my questions. Have they read you your rights?"

"They just did that. That's why I'm calling you. Said I had the right to an attorney. Well, you're sure as hell an attorney."

"Taylor, just yes or no. Have they booked you?"

"I'm not sure."

"Yes or no! Have they fingerprinted you?"

"Yes."

"Is this the first call you've made?"

"Yes."

"Have you said anything to them?"

"You know me better than that. All I've told them is the truth. Here I am, being nice little Miss-Let-Me-Tell-You-About-How-Screwed-Up-G.G.-Fucking-Guidry-Can-Be and they accuse me of killing the son of a bitch! Not that he didn't deserve it, of course."

"Taylor! Open your ears and close your mouth!"

What had she gotten herself into? I couldn't believe what I was about to do. She was sucking me back in.

I was plunging headlong into disaster and couldn't do a damn thing about it.

CHAPTER 16

"YES OR NO," I CONTINUED, "is the only thing I want to hear you say. I'll be there in a half hour, forty minutes max. Do you understand? Say nothing else until I get there. All right?"

"All ri…Yes."

I hung up the phone and put on a clean shirt and slacks. Fingerprinting meant arrest. Finding a judge to set bail wasn't going to happen for hours.

I grabbed two books off the shelf, and drove as fast as I could to the St. Bonaventure courthouse.

Back down the expressway.

Back through the woods and fields.

Back across the St. Bonaventure bridge and along the road parallel to the cane breaks.

The jail was upstairs in the old wooden building, on the floor above the courtroom. Sitting at the desk outside the interrogation room was Sheriff Isaiah Brown.

To find the Sheriff here at this hour was not good. He loved headlines. He wouldn't be here in person unless he was planning to do something to hit the morning news shows.

He informed me, with no small degree of satisfaction, that Taylor was under arrest for the murder of G.G. Guidry and that he didn't care when the judge came in. Taylor could sit there all day as far as he was concerned, because the news crews were on their way, and this case was going to propel him right into the Louisiana legislature.

That's when I first found out that G.G. hadn't drowned in the retaining pond, as the newspaper story had implied. That's when I found out that G.G. had been shot. Three times.

If it was a murder inquiry he was conducting, I pointed out to the Sheriff, with just the right amount of derision in my voice, then whether he liked it or not, the United States Constitution still applied, even here in "his jail" in St. Bonaventure. I had a right to consult with Taylor. Alone. Unsupervised. Without prying eyes or ears.

The Sheriff fumed, but the last thing he wanted was a faulty arrest and interrogation, so he finally agreed to let us meet in a back room, although he pulled his chair up outside the door and had one of his deputies stand next to him, hand ostentatiously on his holster.

Once the door closed, I told Taylor to say nothing. I had brought two old novels with broken spines, their pages brittle and yellowed. I handed her one and took the other.

It was hours later, almost 10:00 a.m., before the Sheriff knocked on the door and indicated that the judge had agreed to speak with me on the phone.

CHAPTER 17

W E WERE BACK AT MY house, and I could scarcely believe how screwed up things had become. "You told me you wanted G.G. dead, but you went around telling others that too? You even told the teller at the bank when you found out the accounts had been cleaned out?"

"Schex, you know that was just an excess of emotion."

"It was an excess of excess, Taylor. They've got your statements to the teller. They've got you ranting at the Cotillion about G.G. taking 'your money' and fooling around with Millie Sue. You must have made quite a ruckus in that parking lot. Apparently, a lot of people from the ball overheard, people who seem to have no love lost for you. And they've got G.G.'s body. I'd say you're in an excess of trouble."

"Schex…."

"Taylor, it was all I could do to get you released. Judge Rochbauve is not known for being lenient. 'Course it didn't hurt that Francine's youngest sister and I had gone to law school together, but it was still tough to get her to set the bond at something reasonable. Now it turns out G.G. was murdered. Body partially eaten away by the chemicals in the holding pond, but not so much as to disguise the three bullet wounds the coroner found. The media will be giving this new angle plenty of play. Taylor, considering all that, you're damn lucky I was able to get you out on any bond, much less one you could afford to post. You owe me. You owe me big."

"You're right. I'm deeply in your debt."

She sounded as if she meant it. She sounded as if she were grateful. "You'll defend me, though, won't you?"

I knew it. Whatever I did, it was never enough. She always wanted something more.

"Absolutely not."

She looked up at me with pleading eyes, glistening with earnest-appearing tears.

"Don't start that with me, Taylor. It won't work."

"But you tried lots of cases with and for Catch. Big defense wins. You *could* do this for me, *if* you really wanted to."

Consistency was never one of Taylor's strong points. She had belittled me earlier, claiming that she had sent Guidry to me because I was a cheap lawyer with no scruples who would do whatever he asked. Which, in fact, was pretty close to the truth. But now she wanted me to be her protector in court, and to do that, she brings up Catch? Taylor and Catch had conspired to ruin my life. It had been a successful conspiracy.

"You made your choice when you went with him. I won't have his ghost hanging over me in the courtroom."

"Schex…" Her voice quivered again. She had quivering down pat when she needed it. "You've got to help."

I had a right to be cold and brutally honest with her after all these years. More honest with her than she had ever been with me. "The charge is murder. Second degree right now, otherwise you wouldn't be out on bail. But, I expect they may change that to first degree. Who knows what they'll come up with in the next few days or weeks? Who knows what you've said about G.G. to others?"

She was crying now, heaving softly.

I felt no pity. I wanted to hurt her. For years I had conjured unworkable schemes to make her suffer, to make her pay. "Prosecutors dream of defendants like you. Scorned woman. Missing money. Hazardous fumes. Sex. Violence. A St. Bonaventure jury will lap it up."

"But I didn't…" she cried.

"Don't tell me anything. I'm not your husband anymore. I'm not your lawyer. And I'm not going to be your lawyer."

She wept. She grabbed a dishtowel and put it to her face. Her body jerked convulsively as the crying grew louder. She put part of the dishtowel in her mouth and bit down on it to try to stifle her sobs.

I had seen it all before. I didn't do a thing to comfort her. I just sat and sipped my coffee.

She saw I wasn't buying her act, so she simply stopped. The tears ceased immediately.

Taylor wiped her nose with the dishtowel. She folded it into a neat rectangle and placed it on the counter. She pulled out her pocket mirror and checked to make sure her mascara hadn't run. Satisfied, she looked up at me. "If I've treated you badly over the years," she said quietly, "I apologize."

"True. You have treated me badly. But, I don't accept your apology."

"What do you want? You want me to grovel? I'll grovel if that's what it'll take."

"I don't want anything from you. There's nothing you can do for me after all you've done to me. Go home. The police will be watching. They'll come with a search warrant if they haven't already been there."

"Please, Schex, just find the money. Or, at least, get me a lawyer who can help."

Try as I might to suppress it, there was something still there, some feeling left beneath all the hatred and rage. There was no pain in seeing her suffer, but there wasn't the pleasure I had expected.

I walked over to the table, flung the dishtowel into the sink, and ushered her out the kitchen door to the driveway.

As she exited, she brushed past me, putting her hand on my arm and stroking it. "I would be so grateful. *So grateful*, you understand."

She leaned up and kissed me on the cheek.

She was still a damn attractive woman.

I didn't want to think of her in that way, but I couldn't help it.

CHAPTER 18

WHEN I WAS WORKING AT the law firm, there was always someone around to bounce ideas off of. Even during my short time at Old Parish Mortgage, Hubbard Estes – as useless as he seemed – could be counted on to pontificate from time to time. Some of his advice, occasionally, was marginally useful.

To whom could I talk now about this mess? Despite knowing Taylor as well as I did, and despite being the victim of her lies and deceptions, I still couldn't believe that she had murdered G.G. And, whether she had or not, she needed a top rate lawyer, and that was going to cost a bundle. What was G.G. doing with all the cash anyway? Why did Taylor seem to know only about $1.6 million? Or did she know about it all and was testing me? Whose cash was it, really? G.G.'s? The corporation's? Someone else's?

That's why, late Thursday morning, I pulled into the visitor's parking lot at the LSU Law School. It was a portal to my previous life, when I was a student with nothing more pressing than the next class, the next exam, and the next party.

Summer school was in session, but morning classes had ended. Students were scattered in the library or talking quietly in empty classrooms, keeping out of the summer's torrid heat.

I took the elevator to the top floor and went to the end of the hall, to the "Emeriti Warren," where the law school provided a group of small offices for retired faculty to linger. I was seeking Professor Artemis Calandro.

I knew he was in from the tobacco smoke that wafted into the hall. Although the law school's official policy was "No Smoking," no one dared enforce the rule for Calandro.

"Come in, come in. Await not!" His voice was as strong as ever.

He was sitting behind a desk covered with open books and stacks of paper, looking much the same as he had when he taught me five years earlier: Thick gray hair in a crew-cut. Heavy gray mustache. For more than four decades students had referred to Calandro as "The Red Knight," a reference to both his formerly red hair and to his legendary verbal jousts in the classroom, where he would thrust barbed witticisms at hapless students who had failed to master the material to his level of satisfaction.

Half-smoked cigarettes were piled in ashtrays. Bound legal works lined the walls, including at least three dozen volumes he had written. Other books were jammed against the ceiling and threatened to spill off the shelves. An insulation of words and pages.

I told him that I appreciated his making time to see me.

"Time, my boy? A possession which many aspire to have and which most waste. You've taken time to come to..." he gestured around the room, "my scholar's hovel."

He lit a cigarette and exhaled a cascade of smoke. "And your time is filled with...what?"

"Mostly civil cases. Some transactional work."

Calandro narrowed his eyes and looked over the top of his glasses, just the way he used to in class. "And you're here, my boy, because...?"

"I've often thought about the classes I had with you. Evidence, civil procedure, contracts, corporate law."

Calandro tilted his head to one side; the cigarette dangled down.

"And I've often meant to come by and thank you."

Calandro sat forward in his chair, crossed his arms, and rested his elbows on the open books. "Come, come, Mr. Schexnaydre, I'm retired, not retarded. Fine record. Good student. I remember you. Went to a big law firm, as I recall. And then, as far as I can tell, you dropped out of sight."

Calandro took off his glasses and spun them in his left hand. "Surely you didn't show up just to thank me. Usually, when former students call, particularly when they've not been in touch with me since graduation, they want free advice. They want this fount of wisdom to shower them with solutions to problems that confound their limited intellect."

Limited intellect! I had been on the Law Review. Top 10% of the class. But, I held my tongue and plunged ahead. "Well, actually, this involves a corporate issue."

Calandro leaned back in his chair. "An interesting and completely vague formulation. Does the corporation have a problem? Is it an issue involving corporate law?"

Calandro closed his eyes. "Am I to guess the question that you have, or are you able to articulate it with at least some modicum of exactitude? Mr. Schexnaydre, how could you have emerged from my courses, with the grades I gave you, incapable of extricating the crucial legal issue from a morass of facts?" He leaned back once more and closed his eyes again.

"OK." I was going to be as succinct as possible. He was playing with me and I didn't like it, but he was the one man I knew who might be able to help. "Corporate assets are partially in cash. The principal shareholder is dead. The corporate president is charged with a crime, possibly in connection with corporate activities. And the president wants to use the corporate assets to finance her defense."

"Do I hear a query? A possible hypothet?"

I had to put up with this in law school; I didn't have to do it now. "Professor, I came here to ask for your advice. You just want to spar. I don't have the time or patience for that."

I headed for the door.

"Sit down, Mr. Schexnaydre. There is something in your situation that may spark a glimmer of interest for me."

I paused, still standing in the doorway.

"I get it. I understand, Mr. Schexnaydre. You have an issue with a conflict of interest and privilege, don't you? You're worried that if the corporate assets are used to defend the president, then other shareholders might complain, perhaps because the president shouldn't be defended. Or maybe there isn't a proper indemnity clause in the corporate documents. Or maybe there are other stakeholders who must be considered before the assets are spent. Do I have that right?"

Oh, he had it exactly right.

"Now, I take it you had dealings with the now-deceased principal shareholder. I can see from your expression that I'm on track. So, your next issue must be the privileged and confidential communications he... it is a he, correct? Good. The confidential communications he gave you. The attorney-client privilege doesn't have to cease with death, so the fact that you mentioned he was dead means that he told you something about assets that you're reluctant to reveal to the corporation. And that must mean that you don't know who owns the assets he talked to you about."

I sat down, astonished. I had given him a couple of sentences outlining the barest minimum of the situation, and he had extricated the precise details of my problem.

Calandro, forgetting the half-smoked cigarette he had placed in the ashtray a few minutes earlier, lit another one. "So we have four questions. First, the presence of a privilege and whose privilege it is. Second, the waiver of a privilege and who can waive it, if anyone. Third, the use of funds, which may or may not be the corporation's, and which, fourth, may or may not be inextricably interrelated with the existence or waiver of the privilege."

Not only did he identify all the issues head on, he was able to come up with four specific questions that had to be addressed.

But, rather than answering him directly, I tried to pose the issue I had been mulling over. "Professor, the problem is...well, assume the money, or at least a part of it, belongs to the corporation. If I give it to the current president, assume she'll use it for the defense of the criminal case, and..."

Calandro held up his hand. "Don't tell me anymore. We don't have an attorney-client privilege. Anything you tell me could be discoverable."

Calandro set his just-lit cigarette down on the edge of his desk, reached into a drawer, pulled out a bottle of Pinch, and poured a hefty amount of the scotch into a cafeteria glass. "Want some, Mr. Schexnaydre? No? Too bad. Nothing like being retired to take the worry out of having a drink before lunch."

He took a sip and then picked up the cigarette again. "Of course, anything I speculate about will merely be my mental perambulations. If – and, of course, I am only speaking hypothetically – if I were to speculate randomly, I might speculate that an attorney who represents a corporation owes his duty to the entity, not to any particular person. And if I followed that path – that hypothetical trail, which of course I wouldn't do – I might speculate that since one always must act in the best interests of the corporation, one must always presume that the corporation and its officers are acting properly, unless one knows otherwise or suspects to the contrary with a reasonable degree of certainty. I might even speculate that a corporate officer, charged with a crime – a crime that, of course, is not against the corporation – is entitled as a matter of implied right to indemnity by that entity."

"Great," I interjected. This was the kind of information and clarity of thought I needed right now, but it turned out I had interrupted him. He signaled me to be silent.

"Mr. Schexnaydre, it's only hypothetical speculation, in which it would be improper to engage. On the other hand, such hypothetical results may not be appropriate. After all, one might speculate that the best interest of the entity is not furthered in defending corporate officials but in preserving the assets for the use of either the shareholders upon liquidation, or for the use of corporate creditors or other stakeholders. And, if that was the case…"

I had thought that the Red Knight had provided useful information, but here he was taking both sides of the issue, and making each side seem completely plausible.

"…if that was the case, corporate assets, one might speculate, should not be squandered in a proceeding that does not directly aid the corporation. Indeed, one might question what right an officer has to demand indemnity in the absence of an express clause to that effect in the corporate articles or by-laws. After all, it is the entity that one should protect, not the individual."

Calandro picked up a book from the shelf, leaned back in his chair, and put his feet on the desk. It was a signal that our meeting was coming to an end.

"Of course," Calandro added, pointing at me with his cigarette, "all this assumes that the funds are the corporation's."

The Red Knight had ridden again. There were two answers, entirely opposite, that he could explain and defend with equal vigor. Whichever one you chose, he'd attack. There was no single answer. There was no simple solution.

"I think I've speculated enough." It was a statement of finality from the Red Knight. Class dismissed. "It's probably time you spent some hours in speculation yourself. The most interesting answers, as you know, are those one comes to on one's own."

I reached out to shake his hand, but he was already immersed in a book. So, I simply left, leaving the door half ajar as I exited. "Thanks," I said, and then I added, murmuring under my breath to myself, "...as if that really helped."

I was surprised to hear Calandro's piercing bass voice booming after me. "I'm retired, Mr. Schexnaydre, not deaf. Thanking me is appropriate. Thinking for yourself would be even more appropriate."

CHAPTER 19

PROFESSOR CALANDRO HADN'T ANSWERED ANY questions, but he had clarified the issues, so by the time Taylor reappeared at my house that afternoon, I was ready. I had arrived at a new plan and had already started executing it.

We headed to the conference table in the living room. It was the hottest part of the afternoon, and the temperature and humidity had both hit ninety-five. My aging central air conditioning unit struggled. A barely adequate flow of cool air wheezed through the ceiling vents.

Taylor sat straight-backed in the chair in a ruffled white silk blouse and bright pink slacks that clung to the slim figure of which she was so proud.

No pleasantries. She came right to the point. "Come on, Schex. I'm here. You've had your time for thought. Where's my money?"

"First, assuming that there is any money, it's not 'yours.' That's for certain. Even you told me that it belonged to the corporation."

"So, you do know where it is. Don't give me any legal shit. I *am* the corporation! G.G.'s dead. He and I were the only shareholders. Give me the damn money."

"Demands? While asking me for help? You've got it all wrong, Taylor. If you want my assistance, you'll be polite. And, you'll do exactly what I tell you to do."

I could tell that she was taken aback. Good.

"The first thing I'll need are all the corporate documents. The articles. The by-laws. The minute book. The stock register."

"Why?" She feigned meekness, but there was a steely harshness in her eyes.

"You've told me that all the papers were in the den at your house. You said you went through the corporate books after you heard the checks had bounced. You said the books were in order. Well, now I've got to see if they are. Until then, I can't tell you anything or do anything for you. And only after I'm satisfied will I think about helping you."

Taylor smiled bitterly. "Lawyer shit talk! You have be 'satisfied' before you can 'think about' helping? Well, life isn't thinking. Life is acting. Doing what's needed when it's needed. I don't need someone to read a lot of legal mumbo paperwork. I need someone to defend me. Someone to stand up for me in court. Someone to get my money back. Someone to protect my rights in Camellia Industries – it's worth a hell of a lot, and I'll not have it taken away from me without a fight. So, thanks for 'thinking' about helping, but that's not enough. It's not near enough. I need action."

I didn't get angry. I didn't respond immediately. I simply sat there, holding her gaze. At last she shifted her weight, and then, when I knew the silence had become uncomfortable for her, I said, very calmly, "Do you want to hear what I've done this afternoon or not?"

Taylor crossed her arms in front of her breasts. "Well?"

"I've already talked to Lolleana Marston about taking your case."

"You spoke to Lolly?"

"Yes."

"Lolly seemed a flake in college, always off on some left-wing liberal cause."

"She's not a three-button suit, I grant you that. But, given your situation, I think it's to your advantage in court to have a woman defend you. And Lolly is one of the best around of either gender."

"So she'll take my case?"

"She will, if…"

"If what?"

"If she gets her fee up front. Non-refundable."

"Her fee? How much?"

"$775,000."

Taylor rocketed out of her chair and stamped her heels. "Three-quarters of a mil? Non-refundable! What the fuck is that? That's almost half of all the money that was in the accounts. What does she want to do? Get rich at my expense? Even Catch was never able to get a fee like that up front."

"Catch didn't have to defend someone whom the state might try to send to the electric chair."

Taylor's eyes narrowed. "What's this about the electric chair? The charge is second degree, that's what you said. That's what the judge said. And I didn't do it. I sure as hell wanted to kill him, but I didn't."

"Don't tell me. I've told you, I don't want to know. No client confidences. I'm not defending you. No waiver of any potential privilege. You'll have a privilege with Lolly, not me. Lolly thinks…now hear me out…Lolly thinks the D.A. is going to upgrade the charge and then try to get you to bargain back down to second degree. She already knew about the case when I called her. She has sources everywhere. She thinks they may have some additional evidence. You'll have to ask her. After you pay her fee."

"But $775,000?"

"Given what you're looking at, I think seven-seventy-five is reasonable. She's doing this as a favor. To me. To you. Believe me, it's a bargain, three-quarters of a million dollars versus the chair or life in prison."

"What kind of bargain is that? G.G. took $1.6 million, maybe more, and I don't know where it is, although obviously you do. Lolly gets hundreds of thousands. Where does that leave me? I can't live on what's left for the rest of my life."

Taylor was now pacing the room, seething. "This is moving me backward financially, not forward. And I've got to keep moving in the right direction, Schex. So where's the money G.G. stole from me?"

"Money belonging to Camellia Industries?"

"I MEAN THE GODDAM MONEY THAT'S MINE!" She was in a rage.

It felt good, after all these years, for me to be the one who was finally in control. "If I'm sure it belongs to the corporation, you can have it," I said, calmly. Just have to slowly extend the filament and let the fish circle the bait. I had unspooled my reel precisely as planned.

She took a deep breath and tried to regain her composure. She lowered her voice, but the urgency and anger were still there. "Well, I'm telling you. Without me, there won't be a corporation. Without me, the permits may not be renewed. Without me, it will all fall apart next week at the injunction hearing. The plant's already shuttered because of that temporary restraining order. If I can't get it up and started, if I can't beat the injunction, if the State won't do what G.G. said it was going to do, Camellia Industries won't be worth squat. Someone's got to be in court for the injunction, someone besides the plaintiffs and the State. Someone has got to file some papers, some briefs, some legal shit on my behalf. Hell, I'll do it myself if I have to, but Camellia Industries has to be protected. It's all I have now."

She had taken the hook. Now, all I had to do was set it. "Well, you won't be there next week to do it yourself, even if you had the legal skills, which you don't."

"Why the hell not? I watched you and Catch enough."

"The reason is that there's going to be an arraignment in St. Bonaventure. You've got to be in court to enter your plea. And if you try to do that without a lawyer, they're going to make an effort to revoke your bail, which they may try to do anyway. You need a lawyer there, so you need to retain Lolly as soon as possible."

"Well then, I don't need one lawyer, I need two, don't I? One for St. Bonaventure and one for Camellia Industries. Both next week." She thought a minute. "Oh, I get it. You won't handle the criminal case, but you want to represent Camellia Industries at the injunction hearing, right?"

The fish had been snared.

"I see it now, you bastard. You lawyers are sucking me dry. Fuck!"

She paused to consider her options. At last she said, unhappily, "I've got to have it, or whatever will be left of it after you and Lolly finish raiding what's rightfully mine. So I'll get you the books, but you sure as shit better get me the money."

"First the corporate records."

"I told you, I'll get them to you."

"No, Taylor. No more stalling. Let's go over to your house. Right this minute. We really don't have a lot of time to waste."

"They're not there."

Now she was playing with me.

"Don't look at me like that, Schex! I had them, all right, but when I heard about G.G. I thought it best to get them out of the house. Spider has the books."

CHAPTER 20

WHY HAD SHE GIVEN SPIDER the corporate books? Taylor had several explanations, none of them satisfactory. She was afraid of them being stolen while she was out of her house. No one would tangle with Spider. The paperwork was a mess.

But she wasn't making any sense. If the books were important, why didn't G.G. take them along with the checkbooks and ledgers? If the paperwork was a mess, why worry if anyone was going to steal it? If protecting the books was important, why entrust them to Spider? Why would Spider do anything for her if he owed his allegiance to G.G.?

But, when Taylor said, "Spider may have worked for G.G., but he'll do anything for me," I sure believed that. Taylor could twist almost any man into knots if she put her mind – and body – into it.

In the end, it didn't matter why she had given the books to Spider. I had to see them, because only by doing that could I legally get my hands on a substantial portion of the cash. Professor Calandro had indicated the way, in his usual circuitous fashion, and I had figured out how to get back at Taylor while 'helping' her, stripping her of the bulk of the $1.6 million she knew about, and keeping the rest – the $2.8 million – for myself.

I wasn't going to represent Taylor in any criminal case. Nothing but trouble there. Whatever I'd recommend, she'd second-guess. Can't have a defendant sitting in the courtroom, facing a jury who holds her fate in their hands, seething at her lawyer because she disagreed with some tactic. Can't have a criminal client who doesn't think her lawyer is dispassionate, who is always asking herself if her lawyer has some ulterior motive to get even because of past slights.

On the other hand, representing Camellia Industries was perfect. It was all in the clues that the Red Knight had given me. The $1.6 million would evaporate into legal fees, and no one would suspect me if Lolly was demanding far more than I. I'd start with $50k and bill the hell out of Camellia Industries until the rest was gone, assuming Taylor really owned it. Which is why I needed to see the corporate books.

It was perfect. Cleanse the funds she knew about, keep the $2.8 million she was ignorant of, and then, carefully, retreat into a life of leisure.

So, I told Taylor I agreed. Once I saw the books and was satisfied, I'd find a way to get her the roughly $1.6 million G.G. had taken from the bank accounts.

Taylor was unhappy that she'd have to pay the upcoming legal fees out of these monies, and she set down three conditions.

First, Spider lived in St. Bonaventure Parish, so she'd arrange for him to meet me in the parking lot of Poirrier's Market to hand over the corporate books.

Second, Taylor informed me that there was going to be a public meeting that evening at St. Bonaventure High School. Camellia Industries was going to be discussed. If I was going to represent the corporation, I needed to be there to hear what was said by those who showed up. The State was opposing the court-ordered shutdown, and state officials were supposed to be there to explain why.

Third, I had to tell her everything I heard.

None of that was a problem for me. It maintained the illusion that I was helping Taylor look out for her own best interests. I wasn't going to have to scrounge for work after all this was over. All I had to do was to look at the corporate books and maintain the façade of representing the corporation until the State defeated the injunction.

It was settled. I'd pick up the books from Spider at Poirrier's, go on to the high school, and reconvene with Taylor afterwards.

CHAPTER 21

THERE WAS NO SIGN OF Spider when, late that afternoon, I pulled into the lot of Poirrier's Market.

Parking my car, I approached the storefront and examined the hand-lettered signs in the window. "Hot Boudoin and Andouille." That was appropriate; a south-Louisiana market should sell sausage. "Turnip Greens – 19¢/lb" read another. Other signs touted crawfish, fresh crabs, oysters by the sack, shrimp, pork chops, and ham bones. They crowded against one another, taped on the inside of the large windows, covering almost every available space. What caught my eye, however, was the poster proclaiming: "H. Lazcarè. Tonight. 8:30."

I went back and sat on the hood of my car, watching the crowds that flowed in and out of the building. There was a large metal awning that stretched from the roof, shading and sheltering the doors at either end of the concrete block building and extending over concrete islands containing six gasoline pumps.

Stout ladies in summer dresses entered the door on the left and departed later bearing paper bags filled with groceries. Teenagers congregated near the side of the building, smoking. Sunburned men in cutoff shirts, torn jeans, and several days' worth of stubble exited the market carrying six-packs of cold beer. They leaned against their pick-up trucks, drinking and talking.

It was at least an hour and a half from sunset, and the day's heat still hadn't abated. I craved a cold beer and went inside Poirrier's to see what kinds they stocked and buy a couple of bottles. It was my first time in the market. The high-ceilinged building was split in two by a six-foot wall. To the left of the wall was the grocery store. To the right was a large, curved bar. Beyond that were more than twenty tables covered with brown butcher paper. At the far end of the room was a dance floor, and beyond the dance floor was a small, raised stage made of wooden skids.

A few minutes later I was sitting on the hood of my car, finishing my second beer when, from behind, someone tapped me on the shoulder.

I spun around. I hadn't heard anyone approach. Spider was standing there, eyeing me like a deadly animal stalking its prey.

He said nothing. He merely pointed out his sedan at the other end of the parking lot. I got in my car and followed him, pulling up next to his vehicle.

He didn't speak until after he had transferred five large cardboard boxes, wrapped tightly with sealing tape, from his trunk to mine. His voice was soft but menacing. "Do better than your best! As her lawyer, you make sure that nothing happens to her. You protect her, you hear?"

I corrected him. "Protecting *her* is not my job."

"You're not her criminal lawyer?"

"Not me. No way."

For the first time since I had met him, Spider's features ceased to be impassive. A look of concern came over his face. "She needs a *good* lawyer, anyway. The best money can buy."

Before I could respond, he jumped into his car and drove off at high speed, the rear end of his sedan fishtailing as it sped down the road.

CHAPTER 22

T HE METAL-WALLED GYM AT St. Bonaventure High School was surrounded by cars. Beyond it stretched long rows of one-story brick classroom buildings connected by covered walkways. The official meeting time had already passed when I arrived, but the proceedings still hadn't begun. I climbed up the bleachers and took a seat near the top, next to a steel girder. I was amazed at how many people filled the gym. It looked more like a crowd for a major high school basketball playoff than a public information meeting concerning Camellia Industries. I certainly hadn't anticipated seeing so few white faces and so many black ones.

A lectern had been set up in the center of the basketball court. Behind it, on a raised platform, was a row of folding chairs facing the bleachers.

The crowd was growing restless. Finally, a portly white man in his sixties walked to the podium and tapped on the microphone. It made loud popping noises that reverberated off the metal walls.

He leaned into the mic, his wrinkled seersucker suit hanging loosely over his large gut, and announced: "I know y'all are waitin' for Mr. Herrington, and I'm told he'll be here shortly. So, if y'all be patient, we'll get started in just a bit."

The crowd was not in a mood to be patient. The gym echoed with the din of hundreds of voices.

But, after a minute or so, the tone of the cacophony altered. A distinguished gentleman in an elegant blue suit, white shirt, and red tie entered the gym. It was the unmistakable Carter H. Herrington, IV, radiating self-confidence, power, and wealth.

The conversations in the stands became murmurs as Herrington walked briskly to the podium. Large Gut greeted him and introduced him to the six other white men and one black woman on the dais. Besides Herrington, I recognized only one other person in the group – the St. Bonaventure District Attorney.

They all took their places in the seats behind the lectern, leaning over to occasionally whisper to one another, a team composed of many white men and a single black woman facing a largely black audience.

Large Gut went to the microphone and tapped on it once more, as if he didn't trust his first effort to make sure it was on. The crowd settled into a tense, uneasy silence.

"I know y'all are ready and I appreciate your patience. On behalf of the St. Bonaventure Police Jury and the D.A.," Large Gut paused to dramatically gesture to the group seated behind him, "I thank you for coming to this public hearing about environmental conditions in our parish. As y'all know, as President of the Police Jury, I've always made the betterment of all of our citizens my first priority. My calling in life has always been to help the people of this parish. You people are my constituents and that's why I'm proud to be here, with all of you people."

The black audience in the bleachers didn't care about what Large Gut thought was his calling, and they were offended by his reference to '*you* people.'

Large Gut saw he was losing the crowd. He tried to regain their attention. "Sheriff, I see you out there on the second row. Why don't you come up here and join us? Sit right here with the D.A. and the Police Jury."

I hadn't noticed Sheriff Isaiah Brown in the crowd.

The Sheriff called out, "That's all right. I think I'll just stay out here with the rest of *your* people." The crowd laughed at the expense of Large Gut.

Large Gut gave up trying to work the crowd. He raced through the rest of his introduction. "It's public hearings like this one that are important, and I'm glad that Carter H. Herrington, IV, Secretary of the Louisiana Department of Environmental Health, has been able to join us this evening. Let's all welcome Secretary Herrington."

Large Gut backed away from the lectern and started to applaud as Herrington stood up. The D.A. and the other members of the Police Jury also applauded, but the applause was not contagious. The thin sounds of their clapping barely echoed in the metal gym. No one else joined in.

The tension in the building began to mount.

CHAPTER 23

ERRINGTON DIDN'T SEEM TO MIND the uncomfortable silence that descended following his introduction. He unbuttoned his coat and walked around to the front of the lectern, ignoring the microphone. "Can y'all hear me?" His voice boomed. "Good."

He looked back at those seated in the chairs, acknowledging them. "Mr. President, Mr. District Attorney, and members of the Police Jury." He turned to face the bleachers. "My fellow citizens, I can't tell you how glad I am to be here with you tonight, here in St. Bonaventure Parish."

Herrington started to pace slowly, back and forth along the wooden floor in front of the crowd, expertly evaluating their mood.

"You know, I've spent a lot of time in all areas of this state, and there are few places as nice as St. Bonaventure. I've tried cases in the courthouse here. I've fished in the bayou. I've hunted ducks in the marshes, and I've hunted deer in the woods. This is a beautiful place, and you've got a right to be proud. Proud. Rightfully proud."

Herrington took off his coat and draped it on the lectern. His starched blue shirt with the white tab collar and his crisp and shiny leather suspenders were in marked contrast to the jeans and work clothes in the audience.

Herrington unclasped the gold cufflinks from his sharply creased cuffs and stuffed them in his pocket as he rolled up his sleeves and continued to pace in front of the audience, oblivious to the microphone, his voice filling the gymnasium. He spoke with the skill of an experienced orator – his voice rising and falling, casting a spell.

"I didn't come down here on the expressway – no, I came down on old Highway 90, Huey Long's highway. Huey Long was a populist in the best sense of the word. He built more roads, more bridges, and more schools than anyone else."

There was no response from the audience.

But Herrington did not pause for effect. He pressed on, building his tale. "Huey Long built the very foundations of what our state has become. He gave us a great university. He gave us a great hospital system to serve the needy. He gave us a powerful Public Service Commission. He also gave us great stories about himself, and he told them better than anybody else. We all know about his dedication to helping the little man and little woman, the poor and downtrodden, black and white alike."

The more Herrington talked, the stronger his accent became. He was a politician adjusting to the crowd. It seemed that the tension in the gym was beginning to dissipate.

"Along with his dedication came capacity as well, capacity to help the little man. On top of it all, Huey was a great storyteller. Best there ever was."

Herrington was a master. He had come into a hostile environment and was attempting to charm those present, and not without some success. But his story was still building.

"Well, Huey used to tell the tale of a local politician who couldn't hold his liquor as good as Huey. It seems this local boy had come in from an evening of heavy politicking and heavy partying. The sheriff's patrol had to escort him home and help him up a big, curving staircase at his house. Almost had to carry him up. Got him to the top of the stairs. Got him to the door of his bedroom. Propped him up. Now, this man's wife was there, and she was some woman. No sheriff's deputy was goin' to tangle with her. Least not as long as her husband held office."

Some in the crowd nodded their heads. They knew all about white sheriff's deputies and police officers who let politicians and their families do as they please. They also knew that Sheriff Isaiah Brown, the first

African-American to be elected to that office in St. Bonaventure Parish since Reconstruction, wouldn't let any white politician get away with anything. But they understood that Herrington wasn't referring to Sheriff Brown, because back in Huey Long's day, back in the 1930s, no blacks held elected public office.

"Now, those big old deputies balanced this man by the shoulders, opened the door to his bedroom for him, and then hightailed it down the stairway in the dark. So, there he was, full of liquor, trying to navigate his way through his bedroom with 'nary a light on.

Herrington paused for effect. He knew he had garnered the crowd's attention.

"And then there's this crash. A monstrous loud noise."

Another pause. The audience was filled with expectation.

"Quick as a raccoon skiddles up a tree, his wife had flipped the lamp on and is standin' at the foot of the bed, looking at her husband sprawled on the floor, flat on his back, where he had tripped over a hassock. Now that woman was angry. Good and angry. She's standing there, ready to light into him like fire on kerosene."

The crowd was waiting.

"But, flat on his back, he holds up his hand to tell her to wait a second. And then he looks up at his wife and he didn't miss a beat."

Long pause. Big smile from Herrington.

"'I'm now ready,' he said to his wife, 'to dispense with my prepared remarks and take questions from the floor.'"

The crowd laughed with approval, a clear sign that Herrington was winning them over.

Herrington laughed with them. "OK, any questions…from the floor?"

CHAPTER 24

THE LAUGHTER QUIETED. THE GYM grew silent.

Herrington went up to the front row of the bleachers. "This is a public hearing, and I want to hear from you. I want to know what you're thinking."

He looked out into the crowd and spotted a woman about midway up the bleachers tentatively raising her hand. "You've got a question? Good. I'd appreciate it if you'd stand up so we can all see you. And speak up so we can all hear you. This is important, and we all need to know what you're going to say."

A lady in a print dress stood up. "You say you're proud of St. Bonaventure Parish. Well, I am too. I was born and raised here, but I'm not so sure I want my children to stay here. In their school, just down the road, there are three kids with cancers. Now, that ain't right. Kids gettin' cancers just ain't normal. I can't recall no one with any cancers when I was in school here. There weren't no plants here then, but there're plants here now, and three kids got the cancer. It's because of all that pollution, isn't it? So, my question is…what you gonna do about it?"

She sat down and the crowd applauded.

Herrington walked to the bleachers directly in front of the questioner. His voice was full of compassion and empathy. "You said you were born and raised here. I think that's great. What makes this parish great, what makes this state great, is people like you. But, you raise a good point."

He turned to the entire crowd.

"You've got a right to be concerned, and that's why I'm here. I'm as concerned as you are about these allegations that there are elevated cancer rates in St. Bonaventure Parish And I'm as concerned as you are about allegations of unlawful dumping and discharges into your bayou. DEH has done a great job under my administration, but we've got more to do. Lots more. As long as I'm Secretary of the Department of Environmental Health, we're going to do our best to make sure that the industries that are located here obey the law."

There was no applause.

Herrington did not appear fazed. He walked back to the center of the bleachers and looked at the crowd.

"How many of you work at the plants?"

A few hands were raised.

"Come on, I know there's got to be more than that. How many of you work in the plants, or work for a contractor who does work in the plants?"

Hands were raised throughout the audience.

"And how many of you work on the rigs offshore, or in the service companies that serve the rigs?

More hands were raised.

"Your jobs are important. You know that. We all know that. Your jobs support your families. They let you buy food and live in a decent house. They give you money so you can fix up your boat, so you can buy your fishing gear, so you can get that new rifle or shotgun. You know we need those industries. But I'm not foolish enough to think that these companies should be able to do whatever they want. We need them to run right, to run clean. That's the job of DEH, and that's my job. Together, we can make a difference. We can have jobs and we can have a cleaner environment, both at the same time. That's what DEH stands for. You've got my word on that."

Herrington paused, hoping, I thought, for applause. Instead of that, however, low murmurs began to run again through the audience.

Herrington proceeded on without hesitation. "Questions? I'm hearing you talk among yourselves out there. Why not talk to me? That's why I'm here. With this kind of turn-out, there's got to be a lot of you with questions."

An elderly man to Herrington's left rose unsteadily to his feet. Herrington went over to give him a hand, but the man waved him away and said angrily, in a strong voice, "You say you want the industries to run clean. Well, some do and some'ums don't. Take that Camellia Industries plant. They say they're making some kind of stuff for houses, siding and such, but you should smell that place sometime. It don't smell like the plants I've worked at, and I've worked at more than a few. That smell – that's the smell of death to our community. That's what I'm saying!"

The crowd greeted his remarks with cheers and thunderous applause.

This was what I had come for. To observe anything that arose about Camellia Industries.

Herrington calmly waited until the noise subsided. "Excellent question," Herrington complimented. "Odor is an important clue, sometimes, in helping us to catch polluters. We've got some strong laws in this state, and I intend to enforce each and every one of them."

Herrington's comments were greeted with disbelief.

Another man on the front row stood up. "You didn't answer Cornell's question. He asked about the Camellia Industries plant. We've been complaining about that plant for a long time, and yet your Department issued a permit that allowed it to continue operations. We want to know what's going on."

The air filled with the crowd's approval of what had just been said.

I recognized the man who was speaking. Fireworks were about to begin.

CHAPTER 25

ERRINGTON SMILED AT THE QUESTIONER. "Mr. Doucet. I hadn't noticed you, but I should have. I'm pleased to have you here. You've been a strong voice for this Parish."

Herrington was outwardly gracious, but I knew Rad was the last person Herrington wanted to see tonight. Herrington had come to charm the crowd. Rad had come for another purpose.

I went to law school with Octavius Radolphus "Rad" Doucet. He had developed quite a reputation since then. President of the Louis A. Martinet Society, the state's association of African-American attorneys. Active in a number of environmental organizations. Always calling a press conference about some injustice he had uncovered, some new lawsuit he was going to file, or some protest he was planning to lead. Rad had been quoted in the newspaper article about G.G.'s death. He was the lawyer who had gotten the TRO against Camellia Industries. If things worked out the way I anticipated, I'd be in court next week, facing off against him, representing Camellia Industries.

"What about the permit?" Doucet pressed Herrington. "Why was it issued?" Doucet was in his cross-examination mode.

"Mr. Doucet, as a lawyer, you're well aware that DEH's rules and regulations deal with just such issues, and I know you must be aware that the permit was issued in accordance with those regulations." He smiled again and scanned the crowd, looking away from Doucet and towards the upper bleachers. "I know there're more questions out there."

But Doucet didn't sit down. "I've got another question."

"I'm sure you do, but one aspect of a public hearing is to give everyone a chance to speak, not just one person." He gestured to the bleachers, attempting to elicit a response from anyone other than Doucet.

Doucet took a step forward onto the basketball court. "Since I can't get past your staff to get an appointment with you, I figure this is a good time to ask all my questions and make all my comments." Doucet looked at the faces on the bleachers for support, and they gave it to him. Shouts of "let him talk" and "answer his questions" came from the audience.

Herrington, sizing up the situation, graciously smiled and stepped back to listen.

"On behalf of the members of PLEA, our Parish and Local Environmental Action Committee, I sent you a letter of complaint. Your office sent a canned response. Then I sent you a petition signed by over three hundred St. Bonaventure residents, a petition against your granting permits both for future plants and for expansion of current plants. All you did? Shoot back another form letter. How can you stand there and say you enforce the laws when you continue to issue permits to operations like Camellia Industries?"

Herrington moved to the lectern and nestled up against the microphone. His voice enveloped the gym and boomed over Rad's unamplified questions. "Glad to provide you with a response to all queries, Mr. Doucet, even though I'm certain that your organization's petition is not an accurate portrayal of the real concerns, thoughts, and desires of the thousands and thousands of hard-working citizens of this great parish."

Herrington spun out information quickly. "Let me tell you about these regulations. They're carefully drawn, and they ask for information about things like acenaphthene, and benzo fluoranthene, and butyl benzyl phthalate, and dichloromethane and tetrachloromethane. And none of that stuff with the long, fancy names was shown to be in the manufacturing or output processes at Camellia Industries. And when it's not shown, the regulations don't give me a basis to deny a plant a permit."

Herrington thought he had disposed of the question. He was wrong.

Doucet now turned to face the crowd. "He can get his mouth around jawbreaking technical terms. He's very good at all this hot air. But, you'd expect that from a *politician*."

Doucet jumped onto the platform and grabbed the microphone. "You didn't mention toluene, or four-methyl phenolnaphthalene, or any of the xylenes, or dichlorinated phenol…but that wasn't the point, was it, and you know it. The point is the utter failure of DEH to protect the African-American citizens of this parish. You're full of big talk about how important this parish is to you, full of your hunting and your fishing. But you don't know what real importance is. My great-granddaddy hunted and fished here too, but he didn't do it on some white man's recreation weekend, or because he wanted to mount some green-billed mallard or three-pointed buck on the walls of some cypress-paneled den. No, he did it to feed his family. And his grandfather, my great-great-great-granddaddy, fished when he could to feed his family, but he couldn't have hunted here – he was a slave, picking cotton, and if he'd had a gun to fire, they would have hunted him down for being 'uppity.' So, don't tell us about your attachment to this parish. The families of many of those here tonight, like my great-great-great-granddaddy, were attached to this parish…by shackles."

Voices from the crowd yelled out "that's right" and "tell it," chorusing their approval.

Doucet's voice filled the gym with power and indignation. "You look at where these plants are being built. They're not next to some white subdivision. They're not impinging on your property values. Where are they? They're next to *our* homes."

The crowd applauded. Doucet glanced over at Herrington, who was sporting an expression that came across as bitter rather than compassionate.

Doucet continued to build his case. "These plants hurt African-Americans. They're bringing death and destruction into the homes our families have lived in for generations. They're raining down pollution from their smoke stacks. They're lighting up the sky with flares that emit gases, flares that burn like the fires of Hell. They're dumping chemicals into our streams and polluting the waters we drink from. *We* – not you. *Our* homes, not yours. *Our* children. *Our* families. *Our* heritage. And you have the audacity to stand here and smugly talk about 'regulations'? Well, I'll tell you what kind of regulations these are. If they allow such things to happen, they're racist, plain and simple."

The crowd was punctuating each of Doucet's sentences with shouts of approval.

Herrington raised his hands. "If y'all will be quiet, I'll be glad to respond."

The crowd started to quiet down, but Doucet would have none of it. Facing the bleachers, he asked, "What do you want to be quiet for? To listen to him tell more political lies? What's he going to say? Nothing. Is he going to cancel the Camellia Industries permit?"

Rad turned abruptly to Herrington. "Are you? Are you also going to shut down Big Mudcaster Enterprises, or FlowPipe Chemi-Petrols, or any of those other companies on the river that are just as bad?"

Herrington continued to signal to the crowd to be quiet and sit down. "We certainly can talk about these things and air our differences."

Doucet ignored him. "He's not going to do anything but jaw at you. Don't let him. Tell him we want action. Tell him we don't understand why the St. Bonaventure D.A. has said nothing – not a single word – against the plant. Tell him we don't understand why the DEH has filed papers in our injunction suit against Camellia Industries, papers *defending* Camellia Industries and the permits that have been issued. Tell him we don't understand why they have claimed we don't have 'standing' to bring this suit. Tell him we don't understand why DEH, if it is so interested in the environment, is raising a whole host of other 'legal' issues to try to kick our suit out of court. Tell him we don't understand why DEH is paying its lawyers to defend Camellia Industries and to fight *against* the citizens of St. Bonaventure Parish."

The crowd was now Doucet's. They cheered him on. They called out "yes" and "you're right" and "amen" at each of his pronouncements. They stamped their feet with approval.

Doucet continued on with even more fervor. "Tell them NO. Show them all, that we sure as hell have *standing*. Get on your feet. Come on, stand up for your rights!"

The wooden bleachers groaned as person after person rose.

The crowd stood, shoulder to shoulder, cheering.

Doucet urged them on. "Camellia Industries is nothing but a hazardous waste processor, spreading poisons! Yet, DEH still takes the position that Camellia is just a plant compacting trash into building materials. There's plenty that's trashy, all right, and it's not only the Camellia Industries plant. Tell this white man. No compaction. We want action."

The crowd stomped, clapped and yelled, louder than ever.

The D.A. and the male members of the Police Jury were now on their feet too, backing away from their chairs, looking concerned. The black female police juror, however, walked toward the bleachers, smiling, to align herself with her constituents.

Doucet started a chant. "No compaction, we want action! No compaction, we want action!"

The crowd picked up the refrain. It rang throughout the gym. "NO COMPACTION, WE WANT ACTION! NO COMPACTION, WE WANT ACTION!"

Again and again they yelled it, louder and louder, stomping in rhythm, a cacophony cascading off metal walls, echoing and reverberating, continuously building in intensity.

Herrington gave up. He, the D.A., Large Gut, and the other male members of the Police Jury scurried out the rear door to the applause and laughter of the crowd.

Doucet raised both hands in victory.

CHAPTER 26

I FOUND TAYLOR SITTING IN HER red BMW convertible, top up and air conditioning blasting, on the shoulder of the road about fifty yards from Poirrier's parking lot, just where she said she would be.

I quickly explained to her that I had met with Spider and told her what had happened at the meeting I had just come from.

"Dammit, Schex. You see why I need you to be in court this coming week to protect Camellia Industries. You've got to do it."

Everything was going as planned. She was trying to convince me, and she was thinking that this was all her own idea.

"You've got the papers from Spider," she continued. "That's all you need. Just protect Camellia Industries and beat the shit out of these environmentalist fuckers in the courtroom."

"I'll look at those papers tonight, no doubt about that."

"Good. Then it's settled. You'll look at the papers and get satisfied with whatever legal crap you need to figure out and get me the money. I can meet you at Lolly's tomorrow morning by ten-thirty, and we can get that taken care of as well."

'All taken care of' is just what I had planned.

She was no longer looking at me. She was gazing down the road toward Poirrier's. Its parking lot was full, packed with pickup trucks and motorcycles, two-door coupes with rusted side panels, tricked-out cars with racing vents, and old sedans in various states of disrepair. On the left side of the building, where the market was located, the windows were dark, but on the right side all the lights were on and people were streaming in the door.

Taylor left her BMW and started walking down the road to Poirrier's. "Come on, Schex. The night is still young. Buy me a beer. I need a drink."

Taylor's picture had been on the front page with a story about her arrest. Being seen in a bar the evening after she had been arrested wouldn't help her case.

"What's that look on your face? You don't approve? Well, fuck you. I want a drink. You've told me you won't be my personal lawyer, so I don't need your approval, as if that ever meant anything to me, which it didn't. You worry about Camellia Industries. I'll take care of myself. So, are you coming inside with me?

Let Lolly deal with the fall-out in the criminal trial. The $775,000 was all that Lolly was going to get. The bulk of the rest of the money was going to legally flow into my pockets, one way or the other. The more trouble Taylor brought upon herself, the clearer the path was for me.

I followed her into Poirrier's, which was jammed shoulder-to-shoulder. The listless wooden fans hanging on long metal poles from the high ceiling did nothing to cool the place down or disperse the haze of smoke that hung in layers.

We found a spot at a small table in the back of the room, but no matter where Taylor was, she couldn't avoid being the center of attention. She invited it. The men at the adjacent bar ogled her in her skin-tight jeans and the form-fitting denim shirt that accentuated her athletic figure.

As I put cash down on the bar and grabbed a couple of beers, a man's head appeared above the crowd at the front of the room. He was standing on the stage, but no one paid any attention to him.

The man put his fingers to his mouth and blew a piercing whistle into the mic, causing the speakers to scream with feedback.

The barroom chatter ceased.

"Now," the man said, with a thick Cajun accent, "I got a treat for y'all t'night. It's what y'all been waiting for."

Dozens of boots pounded approval on the wooden floor.

"Y'all may be waitin' for beer. We got plenty 'a dat. And y'all may be waitin' for food. We got plenty 'a dat too. Don't forget 'bout our specials, ya' hear? We got dem fried oysters, dem fried catfish, and dem soft-shell crab. We even got da last 'a da soft-shell crawfish in the back. So, if y'all are hungry, order ya' some 'a dem critters now."

The beer bottles clanked in response. Get on with it.

"I hear ya. Now, in Louisiana we got all kinds 'a critters. Critters ya can eat, and critters that'll eat ya. We got dem in da marsh and in da swamp, in da woods and in da fields. But 'a all da critters out dere, da meanest and nastiest of dem all – other den a Louisiana politician – is da bear. It lives along da edge of the swamps and it hunts in da woods. It's a powerful mean hunter. It's a powerful mean creature. Got dem powerful paws and powerful jaws and powerful appetites. And we got a powerful lot 'a bears in dose woods. Right?"

The audience agreed by once more rapping their beer bottles against the edge of the tables.

"But, we got da biggest and most powerful 'a all da Louisiana bears right here on our stage t'night."

A pulsating rhythm began. Bottles against bottles. Knives against bottles. Bottles against tabletops. The crowd knew what was coming.

"Some people, dey like dat grizzly bear."

More noise.

"And some people, dey like dat black bear."

The crowd grew louder.

"And some people, dey even like dat brown bear."

Louder still.

"But dere's not nobody dat don't like dat Hebert." With his Cajun accent, Hebert was pronounced as 'A-Bear.'

The crowd exploded, and the man on the stage yelled into the microphone to be heard above the commotion, "And we got him for you. Dat's right – Hebert Lazcarè!"

The noise was intense. Screams. Whoops. Hollers. Wild applause as an immense man entered from behind the stage. He was thickly bearded, dressed in a white shirt and red suspenders attached to baggy jeans. He was carrying something under his arm.

I recognized him. Red Suspenders. The man who had turned me away from the Camellia Industries gate.

CHAPTER 27

HEBERT LAZCARÈ TOWERED OVER THE three younger men who took their places on the stage, behind the drum set, bass, and fiddle that awaited them.

Lazcarè hoisted the straps of his small accordion and rested the bellows on his ample stomach. He gave three beats with his boot on the wooden stage, and the four-piece band took off in a whirl of notes.

Lazcarè sang in French, nuzzling the microphone. The fiddle danced around the melody. The bass player sang harmony on the choruses, and the drummer beat out a simple waltz rhythm.

The dancers filled the small area in front of the stage. They moved in a circle. Grandmothers gracefully glided along, some escorted by their husbands and others by their grandchildren. Toddlers held their parents' hands – twosomes and threesomes moving with the counterclockwise flow. In the outer rim of the circle, couples in their teens and twenties performed intricate steps, never letting go of each other's hands.

Waitresses, who almost seemed to move in time with the music, wove their way through the packed room bearing wide cardboard trays piled precariously high with boiled crawfish and crabs.

The crowd knew the song and sang with the chorus. I recognized it. *Jolie Blonde.* My parents and their friends used to sing it when I was growing up back in Des Allemands. The song, in French, is about a beautiful heartless blonde. Like Taylor. The words mean 'look at what you've done, you pretty blonde; you've left me to go away with another. What hope and what future have I?'

Some of the dancers spread sand on the floor from the buckets placed near the walls, the better to shuffle, and Lazcarè and his band continued on into a Zydeco two-step.

Above the music, I thought I detected a murmuring behind me at the bar. I craned to see what was causing the commotion. It was a black man accompanied by a white woman. They had entered Poirrier's white enclave, were ordering drinks, and the bartender was reluctantly serving them.

The black man looked around, scanning the room. I tried to avoid his gaze, but it was too late. Rad Doucet had seen me.

CHAPTER 28

R AD AND THE GIRL ON his arm worked their way over to our table. He reached out to shake my hand. I politely complied.

"Schex," Rad said, "running into you here? Who'd have guessed? Weegie, I want you to meet my law school classmate, Schex Schexnaydre. Haven't seen you in quite a while."

"Guess you weren't looking real hard at the gym then," I said, "spending all your time working up the crowd. Some things never change, do they Rad? You always loved to preach. You were in your element tonight."

"You were there, Schex? Well, wonders never cease! First, Carter Herrington thinks he can sweet talk a crowd down here in my territory, and then you show up. Certainly not a coincidence, I bet, not with Taylor Cameron here with you. Hello, Ms. Cameron; I recognize you from the newspaper photo, although it didn't do you justice. This is Weegie Melton, and we'll just join you, if that's all right."

Once Taylor left me and my career tanked, I slid below the quality rungs on the romance ladder. I had dropped down to one-night stands with cheap skanks whose primary attributes were enhanced breasts and unenhanced brains.

Weegie Melton did not fit any of these categories. She was petit, small-breasted and fine-boned. Her oversized grey T-shirt, worn khakis, and scuffed hiking boots accentuated her natural beauty rather than disguising it, and intellect and refinement seemed to project outwards in her every movement.

"Schex, last time I heard," Rad continued, pulling up two chairs and squeezing himself and Weegie in at the table, "you had left that big firm and had been working for some financial something or other that closed. If you were at St. Bonaventure High School tonight, you must have been there on business, and seeing Ms. Cameron here I can bet what that business is."

Taylor took a sip from her bottle and said, with an icy sweetness, "Mr. Doucet, I certainly know that you think you can stick your nose into my business, getting temporary restraining orders without notice. I heard that you made a speech against my company tonight, creating a commotion and disrupting a meeting. It's so nice to see that you don't confine your repertoire to instigating trouble in the courtroom."

Rad shot right back. "'*Confine* your repertoire'? That's a fancy turn of phrase designed to insult. Well, no fancy language will save Camellia Industries in court when I get that permanent injunction shutting it down for good."

Taylor's eyes glinted steel, but her smile remained fixed.

This conversation had no way to go but in the wrong direction. I couldn't risk Rad taunting Taylor into saying something I'd have to explain in court next week at the injunction hearing. I pushed my chair back from the table. "Sorry that we have to depart, but…"

"Why hurry?" Rad responded. "Come on. Let me buy a round. Here, I'll start again, and I'll even change the subject. Did you know that Weegie here is the renowned Washington, D.C. coordinator from EarthResponsible?"

"Really?" said Taylor, injecting saccharine irony into every word. "Is 'EarthResponsible' a euphemism for a liberal do-gooder group of environmentalists who team up with local scum lawyers to support shutting down plants that give employment to hundreds of folks?"

I hit Taylor on the thigh under the table, trying to get her to shut up. She just glared at me.

"Actually," Weegie responded calmly, "I'm coordinating a group that's visiting the state on an environmental inspection, among other things. In fact, tomorrow morning, at eight sharp, we'll be getting a tour of Wholesale Flesh and Fur. We're going to see the whole operation."

The mention of Wholesale Flesh and Fur reminded me again what a failure my life had been until G.G. appeared at my door.

"Do you think," Weegie continued, addressing Taylor, "you could set up a tour of Camellia Industries? If and when it ever reopens? I'm sure our folks would love to see it."

"I bet they would!" Taylor said. "Not a chance in hell!"

I stood up, pulling Taylor out of her chair. "Hope you and your group have a good trip. Well, we've really got to get moving...."

Taylor made a show of linking her arm in mine. She said loudly, "Schex, I bet if I offered a big enough settlement, he'd dismiss the temporary restraining order in a second in exchange for his contingency fee. Well, you'll show him in court, Schex. You'll show him how to knock out a claim that's nothing but air and insinuation. Were you counting your money already? How much are you getting? Fifty percent? More?"

Rad looked up at her. "Here I am, trying to be nice. But you want to cast aspersions on my integrity? All right, lady. Let's talk. Let's talk about putting plants where they harm my people. Let's talk about racism."

Taylor was indignant. "Racism? You're fighting a war that already has been won. Look around."

She pointed at the dancers and the band and bartenders and those eating at the crowded tables, all white. "You're here. No one has denied you a drink. No one has denied you a table. There's no sign saying 'We Reserve the Right to Refuse Service to Anyone.' The civil rights battles have been won."

Rad sighed. "When Justice Thurgood Marshall was asked by a white reporter why there was still a separate black lawyer's organization – separate and distinct from the white establishment American Bar Association – when he was asked why it was separate 'at this late date,' Justice Marshall's response was, 'It's not that late.'"

Taylor shot back. "You're so last century. Now, just how many decades has it been since Marshall was on that court?"

I again tried to urge Taylor toward the exit, but Rad stood up and blocked our way. "There's racism here. Right now. You're blind to it. Let me open your eyes."

CHAPTER 29

RAD GRABBED TAYLOR'S HAND. "COME on. I'm going to teach you a Creole step to go with Cajun music."

Taylor resisted but Rad was insistent. To avoid making a scene, she allowed herself to be drawn toward the dance floor where couples were already moving to the Zydeco music. A waitress was weaving around the dancers, a metal bucket in her hands, tossing more sand on the wooden floor.

Rad put his arm around Taylor's waist as they walked. Eyes turned. The crowd parted to let them through. Rad held Taylor tightly to him as they joined the circular movement of dancers.

I went back to the table and sat next to Weegie. There was nothing I could do now to extricate Taylor from Rad's grasp without causing a disturbance. Besides, I knew that Taylor was a great dancer and would quickly put Rad to shame. So, I used the time to ask Weegie more about her planned tour, but she simply smiled and said, "No, watch this."

I was surprised. Once they were out on the floor, Rad moved agilely around Taylor, leading her in an intricate pattern through the dancers. No one left the floor. No dancer stopped. The music didn't change. But the mood of the room did. It grew noticeably quieter.

People at the tables pointed and spoke in low whispers. Dancers created an invisible enclosure of space around Taylor and Rad on the dance floor, a barrier between the mixed-race couple and themselves.

As the number ended, Rad spun Taylor. She did a triple turn and started to dance away from him, but Rad put his arm around her waist and walked her back to the table, accompanied by turned heads.

Taylor didn't sit down. She grabbed her beer off the table and said, peremptorily, "I agree Schex, it's time to go."

The music started up again. Now that Taylor and Rad were off the dance floor, the room returned to normal. The dancers crowded in around each other. The Cajun squeezebox of Lazcarè wove its magic.

"You see," Rad said, "this society's not colorblind. It's color conscious. Color is not something they ignore. Color is everything. Oh sure, they'll serve me. And they'll seat me. But they still see my skin, not me. I'm not a person to them. I'm a *black* person. That's the difference. That's racism. Did you see the way they looked at me dancing with a white gal?"

Taylor snapped back. "You think you're the one in charge here? Men! You're going to use me as an example? What's this supposed to be? Lie back and enjoy it lady? You drag me on the dance floor. You treat me like an object. You treat me like I'm nothing. You treat my Camellia Industries as if it's evil. Well, fuck you and fuck your organization and fuck your high and mighty ways."

She turned on her spiked heels. "Schex!"

As we departed, the gravelly voice of Hebert Lazcarè sang the song's refrain over and over:

> *"C'est que c'est le premiere?*
> *L'Oeuf ou poulet?*
> *Eh las bas.*
> *Laissez les bon temps rouler."*

What came first, the egg or chicken? Who cares? Let the good times roll.

Laissez les bon temps rouler. Louisiana's unofficial motto. Let the good times roll.

But G.G. was dead, Taylor was facing a murder charge, Spider was off to who knows where, and Rad Doucet was leading the move to shut down Camellia Industries.

The times were rolling along all too fast, and the only good thing left was for me to legally get as much of G.G.'s $2.8 million as I could before Taylor found out about it.

CHAPTER 30

I CHECKED MY DOOR AS I entered the house. It was locked, just as I had left it.

Once inside, I made sure that the back door was still latched and all the windows were undisturbed. Everything was fine.

Only then did I bring in the boxes Spider had put in the trunk of my car. Each appeared to be identical. Cardboard, unlabeled, sealed firmly with tape. Using a knife, I slit the tape and opened them.

Three of the boxes held file folders. The fourth held stacks of old bank statements bound with rubber bands. The fifth was filled with loose papers, like trash ready to be taken to the curb.

The file folders were relatively easy work. Contracts for equipment purchases and leases. Construction documents for various parts of the plant. Letters to parish officials requesting this and that. Brochures from companies selling machine tooling devices, incineration ovens, and conveyor belts. The ordinary dross of industrial business.

There were a number of forms and applications for various types of bond financing, with documents relating to potential loans through commercial mortgage-backed securities pools and real estate investment trusts. There was correspondence about applying for loans. But, there weren't any actual loan documents, not even a letter confirming that a loan application had been approved.

Then there were the insurance files. I reviewed these quickly. All the casualty, extended coverage, and liability policies were current. G.G. had maintained a full scope of coverage. The loss payee on all the policies, however, was only Camellia Industries; there was no lender listed as an additional insured. Did that mean there was no mortgage on the plant? These materials didn't answer that question.

Then there were the files containing bank statements with images of processed checks, but these were all at least a year old. Nothing current. When Taylor first came to see me – was it only two days ago? It seemed like much longer, but then any time spent with Taylor can seem longer than it is – she led me to believe that the business only had accounts at one bank, and that was the one G.G. had cleaned out. But, there were files from a number of different financial institutions. That was unusual. A business gets lower loan rates and all kinds of extra services when it places all its operating accounts, payroll accounts, and cash management accounts with the bank that is granting it line-of-credit financing.

Most of the accounts were in the name of Camellia Industries, although there were accounts of other corporations whose names I didn't recognize. Why were these mixed in with the Camellia Industries' files? I couldn't figure that out.

There was only one box left, the one that looked like it had been used as a trash bin. It was crammed full of receipts. Hundreds of them. Cheap paper; scrawled handwriting, mostly in pencil, some with smudged ink. Receipts with no dollar amounts listed, no itemization, just cryptic numbers and letters, like "150 sy" and "25 bb" and "3 t."

When I had been with Walker, Thibodeaux, LeBlanc & Adkinson doing litigation with Catch, many of the cases involved accidents, liens, or contracts at petrochemical plants. The plants were always worried about being sued by someone, and they carefully tracked everything that came in and went out. Every shipment had a detailed log of contents, supplier, and source. Today, most everyone keeps things electronically. But, apparently not G.G.

These receipts were strange. They had no addresses, no dates, no phone numbers, no names. A paper trail without a guide.

I dumped the entire contents of this box onto the conference table to see if there was anything else among the receipts.

There it was. The corporate binder had been hidden at the bottom of the box. This was what I had been looking for. It contained tabs for articles of incorporation, bylaws, minutes, stock ledger, and stock certificates. I glanced through them all quickly, confirming that the only two owners were G.G. and Taylor, each with a 50% interest. The bylaws gave each owner the right to purchase the shares of the other in the event of death. And there were two stock certificates, one in each of their names, each for 500 shares of Camellia Industries.

So Taylor had been telling the truth – she was a 50-50 owner. But, with a first right on G.G.'s shares, she also had a motive to get rid of him.

I didn't care about Taylor's criminal case. I had all the information I needed about the corporation so that I could put my legal straw into Camellia Industries' jeroboam of money and suck away.

I put the corporate binder back in the bottom of the box and started jamming the receipts back on top. As I did so, I noticed something strange. There were several that, unlike the other receipts, were printed on light red paper, with only shipping amounts. No dates. No names. No phone number. Only a tiny stylized crawfish in a circle in the upper left-hand corner of each slip and the letters "WFF" in bright red across the top, and below that, "SBP."

Damn! There was no mistaking what these were. Receipts for shipments without detailed information meant that someone didn't want things to be tracked. But "SBP" meant St. Bonaventure Parish. And WFF? The stylized crawfish gave it away. It was the logo of Wholesale Flesh and Fur.

CHAPTER 31

FRIDAY

O N A MAP, ST. BONAVENTURE Parish looks like a thirsty salamander slinking toward the Gulf of Mexico. Its snout is far south in the brackish marshes, but its long, curved tail stretches ninety miles north, almost to West Baton Rouge Parish.

Wholesale Flesh and Fur is just about at the tip of the tail, and the quickest way to get there was not on the interstate but rather across the old Mississippi River bridge that Huey Long had built high enough to let the main river traffic through, but low enough so that ocean-going vessels could get no further than Baton Rouge, all in an attempt to save and stimulate the city's maritime trade. The metal used to be pink, stained by the tons of bauxite imported from Jamaica for aluminum. The Kaiser Aluminum facility used to sit right at the foot of the bridge, and the bauxite dust had permanently discolored everything within a couple of miles of the plant.

It has all been repainted to remove the stains, and I planned to use G.G.'s money to remove the stains of sorrow from my past, left there by Taylor and Catch.

At last I got to St. Bonaventure Industrial Park where Wholesale Flesh and Fur was located. Reflections from dozens of metal-roofed buildings shimmered through the early morning haze.

Wholesale Flesh and Fur was at the rear of the Park, backing up to the bayou and the swamp beyond. Fencing topped with razor wire surrounded the facility except for a small visitor's parking lot marked by a sign – a red crawfish in a circle, the same design that had been on the delivery tickets. There were at least four big buildings in the complex that I could see.

A small bus was just unloading as I pulled in. Weegie was leading at least two dozen people, all middle-aged or older. Even though Weegie was dressed in overalls and hiking boots and had her hair tied back in a denim scarf, she was even more attractive than I remembered from the night before.

This was better than I had hoped. I had planned to just walk in and ask for Trey, but now I could blend in with the tour group and, perhaps, get more information than Trey might have been willing to give me.

I caught up with the tail-end of the group. Weegie was preoccupied and had not yet turned around to notice me, but a woman with a broad-brimmed straw hat said as I approached, "You're a bit late. Did you miss the bus? I didn't see you at the hotel last night or this morning."

"Oh, I'm from Baton Rouge," I said. "Just thought I'd join y'all on this part of the tour."

The woman hit her husband on the arm. "I told you, Morris, they really do say 'y'all.'"

Morris grunted.

"We're from San Diego," she announced proudly. "This is our *third* EarthResponsible tour!"

She paused to wipe her brow with her handkerchief. "This is our first time in Louisiana. Is it always this hot here? Even so early in the morning? And the bugs. Ugh! They crawl. They fly. And walking here's like trying to exercise in a sauna, what with all this humidity. It's not like San Diego at all, is it, Morris?"

Morris grunted again, non-committally.

Only when we approached the front door did Weegie turn to face the group. That's when she saw me. She ushered the group though the door, grabbing me by the arm as I started to enter. "What are you doing here?"

"Well," I said, "last night you announced you were giving a tour here. Thought I'd drop in to see what brings your tour group all the way down to these parts." I tried to make this sound as plausible as possible.

I hadn't charmed anyone in years, but that didn't mean I didn't want to start trying again. I'd try with Weegie. No harm. "Is there a problem if I tag along? After all, I'm sure that you, as a tour guide, wouldn't object to having another customer. I'll gladly pay whatever the tour company charges."

"I'm not a tour guide. I'm a Coordinator," she said.

I had offended her by misperceiving her role. "I stand corrected. Coordinator."

"Standing corrected is good for the posture," she said with a smirk. "Step inside with the rest. Maybe you'll learn something that will make you more environmentally sensitive."

"So this is sensitivity training?"

She looked at me quizzically and then gave a wry smile. "All right," she said, acknowledging my poor joke. "In a way, I guess it is. EarthResponsible's tours are part of our overall fundraising and grant efforts. We use them to raise money so we can continue and hopefully expand all of our worthwhile projects. Tour participants have a way of becoming EarthResponsible donors. Perhaps by the time we're finished I can hit you up for a donation."

I thought that might be interesting. Since she planned to hit on me, I figured I might, given the right opportunity, try hitting on her.

The two of us entered a narrow waiting room with only four chairs. The group was milling about on the ripped indoor-outdoor carpet. An alarm, triggered when the front door opened, continued to chime, but no one was in the receptionist's cubical, which was made out of the same cheap paneling that covered the walls.

At last, the inner door opened. A small Asian man in jeans and a white lab coat entered. "I'm Kuo Htay, the production manager. On behalf of Wholesale Flesh and Fur, let me welcome all of you visitors from

EarthResponsible. We normally give tours in the afternoon, but Mr. Trey said you'd be here at eight and you're right on time."

Weegie shook his hand. "Weegie Melton, EarthResponsible. We're happy to be here, Kuo…" she mangled the pronunciation.

Kuo smiled. "Everyone does that. Can't get their tongues around the sounds. Call me Kirk, everyone does. It's easier."

"OK, Kirk."

"Mr. Trey said that you're to get the run of the place. The first-rate, in-depth, no-holds-barred explanation and inspection." He raised his voice so everyone could hear. "Mr. Trey is very proud of the way we run this facility. It's the finest in the state – and in the region. Just follow me. You're in for an eye-opening experience."

CHAPTER 32

IN SHARP CONTRAST TO THE shoddy waiting room, the interior of the plant was gleaming. Corrugated metal walls, almost iridescent, stretched up at least thirty feet to the steel trusses that crisscrossed under the aluminum roof. Huge black ducts wove overhead, punctuated by grates dispensing a constant flow of cool air. Pipes in bright reds, greens, yellows and blues were braided through the metal work, connecting to large chrome cylinders on the ground, to vats that squatted along the walls, and to color-coded spigots over bronze assemblies.

Thirty or more women, all Asian and dressed, like Kirk/Kuo – whatever his name was – in jeans underneath thigh-length lab coats, were on either side of a metal platform. At one end, slowly moving down the rollers, were long rows of aluminum trays piled high with crawfish.

"We're running two shifts right now, because it's the end of crawfish season," Kirk/Kuo said as we walked past the ladies. Their fingers moved swiftly with no wasted motion, reaching into the piles of crawfish on the tray and peeling the tails in a single movement.

"Come on outside first, and I'll try to show you how all this works. Mr. Trey said you need to understand how we support the things that EarthResponsible stands for."

We followed Kirk/Kuo through the length of the building, past more walls with double metal doors, past locked metal doors, past more machinery and equipment, through hanging strips of plastic and out another series of doors, finally emerging onto a concrete loading dock that ran along the side of the building and terminated in a landing on the bayou.

Everyone's glasses fogged up from our encounter with the warm morning air. "Happens all the time," Kirk/Kuo said. "We have to keep the humidity low in the building. Look over here."

Kirk/Kuo pointed to the conveyor belt system that ran in two sections, one from the area where tractor-trailers backed up to a loading dock, and one from the landing where boats coming down the bayou could tie up.

"All of this feeds the farm-raised crawfish into the separating sieves. We try to buy only from Louisiana growers, although the Mississippi growers think they can raise them. But what do they know? Half of them still call a 'crawfish' a 'crayfish.'"

"So they're grown in aquaculture, like catfish?" Weegie asked, both for her own benefit and on behalf of the rest of us on the tour.

"Not so deep. More like modified rice fields. In fact, many are raised on what used to be rice fields. Sometimes, on flooded fields used at other times of the year for soybeans. We're almost at the end of the season.

Kirk/Kuo pointed to several refrigerator-sized wire tubs tilted on an angle. "We run water through them and sort them. We've got five sizes of sieves. Only two are up right now. Put crawfish in, start the water, and they just slosh through. The big ones stay in the main drum. The smaller ones drop through to the next. The pieces and debris drop out the bottom," he said, pointing to a trough that ran through the loading area, "and we dispose of all that."

That stuff being disposed of had to be shipped somewhere. But so what if this went to Camellia Industries? There was nothing toxic about crawfish. No need for an injunction to shut down a company for taking crawfish waste. You could bury it in a hole or grind it up and fertilize fields.

Kirk/Kuo continued leading us through the building. "Once they've been sorted by the sieves, we turn the tubs upside down. The crawfish go right into the pots."

We accompanied him back into the cool interior of the building, where we followed the path of the conveyor belt and ended up in front of tremendous containers. They were as tall as I was, and the streams of rising steam were whisked up into vents that hung from wires.

Kirk/Kuo shouted to make himself heard. "These are our boiling canisters. Each holds four hundred gallons. We can process up to two tons of crawfish a day if we have to. Just wait a minute, but step back so you don't get splashed. We're about at the end of one of the cycles.

A soft, electronic bell went off and machinery next to one of the containers whirred. A pulley in the ceiling, its thick chain clanking, turned and lifted a gigantic mesh basket, filled with glistening red crawfish, from the huge vat, pouring them into another tub.

"Once they cool down, the ladies over there peel them and then we package the tails. Twelve-ounce and sixteen-ounce packages for stores; four-pound packages for restaurants. Fresh crawfish. Can't beat it. We also flash freeze the smaller sizes for use throughout the year – the season, even though the growers have extended it, can't last all year, but the demand for crawfish surely does."

"I have a question!" It was the woman on the tour who was still wearing her broad-brimmed straw hat, even though we were indoors.

Weegie whispered to me, "That's Myrna. She and her husband are quite a pair."

Myrna pointed to the Asian women who worked the piles of red bodies, and asked "Do *they* live around here? Morris, *they* don't look like they belong here, do they?"

Morris grunted again.

The women on the line pretended not to hear the question or the tone with which Myrna spoke. They merely carried on, efficiently eviscerating the crawfish, putting empty shells on one conveyor belt and expertly extracted tails on another, ignoring Myrna's implied insult.

Kirk/Kuo responded with a tinge of sadness, "They, I, we – we're all living here now."

"Here being St. Bonaventure Parish?" Myrna inquired. "I didn't see a lot of houses or apartments on my way over from Baton Rouge. Is there a town or neighborhood nearby I missed? This is really in the middle of nowhere, isn't it? I mean, do people really live out *here*?"

Kirk/Kuo tried to ignore her insensitivity. "They live here, *here* being the United States."

Myrna hit her husband in the arm. "Morris! He knows what I mean. He's making fun of me."

I could see that Kirk/Kuo was not going to bother to explain to Myrna that south Louisiana was filled with the second, third, and now fourth generations of those who had escaped from Vietnam as boat people, or who had gotten out through Laos or Cambodia. They had come here because they knew about fishing and seafood, and because the climate and the waterways reminded them of home.

As we entered the next room, Kuo flipped a switch. Overhead doors came down, sealing off the crawfish picking room and relieving the women on the production line of having to endure more of Myrna's insensitive comments.

Kirk/Kuo corralled us towards a set of double doors. "This will be our last stop. I think this is the part you'll probably remember most. That's what everyone says after we take them through this next section."

CHAPTER 33

IRK/KUO OPENED THE STEEL LATCH. This room was a good ten to fifteen degrees colder than the crawfish and shrimp processing areas.

The doors slid shut behind us. We were in another metallic room. Racks of tall cylinders, each marked with a skull and crossbones inside a yellow triangle – the symbol for toxic chemicals – were propped against the walls. The center of the area was filled with wide stainless-steel tables on wheels. Each table, at least fifteen feet long, had a deep trough that emptied into drains in the floor. The roof was lined with overhead rods along which ran pulleys dripping with chains, each of which ended with a thick two-foot long hook. A modern-day Inquisition could have been held here.

"This," said Kirk/Kuo, rubbing his hand across the top of the slightly convex surface of one of the tables, "is what you've all heard about."

The group gathered around him. They didn't want to miss anything.

I hung back. There was nothing here I hadn't seen in other places. This was just fancier.

"Alligators are an endangered species," said Kirk/Kuo, "but not here in Louisiana. And Mr. Trey is a big supporter of EarthResponsible. I'm told he contributes lots."

"That's what they say," said Weegie, fingering one of the hooks that hung low over the table; it swung gently back and forth on its chain as she touched it.

"Nutria are not endangered. Neither are most snakes. We process them all. Nutria used to be big in the fur trade, but that's dropped off a lot. Almost can't give it away now. Still, we do some nutria. Some muskrat too. We treat the pelts in the next room. But here's where we do skins. Reptiles some, but mostly alligators. We process them. Harvest the meat. Tan the hides. That's what those chemical tanks are for – please don't go near them or touch any of the valves. Nothing wasted in any alligator we get. We handle it all, start to finish."

"You know, before I read the brochure for this tour, I thought you couldn't even sell alligators legally," said Myrna. "I mean, Morris had a pair of alligator shoes, but I made him give them to the Salvation Army when we joined EarthResponsible, didn't I Morris?"

Morris nodded in reluctant agreement.

"As those reading materials we sent out to you explained," Weegie said, "here in Louisiana you can sell alligators if you have a permit." She seemed displeased at the idea that permits would even be issued.

Kirk/Kuo continued his pre-programmed patter. "You need permits each step of the way. There's a short hunting season. Each hunter is licensed. Each alligator is tagged when caught. The Wildlife and Fisheries agents are very strict. They check the tags when the boats and pirogues come in from the bayous. They check the tags again when they come here. And we can't even harvest the hides until the agents are present. There's a shortage of agents right now – they're stretched too thin and we're stacked up, although they should be here next week and then we can start again."

"I don't understand all this. And he talks in a funny accent," complained Myrna to Morris in a voice that was loud enough for all to hear.

Weegie was gentle but firm. "Myrna, why don't we let this nice man finish the tour, and then there will be plenty of time for questions at the end. Here's a pad and an EarthResponsible pen. It would be great if you could take lots of notes so that you can help us all when we get to the Q&A session."

Kirk/Kuo looked relieved and thankful for Weegie's help.

He pointed to some diagrams in frames on the wall. "Having an agent present when we do the skinning is critical, not only because it's illegal to do it without agents around, but also because each year we have to cut the skins differently. These are the patterns for this year. The cut changes from year to year so that any agent looking at a skin can tell in which year the harvest occurred."

Kirk/Kuo walked over to a large stainless-steel door on the side of the room. "Until the agents arrive for the cutting, we keep the alligators in here."

He pulled open the door. Inside was a huge walk-in freezer.

Piled almost to eye level were stacks of dead alligators. Bony-plated backs and deadly faces with ferocious features. Eyes staring blankly. Open mouths with razor-sharp teeth. Vicious claws, bigger than catchers' mitts. Stiff-ridged tails protruding at odd angles.

The group became excited. They pulled out cameras and cell phones, holding them high over their heads, trying to get a good shot of the interior of the freezer. Shutters snapped incessantly.

"Almost fifty of them in here right now," Kirk/Kuo said. "It's all a self-contained system. See those pulleys? We hook up the gators to bring them over to the peeling tables. Skin goes into the treatment tanks for tanning. Flesh goes to the restaurants."

"Restaurants?" asked Myrna, squinching up her face in disgust.

Weegie shot her a look and Myrna immediately quieted down and wrote something in her pad.

"Yes," Kirk/Kuo continued. "Restaurants. Alligator tastes kind of like chicken...swamp chicken. Very good in a stew."

Kirk/Kuo started to close the freezer door, and as he did, Weegie announced, "Alligators are endangered, and but for a quirk in federal law and state politics, their skins would not be 'harvested,' to use the euphemism, to provide high-class handbags and shoes and wallets. Or food for tourists. Don't you let me catch any of you sampling any 'swamp chicken' on this EarthResponsible tour!"

Kirk/Kuo was still trying to shut the freezer door. A frozen alligator carcass had slipped from the side of the stack. Kirk/Kuo kicked at its tail, trying to clear the door jam.

The tail, stiff and frozen, wouldn't budge.

The door couldn't close.

"Stand back a minute. I'm going to have to restack these." Kirk/Kuo went to one of the tables, opened a drawer underneath it, and pulled out a pair of thick gloves. "If you're not careful, you can get caught on the claws or teeth."

With both hands, he pulled at the tail that was jamming the door. He yanked hard, trying to get the offending alligator out of the freezer. He pulled on it again and it moved. As he dislodged it, a portion of the stack inside the freezer shifted.

Backing out of the freezer door and hauling the dead gator with him, Kirk/Kuo let it slide on the floor in front of the group. It was almost ten feet long. One or two of the men prodded it with their feet, marveling at its size and its five-toed front legs and four-toed rear ones.

Kirk/Kuo returned his attention to the freezer door, but it was too late.

The pile inside the freezer had continued to shift.

The gator that Kirk/Kuo pulled out had set off a chain reaction.

The middle of the pile slipped forward.

More tails and claws and jaws flowed toward the freezer door.

The top layer moved as well.

Slowly but inexorably, one body slid over another, and the door was blocked even more than before.

Still the movement continued.

Then, from inside the pile, as the frozen alligators spilled out of the door, something unusual became visible from under the top layer – a man's arm, followed by the head and shoulders to which it was connected. His eyes were glassy and his skin a cold, deadly pallor.

Myrna fainted.

Weegie gasped.

I took a step forward to get a closer look.

It was Spider.

CHAPTER 34

SHERIFF ISAIAH BROWN SLAMMED HIS pad down on the counter in the lunchroom of Wholesale Flesh and Fur. The cheap wire spiral top came undone and the pages started to come loose.

He could engage in all the theatrics he wanted. It wasn't going to faze me in the slightest. I did what Catch taught me. If you're engaged in a battle, you have to *be* in the battle; you can't be anywhere else. You can't let any other thoughts distract you from the immediacy of the moment, whether that moment is the middle of a trial, the critical part of a negotiation, or, in my case, the midst of having a law enforcement officer try to intimidate me into saying something I'd later regret.

So, I put all thoughts of why Spider was dead out of my mind and stopped thinking about who could have killed him and how he had gotten in the freezer. I would deal with all these later. Now, I concentrated on flowing with the moment.

I leaned back in the chair, stretched out my legs, and yawned.

That made Sheriff Brown rant even louder. "You're in a hell of a fix, as I see it counselor. Yesterday morning you're sitting in my office in the courthouse, acting as the lawyer for Taylor Cameron. You're the lawyer who bailed her out. Why the judge would even fix bail on this murder rap I'll never understand. That's strange, I'm thinking. Then you're with Cameron right down the road at Poirrier's, and you admit that you met Spider Louiviere there last night as well. That's even stranger. And then this Spider guy shows up murdered, and you're here when the body is found. Now why shouldn't I hold you as a material witness? In fact, why shouldn't I go to the judge and get her to revoke Cameron's bond and hold you as a suspect at the same time? Give me one good reason."

I remained completely calm. I wasn't on the stand. I wasn't under oath. I could freely ignore any question I didn't want to answer.

"Are you finished with me yet? I've been more than cooperative." Of course I had cooperated. There was no reason not to, given all the witnesses who could identify Spider, Taylor, and me from last night.

"And that's all you're going to say, Mr. Law School?"

"It was a pleasure meeting you again, Sheriff." I got up to leave. I knew that would set him off, and it did.

"Sure, sure, you know all your rights. Got a head stuffed with cases and statutes. Got a fancy degree hanging somewhere. Think you're smarter than lots of us. Well, go ahead. Don't level with me. Play coy and pretend I don't know about your being at the public meeting at the gym."

That did catch me off guard for a moment. I didn't know that anyone from the sheriff's office had seen me at the meeting, or, if they had, that anyone had recognized me. Then I realized I had told Rad and Weegie, and the Sheriff had already questioned her. Maybe she was the source. Or Rad. Or both. My being in the gym was no secret in any event.

I didn't show any reaction, however. I simply started toward the door, but the Sheriff moved to block my way.

I stood my ground. "Why don't you open the door for me, since you're in front of it? I'm sure you don't intend to have a wrongful detention."

"What a crock!" Sheriff Brown said. "You disgust me. Go ahead. Don't let me 'wrongfully detain' you from getting your ass out of here. Just remember, Counselor, you and me are going to go another couple of rounds before I'm finished."

CHAPTER 35

I EDGED MY WAY PAST the Sheriff and into the crawfish processing area we had toured hours earlier.

The ladies who had been working on the assembly line had taken off their lab coats and were talking among themselves. A group of uniformed state police officers, some of them still wearing dark glasses and their tall, broad-brimmed hats, were joking with uniformed members of the St. Bonaventure Sheriff's office. A police photographer, his camera gear slung heavily around his shoulders, was conversing with two ambulance drivers in medical green.

And, coming toward me, were Weegie, Kirk/Kuo, and a husky man with a big grin – Beauregard "Trey" Sanders, whom I had headed out here to see.

Trey paused in front of three uniformed officers, raising his voice to be heard above the machinery. "How much longer y'all gonna be?"

They shrugged their shoulders.

Trey came toward me, right arm outstretched, pumped my hand in greeting. "Schex! Haven't seen you in a coon's age. Terrible thing, Schex, to meet like this. Kirk told me you were here; seems the Sheriff has commandeered part of my plant for his investigation. Hell, come on back to my office. Let's catch up on old times."

Trey's interior enclave was paneled in aged cypress. A large desk, spotless, with only a fancy pen set on its surface, stood in one corner in front of a high-backed leather executive chair. A laptop computer was open on the credenza. Pictures of wildlife hung in expensive frames on the walls. Geese in flight. A nutria raising its head out of the water at sunrise. An alligator coursing through the water. An egret perched on a cypress tree. Each photo was signed and dated, products of a prominent Louisiana nature photographer. Intricately hand-carved duck decoys rested artfully on illuminated shelves built into the walls.

"Kirk called me at home. When I got here all hell was breakin' loose. Kirk told me all about the poor guy in the back freezer. Discovered right in front of Weegie here and her tour. Damn shame. I had hoped to make this a special day for EarthResponsible. I guess they'll remember it, but for all the wrong reasons. Sent 'em all back on the bus. They were as skittish as a turkey during hunting season. I'll get Kirk here to take Weegie back when we're done."

I was sitting on the leather sofa. Trey settled into one of the deep armchairs and Weegie occupied the other. Kirk/Kuo remained standing, awaiting Trey's bidding.

Trey gestured around his office and toward the plant beyond the door. "Look at all this great shit! Who'd have guessed? There we were, years ago in law school, me struggling like hell to understand all that first year stuff and you managing to fly through with high marks. Boy, was my family fried when I bombed out, despite all your help. Damn law school professors didn't seem to care about helping a football star pass. Ol' Calandro's grade knocked me completely out of the running. Really skewered me good."

I humored him. "Looks like it was my assistance that let you down, but the Red Knight seemed to have done you a favor, giving you the opportunity to go into business. You've done quite well for yourself since then."

"'Quite well' ain't the half of it. If I had been a lawyer I'd be slavin' away, night and day, to make a buck. Here, I got other people to do the work." He reached over and gave Kirk/Kuo a heavy pat on the back. "Right, Kirk?"

Kirk/Kuo replied with a dutiful employee's obsequiousness. "Right, Mr. Trey."

"The damnedest thing is this guy in the gator cooler. Horrible. Really is. But we're not going to let it ruin the party tonight, are we Weegie?"

Weegie chose her words carefully. "I don't think the success of a party, even a party for EarthResponsible, can be equated with the death of a human being. I came a long way for all this, but it's not the most important thing now, is it? I mean, we all support the environment, which is another way of affirming life, yet a man is dead."

"Dead. Right in my place. A damn shame. But," he said cheerfully, "life's gotta go on."

"And that's all you have to say? 'Life's gotta go on.'"

"Come on, Weegie, you know what I mean. I'm sad, all right. See how sad I look? Well, shit, it's true that I don't look that sad, but I'm-sure-the-fuck upset. Got the Sheriff's people and the state police and who knows who else crawling 'round my processing plant, poking their noses into everything, shutting down production. Big-haired reporters out there in the parking lot, acting like this was the crime of the century. For God's sake. I saw the body. Bullet through the temple – close range it appeared. Not a big weapon – '22 pistol I'd guess. If someone had been hit with a '38 or a '44, it would have made a mess. But this was small caliber and neatly done. Wish some of the hunters who sell me pelts could do it as neatly."

Weegie crossed her arms angrily. "You're complimenting the murderer and comparing a man to a pelt?"

"You do beat all. For someone who knows so much about the environment, you ought to know something about hunting too, just to even things out. A hunter would know what I meant. A clean kill. Not a long, painful death."

"You mean," Weegie said, shaking her head in disbelief, "not like the slow death that the environment is suffering, the slow death that the residents of Cancer Alley along the bayou are suffering from. Death is death; don't rationalize it away."

"Yeah, dead is dead is dead. But a slow death is worse – for man or animal. It's needless suffering. At least the guy in the freezer didn't have that."

"Not a slow death," said Weegie, "but certainly a needless one."

Silence.

She glared at Trey. "Do you really plan to go through with the party?"

I had been waiting for an opening to bring up the subject of what Wholesale Flesh and Fur had sent to Camellia Industries, besides waste from the crawfish, shrimp, and crab processing. I wanted to ask why their receipts gave no detailed information. I wanted to ask about how Trey disposed of the toxic chemicals in the alligator area, but the conversation kept spiraling further and further away.

"I didn't set all this up not to go through with it, little lady. We're gonna raise big money tonight for EarthResponsible."

Weegie stood up. "I'm not your 'little lady.' I didn't come down here just to raise money. And I'm not at all comfortable about this. I'd like to go back to my hotel now."

"Now, don't get all huffy. You really want to go all the way back to D.C. and tell your boss that you came all the way down here to skip out on the event and miss out on bringing back that big check?"

Weegie paused.

"Now you and I both know that EarthResponsible needs the funds. Probably already got it budgeted for the next quarter."

Weegie pondered the situation. "It doesn't seem right at all. Not right at all. And yet..." She seemed to resign herself to her predicament. "OK. I'll be there tonight to pick up the check at the ceremony."

"That's the way. Kirk, you run along and take this nice lady back to her hotel. On your way out, however, you tell those pickers to stop that yakking and get back to work. We've got a load that's got to be out tonight, and they're gonna have to work double hard to get it out on time."

Kirk/Kuo escorted Weegie out.

Trey, with a big conspiratorial grin, turned to me as the door closed behind them. "What you gonna do? Washington, D.C. woman – thinks she's hard." He gave a boisterous chuckle. "Let me get in her pants. Then I'll show her something hard."

Trey, still amused at how clever he perceived himself to be, went over to the illuminated shelves that lined the walls. He pushed a button and a panel popped open revealing a refrigerator. "Get you a beer?"

He tossed me one and grabbed another for himself, popping the top and slugging it down in a continuous gulp. He settled back into his chair, boots on the glass table. "Kirk works his tail off. Best manager I've had."

"He seems very competent."

"Competent as hell. The place almost runs itself now. Shame I'm gonna have to fire him."

CHAPTER 36

TREY'S FIRING KIRK/KUO SEEMED heartless, but I didn't care. I knew I had nothing to do with Spider's death, but the Sheriff seemed to be trying to pin it on Taylor and implicate me. I had an incentive to find out anything that could help point to the real killer. "If he was involved, why would he open the freezer in front of a tour group or move the gators knowing there was a body in there? So, why fire him?" Ask the question with open curiosity. That was Catch's technique.

"Because he fucked up bad," Trey said. "It was his job to lock up the freezer yesterday. He's supposed to check daily on everything before he leaves. Now, how do you think that body got there? Just crawled in and buried itself among the gators?"

"You think one of the other workers did this without his knowledge?"

"Shit no. None of my employees would dare do anything that would slow down production. They're paid by how much they do. Any pause for any reason, like right now, costs them big bucks."

"So someone inadvertently left all the doors open?" Catch always said that the best way to get an answer is to make an effort to appear more dense than the person you're talking to. Because I was talking to Trey, I had to make an extra effort.

"You are the goddamnedest thing, Schex! You don't know nothing about this business, do you? In fact, from what I hear, you don't know much about *any* business right now, including the law business." He reached into a drawer. "Want some of these peanuts? No? Well look, we lock the freezer doors and drop the shutters to the equipment rooms, but we don't lock the dock entrance when we're expecting shipments. We leave the bays on the bayou open so that the trappers can pull the gators up next to the freezer. If they come in after dark, as they often do, then the next morning we run a tally and put 'em in the freezer. So all the trappers and all their kin – and that about covers this and all of the neighboring parishes – know how we operate. That's why Kirk fucked up big time by leaving the freezer unlocked. I really don't give a damn about the body, you understand – as long as the cops get out of here soon so that we can resume production – the fuck up is that someone could have taken a couple of the gators. Those critters are worth beaucoup bucks."

"I still don't understand." This time it was true. Trey seemed more concerned about losing alligators than having a dead man in his freezer, but I wasn't going there. "If they didn't know the freezer would be open, why bring him here at all?"

"Damned if I know. Maybe he was shot here. Maybe he was dumped here. Everyone around here knows that those alligators in the freezer weren't going to be processed for quite a while. Maybe whoever did this figured they still had a couple of weeks before anyone got down into that pile. Maybe one of them did it. Gators have been here for almost two weeks, waitin' for the Wildlife and Fisheries agents to get here for the skinning. Those trappers don't get paid their money until the cutting is done. Maybe it was one of those Laotian or Cambodian fishermen. They deliver stuff here all the time and have been all over the plant. They've got a grudge against some of the gooks who work in the plant. Something to do with that old war, or maybe with fishing rights out in the Gulf or maybe it's some gang shit. Can't figure out what they get so excited about all the time. Can't understand a damn thing most of them say anyway. Could even have been one of the truckers who pick up the refrigerated shipments – I got to keep on friendly terms with them. Give them a couple pounds of fish or crabs. They like to watch some of the processing when they come. Could have been almost anyone, once the stupid door was left unlocked."

"So you think he *was* shot here?"

"Beats me," Trey said. "Lots of ways to clean up blood here, and lots of blood accumulates in that freezer. Gators are brought in and they keep on dripping until they're froze solid. We put drains in that freezer when we built it. But, anyway, someone got in here and I'll not let this ruin me. Spent too much time building this place up to have some publicity like this shut me down. I've ordered all new locks; ordered an electronic alarm system too, just this morning since I've been here. Here I was concerned that someone could get in and ruin some equipment. Never thought I'd need an alarm system to keep dead bodies out."

Keep dead bodies out? I figured Trey wasn't counting the thousands of carcasses that had graced the plant during 'processing.'

Trey drained a second can of beer, tossed it into the wastebasket, reached out to punch the button on the sideboard, waited for the refrigerator to appear, and leaned back and retrieved another beer, all without getting out of his chair. "So, I gather from what the Sheriff told me – I supported Isaiah in his last two campaigns and give to the Church Youth League he heads up – that you're doing something involving Camellia Industries."

I avoided the question and instead presented Trey with one of the light red invoices that I had taken from the boxes Spider had delivered. "This is yours, right?

Trey looked at it perfunctorily. "Yeah."

"Been doing business a long time with Camellia Industries?"

"Hell yes. Since the beginning. Ten years or so. Uncle Carter got the start-up costs arranged for me. Got me a building loan. Greased all the right wheels. Got me hooked up with Camellia Industries. Couldn't have done it without Uncle Carter."

That would be Trey's uncle Carter H. Herrington, IV, Secretary of the Department of Environmental Health.

"Used to be a bitch getting rid of that stuff," said Trey, "especially all those tanning solutions, and then G.G. came along. It was great. That fat old man sure could fix things. That's what Uncle Carter used to say.

And that gal G.G. Guidry lived with, Taylor – great bazooms and a tight ass. But, you were married to her, so…" he smirked, "you know all about those bazooms."

He was right about that. Of course, it was only later that I found out that Taylor had what my high school friends in Des Allemands called a *sein chaleureux*, a welcoming breast. Her breasts had welcomed more hands than it takes to unload an ocean going vessel. Welcomed other male appendages as well.

In any event, no wonder the State Department of Environmental Health was pushing all-out to defeat the injunction. Uncle Carter was helping Trey, and Trey was disposing of all his used processing chemicals, undoubtedly toxic, through Camellia Industries' licensed facility. At least a facility that was licensed until last week's injunction. And if Trey couldn't dispose of his chemicals, he couldn't continue to operate. Trey needed G.G., and Uncle Carter was helping Trey stay in business. One big happy family.

"Tell you what," said Trey. "Why don't you come to the event tonight?"

"You mean that thing with EarthResponsible that you and Weegie were talking about? I wasn't invited."

"'Course you weren't invited. You don't have enough money. You don't travel in the right circles, Schex. But don't worry. Come on, you can be my guest. It's the least I can do for an old pal. Gonna be fun. We're having a big *cochon de lait* at the Club Champs D'Èlysèes. Roasted pig served by waiters in tuxes, along with champagne in those tall, fancy glasses. Gonna be great. A band. Dancin'. Black tie. Old ladies in pearls. Young gals in those low cut, sparkly cocktail dresses – they bend over and you get a view. It is gonna be *the* place to see and be seen."

I acted as if I was reluctant. No harm being seen with the power clique. With the $2.8 million I'd figured out to get free and clear, I'd soon be one of them. "Well, if you insist."

Trey raised himself out of his chair and led me out. "Then I'll see you tonight. Come around seven. The Sheriff ought to be finished about now, and production is behind."

He looked at his watch. "Damn. Not gonna get to go fishing today. Whole beautiful day shot to hell."

CHAPTER 37

AS SOON AS I LEFT Wholesale Flesh and Fur, I headed back to Baton Rouge to meet with Taylor and Lolly Marston.

Lolly's office, which was several blocks down from mine, bore no resemblance to mine. Lolly's success was reflected in the immaculately restored details of her antebellum cottage and her meticulously kept lawn with flowering plants blossoming from every corner. Skylights streamed sunshine into the high-ceilinged rooms and bathed her antique consoles and cabinets in a warm glow.

When I arrived, Taylor was already there. A young guy sat in a chair on the side holding a tablet computer. After the usual round of greetings and some pleasantries, including introducing us to her associate – Cecil "Beau" Faessen, Jr. – Lolly launched into the business at hand. "This is a joint meeting of counsel. I want everyone to understand that."

"You don't have to be so formal, Lolly; after all, we are all among friends," Taylor said sweetly.

"Taylor, I'll defend you. Spare me the southern belle routine. Beau, take notes."

Beau nodded his head. He was ready.

"Now, we're going to do this by the book. No waivers of any privilege. Schex and I talked about this when he first contacted me, Taylor, and it's going to be tough to keep the privilege intact with two separate counsel, one for criminal work and one for civil. Although there is a joint defense privilege, we're not going to give the D.A. a shot at busting it with some theory that it doesn't apply across civil and criminal lines. Understand?"

"I'm being given a lesson in the law?" asked Taylor, still all sweetness. "Do I have to take a test, Lolly?"

"You have to listen and understand, Taylor," said Lolly sharply. "Judge Rochbauve…"

"Francine?" interrupted Taylor.

"From where you sit right now, Taylor, it's Judge Rochbauve. Remember that. She did you and Schex a favor on the bail. I don't want you to indicate to anyone outside of this room, even inadvertently, whom you may know or how you know them. So let's start right here, right now."

"Judge Rochbauve. I got it."

"The judge gives legal education seminars on criminal procedure and privileges. No way are we going to take any chances. On those things we have to do together, we will, but on everything else we're going to meet separately. Schex and I are going to keep separate files. We're going to lock this down as tightly as possible. Is that understood?"

"Understood," echoed Taylor, with honeyed tones.

"And one more thing." Lolly obviously was not happy with Taylor's simulated attitude of confectionery cooperation. "As a favor to you, and as a favor to Schex – after all, I've known you both a long time – we're having this initial meeting before I've received my retainer. But, this initial meeting is as much as you get for old times' sake. Before we go further, before I do any more work, you will have to pay me my retainer. In full. Is that clearly understood?"

Taylor's false smile remained fixed. "Pay you? Of course. That's the rule. I *pay* you. You *work* for me. I understand everything just fine."

"You'll be just fine and justly convicted if you don't follow my instructions," Lolly snapped. "Now that we've all postured, let's get started."

Lolly looked over at Beau. He was typing quickly, wearing a look of bemusement.

Lolly turned back to Taylor. "Now…" She waited for Taylor to speak.

Instead of responding to Lolly, Taylor turned to me and said, in her most saccharine tone, "Where would *you*, who also work for *me*, like me to begin?"

I wasn't going to let her play me. "OK, Taylor. Begin with the truth. Why did you give all those boxes of corporate documents to Spider? And don't give me any more shit about being worried about their safety. Who, besides you and me, would even care about those books?"

I addressed my next comments to Lolly. "I have the corporate binder at my office. The bylaws give Taylor a right to purchase G.G.'s shares in the event of his death. At book value. And that's a hell of a lot less than market value."

"A motive for murder," Beau murmured.

Taylor snarled at him. "Well, smart-ass, I may have had a motive to murder fucking G.G., but I didn't." Turning to Lolly and me, Taylor composed herself. "I've told you both I didn't, and that's the truth."

"Assuming that statement is correct," I said, "you still haven't answered my question. Who would care about the corporate books, besides you and me?

"Why, 'The Snake's' son, of course. Spider knew about that, which is why he called me after you and I left Poirrier's last night."

"He called you?"

"Sure. I met him later in the parking lot of Wholesale Flesh and Fur."

CHAPTER 38

AS SOON AS I EXPLAINED that Spider was dead, found in the alligator freezer of Wholesale Flesh and Fur, Taylor gasped. Was she visibly upset, or was this another one of her ploys? Beau was so astonished his tablet computer slipped off his lap and hit the floor. Lolly said, "This is going to require an increase in my retainer."

'The Snake' had to be Carmine 'The Snake' Micelli, the don of 'the family' in New Orleans. He ran the unions that serviced the wharfs and the restaurants, and supplied busboys and waiters and truckers. He controlled the drugs that flowed into and through New Orleans, as relentlessly and with as much volume as the Mississippi River flowed through the Crescent City. He controlled the prostitution rings. It was said he controlled a number of politicians throughout the state.

I started in on Taylor. "Why would 'The Snake's' son want the books? How would Spider know about that? Why did you meet with Spider after we left Poirrier's? Why, Taylor, why?"

"It sounds pretty bad, doesn't it?" Taylor's voice had a slight quiver in it.

"It sounds," said Lolly, "like you're going to make the prosecution's case easy and mine difficult as hell," said Lolly.

Taylor buried her face in her hands. "Help me. Both of you. Please! I didn't hurt Spider. I couldn't hurt him. He was like this big teddy bear." She reached into her purse, pulled out a tissue, and blew her nose.

I wasn't buying the sobbing routine. Neither was Lolly. Seeing that it was getting her nowhere with us, Taylor's eyes became dry and her voice cold.

"You all want the truth? Well here it is, Schex. According to Spider, no matter what G.G. said to your face, he didn't trust you. Spider said he had talked to people about you and that you'd only mess up once you found out G.G. and I were involved. He said you were incompetent to do anything beyond putting together some simple corporations. Spider called me on my cell phone, after you informed him you weren't going to be my criminal lawyer. He was actually relieved. Spider told me that he had a way of getting me to a real lawyer, a quality lawyer who could really help. He said he had already made a phone call about that."

Beau had abandoned his cracked tablet and was bent over a legal pad taking copious notes.

Taylor seemed to be piling lies upon lies. "He told you he had made another call? To whom? If it was on either of your cell phones, the cops will track it all down. And you didn't tell me any of that before? Come on, Taylor, Lolly here is trying to help you, and all you do is talk in riddles. How was Spider going to hire a 'quality attorney'? Did he have any money?"

"I have no earthly idea who he called! Come on, I'm trying to tell you what I *do* know, not what I don't know. Besides, he sure didn't have any real money. Why do you think he worked for G.G.?"

"So how was he going to hire you an attorney?"

"He said he had ways."

"And why meet at Wholesale Flesh and Fur? Why not at Poirrier's, or, better yet, back in Baton Rouge?"

"Because he lived down in St. Bonaventure, and because he said he used to meet G.G. at Trey's plant from time to time."

Lolly was confused. "Trey? Which Trey?"

Trey is a common name in south Louisiana. Many sons carried their father's and grandfather's names. Grandpa would be "Senior," father would be "Junior," and son would be "Trey." I explained to Lolly that Taylor was referring to Trey Sanders, owner of Wholesale Flesh and Fur and nephew of Carter Herrington, the head of the Department of Environmental Health.

Lolly continued pressing Taylor. "And what happened when the two of you met?"

"Nothing. Honestly. Really. He just wanted to re-assure me that he was going to take care of me. That was all. It was a two-minute meeting in the parking lot. And then I left."

"Taylor," said Lolly, leaning forward in her chair, "you and I are going to have a conversation, and depending on what you tell me, I'll decide whether I'm going to help you after today. Maybe…just maybe we can stay one step ahead of the D.A., at least for a day or so."

"And the Sheriff too?" asked Taylor.

"No," Lolly explained, "you don't get it, do you? The black Sheriff and the white D.A. down in St. Bonaventure Parish are political enemies. They work together because they have to, not because they like each other."

Taylor was baffled.

"Why," asked Lolly, "do you think you were arrested by the Sheriff before the D.A. could act? Before the D.A. could charge you and call a press conference announcing the charges? It was because the Sheriff was trying to paint the D.A. into a corner. They didn't really have anything on you at the time except your foolish statements about wanting G.G. dead, so the Sheriff had nothing to lose. If the D.A. didn't charge you, the Sheriff could claim to his constituents that it was because the D.A. was trying to protect white people. And if the D.A. did charge you, as he did, then it was only because the Sheriff had acted first. Either way, the Sheriff gets a political plus. So, the D.A. is going to want to counter that. If they find out that you were at Flesh and Fur with Spider last night, the D.A. is going to move to revoke your bail and do everything in his power to use you to grab the limelight for himself."

Taylor looked up hopefully at her. "So, what can we do?"

"*We* are not going to do anything. You're not part of the 'we.' First, I get my retainer, and then the only two things you're going to be occupied with are telling Beau and me the complete truth and then doing as I instruct. Precisely as I instruct."

"Well, don't look to me for the retainer," Taylor shot back. "Talk to Schex. He knows where the money is. All $1.6 million of the money G.G. took from Camellia Industries' accounts."

CHAPTER 39

"LOLLY," I SAID, "YOU AND I need to talk. Privately."

"Beau," said Lolly, "you stay here with Taylor. I want you to go through with her – at least twice, understand? – everything she did yesterday, from sunup to sundown and back again. I want to know when she woke up, when she had breakfast, what she had to eat, when she took a pee. Everything. Take lots of notes. Don't miss a thing."

Lolly and I went two rooms down the hall into Beau's small office and closed the door.

"Lolly, you're right. We have one day, maybe two if we're lucky, before this thing is connected back to Taylor. Defending her is in your bailiwick. I have the corporate books, and I'll arrange for you to get your retainer in a couple of days."

"Schex," Lolly said, "you don't understand the time frame here. I need the retainer. *Today*. Things are really serious, now. I agreed to this meeting with the two of you because we've known each other a long time. And I'll let Beau debrief Taylor for a couple of hours. But, friendship only goes so far, and from what I've heard already, I'm going to be earning my fee. I've learned from experience; get that retainer up front or you don't get it at all. And, by the way, in light of what Taylor just revealed about meeting Spider, the retainer is now an even million dollars, not $775,000. I guarantee you, I'll be earning every penny of it if I am to keep her out of prison.

I was willing to act fast. "I understand. I can have the retainer for you in cash in half an hour."

"No! No cash. Are you crazy? Do you know what I'd have to go through at the bank, filling out those cash reports for amounts over ten thousand dollars? The feds would be all over me, what with all the talk today about money laundering being related to terrorism. If I got that much cash, it would only throw suspicion on me. Look, I spent three years fighting a RICO forfeiture claim where the feds were trying to get my fee, claiming that the monies were the proceeds of my client's 'criminal enterprise.' I'm not going to give them a toe-hold to come after me again. The most I'll take in cash is $8,500. Run the rest of the money through your trust account and get it to me. I'll take a check for the balance. But, I warn you, I always call first to make sure that it will clear. Don't make me withdraw from the case tomorrow morning if the money's not there."

"But, it's already after noon," I pointed out. "I'll just give you the cash and let you hold it, and then we'll take care of the paperwork later."

"I do it by the book, Schex. I don't touch cash in excess of ten K. That's the federal limit on reporting. I don't touch cash at all – that's what you do. I never deposit ten thousand or more in cash into my bank; I deposit checks. I don't care how you do it, and I don't want to know. I just want my check. Today."

CHAPTER 40

ONCE YOU GET TO THE edge of the ledge and start to slip off, knowing that there's no way back, you might as well jump.

Well, I had been slipping every moment since I first opened the suitcase. This wasn't part of my initial plan, but what the hell, I knew from my days at Old Parish Mortgage exactly how to deal with it, even if it meant having to cross over the line a bit. So, I didn't merely jump over the line and off the ledge, I vaulted into potential disaster.

I knew what I had to do. Get the money out of the crawl space. Organize the crumpled bills into packages ranging from $7,010 to $9,880 – strange amounts to throw off suspicion. Avoid using the money in the counting machine wrappers, which would only spark questions. Travel to as many local banks and savings and loans in one afternoon as I could and open several accounts at each one under a variety of titles – all trust accounts for my office. A large flow of cash into an attorney's trust accounts – although not within an exception to the federal banking statute, with its $10,000 cash trigger on forms that had to be filled out – usually wouldn't arouse concern.

But as I pulled into my driveway, I rejected all those schemes. Why help Taylor one more minute? Why give anything to Lolly? G.G. was dead. Spider was dead. My practice was never going to come back. The money from the suitcase might as well be mine. The hell with legalities. Take the cash and run. That seemed a realistic possibility the more I thought about it.

As I entered my front door, however, I was shocked to see that my house had been ransacked. The leather chairs had been cut open, their stuffing flung on the floor. All the shelves had been pulled down and their contents scattered everywhere. My desk had been rifled and its drawers broken. All the file cabinets were on their sides, folders pouring out of each disemboweled metal container.

As I was trying to absorb what had happened, I was grabbed from behind by an iron grip. I was forced back into the hall and then into the conference room and slammed into a chair.

While I was still being restrained by rough hands, a wire was wrapped around my neck. It began to tighten, not enough to cut off my air supply, but enough to keep me fearful that if I moved or struggled, it would tighten more.

The man behind me wrenched my right arm and, slipping a loop of wire over my wrist, bent it behind me. I was shoved forward and then pulled back. My arm was now jammed between my back and the slats of the chair.

He attached the wire around my wrist to the one around my neck so that when I tried to move my right hand down, the noose around my neck tightened.

I endeavored to use my left hand to reach behind me to hit the man holding me, but I was not quick enough. A large, calloused palm shoved my face down against the top of the table. My left hand flailed in the air helplessly.

"Do I have your attention?" a deep voice asked.

I grunted. That was all I could manage with the wire around my neck.

"Good," said Deep Voice. "Now, I'm going to ask you a few questions. I know you'll want to be completely truthful with me, won't you?"

I was yanked back upright. My right hand was crushed against the wooden back of the chair.

"We found the paperwork you had done for G.G.'s new companies, and boxes of Camellia Industries' shit, but where's the rest of it?"

I shrugged my shoulders to indicate that I didn't know what the man behind me was talking about.

"Wrong answer." The wire tightened. The cold, cruel strand cut into my neck. My breath was immediately cut off as the wire constricted the airway above my Adam's apple.

I struggled but I couldn't move.

I tried to twist my body, but I couldn't.

I could feel my heart pounding and the veins pulsing in my neck. I was in good shape. I could jog for miles without being winded, but after a minute or so of unsuccessfully writhing to free myself, it was no use.

I couldn't extricate myself from the man's grasp or from the wire. I couldn't breathe and my lungs began to burn, becoming a vast center of an unquenchable desire for air. Then everything – the need to breathe, the will to resist – started to recede, and I knew I was blacking out.

But, when I had almost lost consciousness and had started to slump down in the chair, the wire around my neck suddenly loosened.

I frantically inhaled, filling the void that just a moment ago gripped my lungs.

I couldn't seem to get enough air. I coughed and could feel the blood ooze down my neck from the wire's cut.

I was panting hard and just beginning to collect my thoughts when Deep Voice spoke again.

"Once more," he said. "The rest of *the things* belonging to Camellia Industries? Where are they?"

I tried to turn toward Deep Voice, but the wire tightened. "Don't move – Just answer the question."

I said nothing, frantically trying to think of a way to escape.

"You are fuckin' gonna die, you know that?" Deep Voice said it not as a threat but as an inevitable fact.

Deep Voice momentarily loosened the wire, but before I could do anything, he brought it under my chin and yanked down so hard that my neck was bent backward. All I could see was the ceiling. Deep Voice remained out of my line of sight.

My right arm was still pinned behind me, and a second man, whom I couldn't see, grabbed my left arm and pulled it taut across the top of the table.

Out of the corner of my eye I caught the glint of a knife blade. A moment later, I felt the blade as it carved a line from my forearm to my wrist in one swift motion. The sensations came in three waves. First, the cutting. Then warmth where the blade had sliced. Then pain. Excruciating pain. I tried not to scream, but I couldn't help moaning from the torment.

"Let's try that answer again," Deep Voice said, "or the next time Ribeye cuts you, I guarantee it will be worse. Where is it?"

What could be salvaged at this point by keeping silent? Only my life. There was no reason not to give Deep Voice what he wanted. I had run out of options. "Up above the ceiling."

I clenched my jaw and gritted my teeth, trying to not give Ribeye or Deep Voice the satisfaction of hearing any further moans from me. "Really," I managed to get out, "there's a crawl space. I'll show you."

"This house ain't got no attic," said Ribeye. "We already looked." He twisted my left arm, turning my palm up and opening the fingers of my balled fist.

Deep Voice said, "Feel that?"

I could. Ribeye was tapping a knife blade on the tips of my fingers.

"Now, if you're not telling the godawful truth, Ribeye will first cut your balls off and then remove each finger, one at a time. So, I'm going to let you get up, very slowly, and you're going to take us to where the stuff is hidden."

The wire was removed from my neck and wrist. My neck, now no longer craned backward, ached as my eyes focused.

Sitting across from me was the one called Ribeye, a guy in his fifties. A slab of muscle with a keg of a chest and a pylon of a neck. A broad, broken nose. A face as flat as a cheap carnival mask.

When I looked down at my left hand, which was pulsing with pain, I almost passed out. My shirtsleeve, which had been white, was maroon, split open from the elbow down. Blood was pouring from my arm, spreading over the top of the table and dripping onto the floor.

Deep Voice pulled my chair away from the conference room table and swung it around, me in it, facing the fireplace. He had maneuvered it so that I still couldn't see him.

I tried not to show how much pain I was in, but I involuntarily groaned.

"Shut up!" commanded Deep Voice, giving me a painful whack on the back of my head.

"Ribeye, go get something so he doesn't bleed all over the goddamn car."

Why were they mentioning a car? I was going to give them what they wanted.

I heard Ribeye go toward my bedroom and then return. He threw the sheet from my bed on the floor at my feet.

Deep Voice came around from behind me and picked up the sheet. Now I saw him. Like Ribeye, he was also in his fifties. At least six foot eight. Linebacker's build. Thick mane of salt and pepper hair pulled back into a short ponytail that hung over his collar. Eyes that showed no mercy. Swarthy complexion.

Deep Voice picked up the bloody knife from the table and wiped the blade clean on my slacks. He used it to cut the sheet into long strips and bound them tightly around my arm. The first layers turned red immediately, but by the time the fourth strip was wrapped, it was a dull pink. When he had finished, my now useless left arm was wrapped from biceps to palm.

"OK. Now where's this fucking attic?"

He helped me to my feet and I showed them the access panel in the slatted hall ceiling.

"Well," said Deep Voice to Ribeye, "what are you waiting for?"

Ribeye grabbed a chair from the conference room. Standing on the chair, he punched the panel loose. With an effortless, acrobatic move, he pulled himself up into the opening. "Where is it?"

Deep Voice tapped the blade against my cheek.

"Under the insulation. Garbage bags."

A stream of insulation poured through the hole, followed by the trash bags, which hit the floor with a thud. Ribeye leapt down from the opening and landed lightly on his feet. He peeked in each plastic bag. "It looks like it's all here. Sure is a hell of a lot of it."

"Get the bags and all the other stuff we found in the car first," said Deep Voice. "Then come back and take this piece of shit. You may have to carry him out."

I guess he did, because the next thing I remember was being in a car in the middle of nowhere.

CHAPTER 41

SATURDAY

AT FIRST, I BECAME AWARE of my arm. My exquisitely painful, aching, burning arm. Then I became aware of the hum of the engine and the wash of the tires on the roadway.

I opened my eyes.

I was propped up in the back seat of a large sedan. Ribeye was driving. Deep Voice sat next to me. When he saw I was awake, he put the flat of the blade of the knife on my ear. "Sit still and there won't be any problems."

To our left, the black of the night sky was giving way to dark blue streaked with luminescent crimson. In either direction, marsh stretched out to the horizon. The water in the ponds and canals reflected the gathering light. The asphalt road we were traveling on was only three or four feet higher than the water level, built up on a mound of dirt dredged from either side of the macadam trail.

The sky lightened some more. White egrets flew gracefully in the early morning light, flapping their wings slowly.

The marsh grass was a pale green. Lilies spread out, choking the open water. Spindly horned beaksedge and delicate lizard's tail rose in clumps from spots along the edges of canals.

I was taken by the beauty and the remoteness, and then I realized that, for a moment, my misery had lessened. I had to concentrate on something other than my arm.

I forced myself to focus not on what I felt but rather on what I could determine.

If they were going to kill me, why hadn't they done it at the house? To avoid leaving a body?

Who were they? I figured they wanted the money, but they also took all of the boxes with the Camellia Industries documents. For what purpose?

Were they the ones who killed G.G.?

Were they the ones who killed Spider?

Were they now going to kill me?

The sky was getting brighter, although the sun still wasn't up. The eastern horizon was turning a crimson red. Above that, blended by the gentlest of palettes, were mauves and pinks which mixed into azure as the stars slowly disappeared.

The car slowed and swerved to the right onto a dirt road. I groaned again from the pain as we lurched and bumped toward the still-dim western sky, my arm radiating agony with each jolt.

The swamp grasses had given way to low-lying land. Palmettos gathered at the feet of cypress trees and formed green islands out of which rose scrub hardwoods.

The car stopped at the end of the spit of land. The marsh stretched out beyond us, severed in two by a wide canal that passed by the edge of this little peninsula. Ribeye got out and, holding a gun on me, motioned where I should go.

I was directed to a small dock on the edge of the canal. My left arm was raw and stiff beneath the strips of bedsheet. Each movement made the cloth feel like sandpaper against my torn flesh.

Deep Voice positioned himself where the dock met the land. I followed his instructions and walked to the end of the dock. Meanwhile, Ribeye removed the garbage bags, the five boxes, and the folders containing the paperwork I had done for G.G. from the trunk, along with both my iPad and laptop.

Ribeye backed the car far under the trees and emerged carrying a machete. He sliced down dozens of broad palmetto leaves and covered the car so that it was almost impossible to see if you didn't know it was there. Then he made several trips to bring the machete and everything that he had taken from my office and placed them all next to the dock.

Then…nothing.

Ribeye sat on a box. Deep Voice stood his ground, watching my every move.

I was tired and lay down on the dock. If they hadn't killed me by now, then at least I could rest a bit.

We were there for a long while.

When I opened my eyes again, the sky was all blue. The sun was above the horizon, the heat was oppressive, and dozens of mosquitoes were swarming above my arm, attracted by the bloody bandages. I tried to swat them away, to no avail.

"There it is," Ribeye said.

I struggled to get into a sitting position and turned to look in the direction Ribeye was pointing. For a few minutes, I couldn't see anything, but then I heard the sound of an engine. After a moment more, I could see the tip of a slanted pole moving through the marsh.

I managed to get to my feet, my left arm hanging down, even more painful than before.

The pole in the marsh was the antenna of a boat. A man was at the wheel, although I couldn't see him distinctly because the sun's glare was reflecting off the windshield.

As it got closer, I realized that what I had seen was the third deck of a large vessel – maybe fifty or sixty feet long. Sleek. White. Clean. On the bow were coiled ropes and a shining brass anchor attached to a thick metal chain that disappeared into a brass-covered hole.

Ribeye helped tie up the boat. I was directed to get on board. I struggled to do so. Ribeye impatiently grabbed me around the waist, hoisted me over the gunnels, and dumped me onto the deck. My head pounded. My arm was afire. It was almost unbearable. I could barely think.

Only after Ribeye had loaded everything else onto the boat did Deep Voice loosen the lines and jump aboard.

The boat backed away from the dock and proceeded down the canal. The vibrations of the huge engines flowed through my body, further aggravating my bandaged arm.

I longed for an end to the pain. I longed for sleep.

I closed my eyes.

CHAPTER 42

I T WAS THE CHANGE IN the engine sound that awakened me. I was stiff. The sky and air were ablaze with light. Sweat poured off my forehead. My clothes were damp with salt spray and perspiration. My arm was throbbing uncontrollably.

Ribeye was nowhere to be seen. Neither was Deep Voice.

Using my good right hand, I steadied myself and slowly stood up, looking aft. I could see nothing but deep blue water with gentle swells humping across its surface from horizon to horizon. No land. No boats. No ships. The sea moved slowly in gelatinous undulations.

I turned around to see what was in front, and, grabbing the ladder to the second deck, I stared in amazement at a forest of tremendous stanchions, each ten feet in diameter or more. They were encrusted with green and blue eruptions, glistening barnacles that climbed fifteen feet above the surface of the water that continually grabbed at them, then ebbed, dripping away. The metal trunks stretched high above the boat, dwarfing it, a grid of beams and crossbars, terminating twelve or more stories up. Far above I could see a platform reaching beyond the edge of the supports, and above that a multi-story metal building as well as cranes and pulleys. I realized we were miles from shore, among the deep-water oil rigs.

Ribeye was standing on the bow of the boat, rope in hand, tossing it at one of the thick metal pipes that formed the lower cross bars. On the second try the rope looped over the top and the end fell into the rising and falling water. He took a long pole with a hook on the end, retrieved the damp portion from the waves, and fastened it to the cleat on the deck.

The engines stopped and there was an immediate quiet. The boat slowly bobbed up and down while moving away from the oil rig, pulled by the current, until the rope was taut.

The ladder in my hand shook. A pair of tennis shoes appeared on the topmost rung above me.

I backed away. I was weaker than I thought. I grabbed the wooden railing with my one good hand and leaned against it, half sitting, half standing.

A man climbed down the ladder from the upper deck. He wore a New Orleans Saints cap, dark hair protruding from its sides and back. His red polo shirt – it had to be an XXXXL – flowed over vast rolls of fat. His cheeks, lips, and jowls were overfull. His face – a pie made with too much yeast. His skin was smooth and tanned, with a faint olive tone.

He appeared to be shocked by my appearance, by my neck scrapped raw from the wire, and by my bloody bandaged arm. Apparently, it was the first time he had come down to look at me. He called out peremptorily, "Frankie! Ribeye!"

Ribeye came from the bow, edging his way along the rail. Deep Voice – Frankie, now I had a name for him – climbed down from the upper deck.

"What did you do?" The fat man clearly was used to giving orders and having them followed. "I told you to retrieve Guidry's things, not to cut someone up. You're not working for Paolo. You're working for me. You do it my way."

They didn't say anything, but I noticed that Ribeye and Frankie threw a knowing look at one another.

"Where is it?" the fat man said, looking around the deck.

Frankie pointed to a hatch next to the ladder.

"The galley? Let's go."

The fat man took my good arm and helped me through the opening. The Camellia Industries' boxes I had gotten from Spider were on a table that was attached to the wall, surrounded on two sides by wooden benches with high backs and red cushions. The plastic trash bags were on the floor. On another counter were the files I had prepared for G.G., along with my iPad and laptop.

The fat man sat me down on one of the benches and settled heavily onto the other. Frankie and Ribeye did not take a seat, and the fat man didn't offer them one. They stood at the foot of the table.

The fat man looked quickly through the boxes until he found the Camellia Industries corporate binder. He licked his index finger and flipped through the pages slowly. He didn't rush. No one spoke. Finally putting these to one side, he picked up the files on the five corporations I had drafted for G.G. and followed the same procedure.

When he was through, he put Camellia Industries' corporate binder and G.G.'s files on a shelf and signaled for Ribeye to move the rest of the boxes, which Ribeye did quickly, stacking them in a corner of the galley.

Next, the fat man emptied the trash bags onto the table. Out spilled the stacks of wrinkled bills I had counted and wrapped with rubber bands, my handwritten scrawl of the amount on each package. Out came the bundled money with the torn counting machine wrappers that I had taped back together after counting each stack. "Frankie, is this everything? Are you sure it's all here?"

"We didn't count it. We just got everything together and brought it to the landing."

I was starting to feel faint again. The boat's oscillations were making me nauseous, and the pain in my arm was pulsing in unison with the movement of the vessel. From the gleaming brass fixture on the wall, I caught a glimpse of my face. It was sickly white.

The fat man commanded, "Put him on the bed in the cabin."

Frankie and Ribeye pulled me up roughly, each movement making the pain and nausea worse. They opened a mahogany door, revealing a bedroom. Red velour wallpaper covered the walls and surrounded the ports that looked out onto the Gulf. On a built-in teak pedestal rested a large mattress adorned in purple sheets and a red silk coverlet. They put towels down so that my bloody arm wouldn't stain anything and then closed the door so the fat man couldn't see.

It was then that they harshly threw me down on the bed, and Frankie punched me in the gut.

I curled into a fetal position, groaning in pain.

CHAPTER 43

I WAS ROCKING IN A HAMMOCK in the summer night. Taylor, in a clinging swimsuit, was seated at a nearby table, the moonlight painting her with a bluish glow. She held a tall slender glass in her hand. The champagne in it sparkled as she raised it in a silent toast to me. Her hair was loose and fell down around her shoulders.

The hammock swung slowly, in long arcs.

The table at which Taylor sat became a bed. She was toasting me from the bed, and I couldn't get out of the hammock to go to her.

I could smell perfume in the air. It was a scent I couldn't quite place. Like flowers. Mechanical flowers. Something metallic, different, strange and wondrous. A perfume with a petroleum base.

I felt an itch in my arm and scratched it.

The pain was startlingly immediate, coursing up to my shoulder.

I was not in a hammock.

I could feel myself awakening. It was not an instantaneous awareness of being awake, but rather that slow revival you experience when you long to return to the comfort of sleep but cannot; when you want to retreat into the dream but every moment draws away another drape, opening the curtains into full consciousness.

I opened my eyes. The cabin was dim and the air smelled of oil and gasoline. Of salt and brine. Of fish.

I struggled to sit up. My left arm was burning and itching where I had tried to scratch through the bloodied strips of sheet.

I managed to walk unsteadily to the galley. No one was there. The table was clear. The cash was nowhere to be seen.

I walked out onto the deck. Ribeye, fishing rod in hand, was sitting in one of the wooden trolling chairs that were fastened to a chrome stand. "He's awake," he said to the fat man, who was reeling in something off the end of the boat.

Ribeye pulled up his line and examined it. A fleshy lump of bait hung limply from a stainless steel hook. "Fuck! Lost it."

The fat man continued his battle. His rod rose up, and he cranked quickly and efficiently. Then the rod lowered again. I could hear the whine of the reel's drag as the fish struggled to free itself. The movement was repeated again. Rod up. Quick cranking. Rod down. Whine of the drag.

The fish moved under the boat. The fat man followed, walking around the deck, holding the line to the left, then to the right, up, then sideways. He played the fish. He worked the rod, a conductor directing a symphony in the sea. Up and down. A legato movement. The fish tired for a moment, and the fat man's hand was a blur as he reeled in the line.

Ribeye stood nearby, with a large net, ready to help.

The fat man bent over and looked into the water. "Damn. Thought it might be. Get the grapple."

Ribeye put down the net and reached under the gunnels. He retrieved a metal pole with an evil-looking prong on the end. He bent over the side of the boat, next to the fat man.

"Ready?"

Ribeye nodded.

The two worked together. The fat man kept the rod parallel to the water, cranking all the time, and Ribeye swung the pole with its curved, sharpened crook like a scythe.

Together they both pulled back and flung a shark onto the deck, writhing and thrashing, the hook and line in its bloody mouth.

Ribeye's metal prong was sticking from a deep wound in its side. The shark's mouth was agape, all teeth and blood and anger.

Ribeye unlatched a piece of heavy pipe from a bracket near the aft railing and walked cautiously around to the shark, which was flopping all over the deck. Ribeye grabbed the end of the pole, which was still protruding from the shark's stomach, to hold the shark in place and used the pipe to club it again and again, each stroke making a thick, resonating thud as he beat the life out of the creature. He worked with vicious efficiency, pounding it mercilessly until the pipe was bloodied and the shark was motionless. Then, giving me a sneer, he hit it one more time.

Frankie had come down from the upper deck holding his knife. In a practiced move, he went over to the shark and dug the metal prong out of its side with a few quick slashes. The end of the grapple emerged, dripping blood over the deck.

The fat man tightened the line. Frankie went to the shark's mouth. He cut out the hook and then grabbed the mangled body by the tail and threw it back into the water. It sailed over the edge of the boat with a rainbow of blood marking its trajectory.

While Ribeye pulled out a mop and bucket to clean up the deck, the fat man pointed to the galley. "Schex…isn't that what they call you, Mr. Schednaydre? I'm glad you had a nap. I think we need to talk."

CHAPTER 44

"YOU CAN'T IMAGINE HOW PLEASED I am to have an attorney like you representing one of my investments."

I didn't understand what the fat man was getting at.

Ribeye and Frankie stood behind my chair, looming over me.

He shoved a wine glass across the table toward me. "Here. Pinot Grigio. Very nice."

"You have something stronger? My arm hurts like hell." If I was going to be killed, I didn't want to end it with a glass of white wine.

"No doubt. Frankie sometimes gets a little too eager. Try this." He reached up to a high shelf and pulled down a bottle. "Lagavulin. Islay single malt. You'll like this. Sixteen years old." He filled a tumbler and put it in front of me.

The scotch was peaty and smoky. I gulped it down. Anything to quench the pain in my arm.

He refilled the tumbler to the rim. "I have read through the corporate documents on the five new corporations you formed. Fine job. Very complete. I've also looked at the Camellia Industries books. Everything is in order."

Why was he playing with me?

"Did you draft the Camellia Industries papers too?"

"No." That was all I needed to say. When faced with cross-examination, answer only the specific question and nothing more.

"But, you represent Camellia Industries, right?"

I shrugged noncommittally. At this point, what the else could I do? I had planned to take the money and leave Camellia and Taylor behind, but now these guys had the money and I had nothing.

Frankie jabbed his elbow into my bad arm, sending an electric shock of pain up my nerves. Everything ached again. My arm. My head. My whole body.

Frankie raised his hand, ready to strike me again if I didn't respond. "Mr. Micelli expects an answer."

Micelli! Confirmation that my situation was hopeless. The fat man had to be Carmine "The Snake" Micelli's son, the one Taylor had mentioned. "The Snake" had been brutal and merciless.

Frankie flipped open a switchblade.

"That's not necessary, Frankie," Micelli commanded, adjusting his Saints cap. "Go sit over there." He pointed to one of the red bar stools.

Frankie took a seat but did not put the knife away. Ribeye backed away from my chair and lounged near the cabin door.

"Come on, Schex," Micelli said pleasantly. "You might as well have a drink. We're out beyond the 12-mile limit. Blue water. International seas. Beyond state borders. Therefore, I feel perfectly comfortable in asking how you like representing Camellia Industries."

How did he know my name? What was the purpose of his questions? He had everything now. Why did he need to ask me anything?

"It's really not a hard question. Either you do or you don't represent the corporation. Surely, you seem to represent Camellia Industries. You watched it from a boat in the bayou. You attended the meeting at the St. Bonaventure Gym. You were at Wholesale Flesh and Fur with Trey the day that Spider's body was found. You were married to Taylor and were with her at Poirrier's."

He sure knew a lot about me.

Micelli leaned forward. "Let's not be coy, Schex. Keeping cash hidden in an attic in plastic bags! Rather gauche, don't you think? So, confirm for me whom it is you represent."

I figured he was going to kill me, regardless of what I said. I took another swig of scotch. "If you know so much, why is that important?"

"Frankie, he has spunk, don't you think?"

Frankie approached, waiving the switchblade under my nose. "I'll slice the fucking spunk right out of him. Just give me a chance."

"Put that away! You've done enough damage already. You and Ribeye go up on deck."

Deep voiced, muscled, ponytailed, short-tempered Frankie let the short fat man, over whom he towered, command him like a servant and huffed out, followed by Ribeye, who slammed the cabin door behind him as he exited.

"Now, Schex," said Micelli softly, "you can tell me. Whom do you represent? It's either telling me, or having me let Frankie work on you some more."

"That's not much of a choice is it?" Why bother to do anything other than lay it all out. "Taylor was going to retain me to represent Camellia Industries at the injunction hearing coming up next week. Not likely I'll be there, is it?"

Micelli ignored by question. "See how easy that was. And the money? That's Camellia Industries' money?"

"That's what some people think." Who could know anything with G.G. dead? All I knew was that it was never going to be mine.

Micelli raised his wine glass and toasted me. "See how simple it all becomes. I ask that you confirm your client, that you confirm your status as an escrow agent for the money. Now it's clear. I am pleased you have been protecting my investments."

"What investments?" I blurted. "I'm not your lawyer. You hire your lawyers by kidnapping them and having them beat up?"

"You'll forgive me, I'm sure, for Frankie's excesses. Of course, you are not my personal lawyer, but you are most definitely the attorney for one of my investments."

I had no idea what he was talking about. "You've got the books. You've got the money. But you have no 'investments.' I checked the books. Camellia Industries was owned 50-50 by G.G. and Taylor."

"Ah, Schex. For an attorney with a degree to have said such a thing! I am amazed. Even I, a mere English major and classics minor – even I, who only made it through the first year of law school at night – even I can comprehend such legal documents. You clearly did not read them carefully."

"Great," I sulked. "This is the quiz before Frankie comes in and finishes me off?"

Micelli's face broke out into a cherubic smile. A smile that said trust me. A smile that was knowing and warm. A smile in direct contrast to his cold, calculating gaze.

Micelli reached under the table and pulled out the Camellia Industries' white three-ring binder, the one with the stock ledger. He opened to the tab labeled "Stock Certificates" and swiveled it around for me to read.

I looked at the certificates as Micelli slowly turned the pages. Two separate certificates, each numbered, each for 500 shares. One in G.G.'s name, one in Taylor's name.

I took another sip of scotch. The alcohol was numbing the pain in my arm, but my head remained clear enough. "See, I told you. 50-50."

"Certainly, but did you read the stock powers carefully?" Micelli turned over the certificates. On the back of each of their documents, G.G. and Taylor had signed the stock power in blank.

Micelli was right. I hadn't read the documents carefully. I had been in such a rush that I had only read the books perfunctorily enough to satisfy myself that the only stockholders were G.G. and Taylor and that the two of them were the only directors and corporate officers.

Undated stock powers signed in blank are like checks payable to cash. Whoever holds the stock certificate is the owner. No one would normally keep signed checks payable to cash in their checkbook. No normal corporation would have stock powers, signed in blank, for just anyone to fill in and claim ownership.

Micelli pointed out another unusual aspect of the stock powers. G.G.'s certificate had G.G.'s signature on it, but, above that, in Taylor's handwriting, was an endorsement of the stock to Taylor. "You see this, don't you?"

I did, and I realized that this only raised more questions. An endorsement transfers ownership. Had G.G. meant for the stock to go to Taylor? Had Taylor gotten him to sign the stock over to her? Had she tricked G.G. in some way to sign the stock power in blank, and then later filled in her own name?

So, who was lying to whom? Did G.G. lie to me? Did Taylor? And what was Micelli's part in all this?

Micelli tapped his thick index finger lightly on the back of each certificate. "And of course you recognize this." On each of the certificates was a stamped inscription in red ink:

"THESE SHARES ARE SUBJECT TO THE PROVISIONS OF A PLEDGE AND SECURITY AGREEMENT, COPIES OF WHICH ARE ON FILE IN THE COMPANY'S OFFICES. THESE SHARES ARE NOT REGISTERED UNDER FEDERAL SECURITIES LAWS OR STATE BLUE SKY LAWS."

Whatever he was going to do to me was going to happen regardless of what I said, so there was no need to hold back. "I didn't read the back of the certificate. You know that already, but I would have seen a security agreement had one been in the binder.

"No doubt. That's because I have the original." Micelli opened a green folder he had retrieved from a locked cabinet and handed it to me. Four pages of single-spaced legal jargon that I understood. This was why Micelli had said that Camellia Industries was his 'investment.' The stamp on the back of the certificates indicated that the stock secured a loan, a loan that had to have been made before G.G. and Taylor signed the endorsements, because their signatures covered part of the stamped text.

The four-page original that Micelli had placed in front of me showed that G.G. and Taylor had given a security interest in all their stock to 'LaCIE, Louisiana Commercial Investment Enterprises, LLC.'

Until whatever loan LaCIE had made to G.G. and Taylor was paid off, LaCIE controlled Camellia Industries.

I pushed the original security agreement back across the table to him, "This is why you needed the corporate books, isn't it? You didn't have the original stock certificates, and without them you were unsure if you could really enforce your security interest. G.G. was screwing with you, wasn't he? Well, now I guess you've got it all. The company. The stock. The money."

"Perfectly correct. And if you represent Camellia Industries and if I have 'it all' pertaining to Camellia Industries – as you said – then you represent my investments. See, there was no reason for your denial earlier, now was there?"

I stared out the window into the azure swells that rocked the boat. How much longer did I have to live? "If you think I'm Camellia's attorney and if you think you own Camellia, then fine. I resign."

Micelli wagged his sausage of a finger back and forth like a metronome. "You're so doctrinaire. What's the matter? You represented G.G., such a paragon of virtue, and yet you suddenly resign when you think I'm involved? You can't imagine how pleased I would be to have an attorney like you."

He was smug.

I was aching in pain, anger, and fear.

The throbbing in my arm was constant and increasing. I was angry at myself for getting into such a mess. Angry at being powerless.

And fearful because I knew my life was about to end. What he had in mind was obvious. I was going to be killed and dumped in the ocean, out beyond the 12-mile limit. No one would ever find out. I would be one of those missing persons whose whereabouts and fate are unknown.

I sighed and said, dejectedly, "You have no power over whether I resign or not. That's *my* decision. So make whatever decision *you're* going to make and get on with it."

"I can oblige on that account." He turned towards the hatch leading to the deck and bellowed, "Frankie! Ribeye!"

CHAPTER 45

"STAND OVER THERE," MICELLI COMMANDED to Frankie and Ribeye as they entered the cabin. "Next to the porthole."

They did as instructed. Frankie had to bend over because of the low ceiling, but his lip curved upward in a grin of anticipation as he pulled out his switchblade.

"Put that away," snapped Micelli.

Frankie did so reluctantly.

Turning to me, Micelli's tone was suddenly gracious. "If Frankie and Ribeye roughed you up a bit, I apologize. Sometimes they are overly enthusiastic."

Micelli looked over his shoulder and said peremptorily. "Frankie, apologize."

Apologize? I thought Frankie was going to lose his temper and lunge at Micelli.

But Frankie did nothing of the kind. He took a deep breath, shook his head in disgust, and said, without any feeling at all, "I apologize."

Micelli signaled for Ribeye to say something.

Ribeye mouthed, "Sorry." He didn't mean it any more than Frankie.

Micelli waived them away, and they went back out onto the deck, grumbling.

After the galley door closed behind them, Micelli leaned over the table toward me. "My apology, unlike theirs, was from the heart. And believe me, they really will be sorry. Made that abundantly clear to them while you were asleep. They were my father's employees, but his way isn't my way of doing business."

So, I was not going to be killed? At least, not just yet? I couldn't figure out what the hell he was up to, but now I was emboldened. "Besides assault, kidnapping, and theft," I asked quietly, not wanting to be heard by Frankie and Ribeye who might be lingering outside, listening, "what is *your way* of doing business?"

Micelli laughed. Not a vicious laugh. Not an evil laugh. But an open and pleasurable one. "Let's see, you think I engage in theft? In violence? Surely you misconstrue my gentle nature."

He leaned back in his seat and gave a toothy grin. "If it were not for me, Frankie would have enjoyed tossing a finger or an ear – one at a time – overboard while you watched the sharks dine on such delicacies. If I was what you think I am, why would I even bother to sit here with you and have this conversation? What more do I need from you? Just your *quiet* assistance."

"Do I have any choice?"

"Certainly." He went to one of the cabinets, brought out a large can of cashews and put them on the table. From another cabinet he brought out a black plastic bag like the one I had used to store the cash in my ductwork crawl space. It contained a package of some sort.

"Action that's louder than words," said Micelli. "There's $513,113 inside. You take it, along with the corporate books. You say nothing about this, and you can do with it as you please."

CHAPTER 46

"YOU'RE GIVING ME BACK HALF a million and the corporate books? Leave with my life? And what do I have to do for this?"

Micelli scooped up a handful of cashews. "You know what has occurred in the modern age? We've lost a sense of magic. We've lost our imagination. Look out that port. We're a speck floating two thousand feet above the ocean floor, surrounded by blue water. There was a time when the world believed that awesome creatures roamed the seas. Great, wondrous monsters. Huge things that swam up from under the waves to destroy vessels with the flip of a tail a hundred feet long. Things that could take wing, darken the sky and, dripping foam, swoop down and bite a great sailing ship in two. And we believed in them. No, belief is too weak. We *knew* they existed. We had never seen them, never heard their roar, but we knew they were there. They simply were. Like giants and gorgons, like griffins and gargoyles, like mermaids and manticores and cyclops and dragons. The world was inhabited with wonder and magic."

He washed the nuts down with a gulp of wine. "We've gotten so advanced. We no longer believe in magic. We test our way through the world. Can you feel it? Can you touch it? Can you detect it? Can you verify its existence objectively? Can you create an experiment that can be repeated and repeated and repeated once more to prove those things you can't see or touch or feel? And if you can't replicate the experiment, then it must not exist."

Micelli pointed to the Camellia Industries' binder. "I discovered magic. I discovered that imagination still exists. And I found it in the most unusual place – in my one and only year of law school."

He put a finger on the binder. "Look at this wondrous creature. A corporation. You can't see it. You can't touch it. You can't hear it. It can't speak. It's nothing, an invisible presence whose shadow is caught on paper. And yet, the U.S. Supreme Court says that it is a 'person.' Just think, all who believe in its existence are touched with its magic, and those who put their money where their beliefs are can be imbued with its genius. It creates a shield, invisible but impenetrable. Investors are covered with a necromancer's cloak, a corporate veil that cannot be pierced. A shell corporation they call it. But it's no fragile shell, easily cracked. It can be as strong and as unyielding as a mountain."

All of this was lost on me. Sure, corporations exist only on paper, and the Supreme Court has said that corporations have a ton of rights, like funneling unlimited money into political campaigns, but what did any of this have to do with Camellia Industries?

Micelli continued on. "Magic existed. For a while. But the magic is wearing thin. Pierce the corporate veil! Pretend it doesn't exist. Use RICO and claim all businessmen are racketeers. It's like a wizard's incantation – say Racketeer Influenced and Corrupt Organizations Act under federal law, and the invisible shield disintegrates."

"Or dies," I suggested. "Like G.G. and like Spider. Corporations aren't magic, and lawyers aren't magicians."

"But of course they are. You're a magician. You transformed G.G.'s thoughts into five entities that sprung out of the ether. Don't you realize that, even as we lose our belief in magic and wonder, our belief in demons grows? Demons that leach into the soil and air and water, waiting to fill us with evil to which we give modern names, like radiation, toxins, or carcinogens. Our belief in invisible evil is so strong we've created a whole industry to deal with our fears. We want fire and water to be summoned to destroy the evil. Fire to burn it. Water to soothe it. Waste treatment plants and incinerators. But, who

Michael H. Rubin

in their right mind would want to run these corporations when the magic that allows you to destroy such evil itself is so weak? Let someone claim that the fire was not strong enough, or that the water was not pure enough, and you have unlimited personal liability. Unlimited! Nothing is safe. Not your home. Not your car. Not your life savings. The corporate veil is cast aside and we are naked. But feed a corporation rather than *run* it – that's where there's still magic. There's enough belief in magic left to think that corporations have some existence, no matter how fragile, and these sylvan creatures must be fed. Their feed is invisible too; credits that transfer over wires, that exist as electronic pollen to be harvested as needed."

It was no good trying to respond. Micelli was going to lecture me. I had to listen as he shot off one metaphorical volley after another.

He kept using the word "magic." The "magic" of corporations to protect lenders from liability when they loan to those who poison the ground, water, and atmosphere as long as they are only creditors and not operators. Yep. Got that. Standard legal rules. So what?

The "magical" first eight years of his life, spent with his mother, sisters, and beloved "Papa" before "Papa" was "ensnared by the evil ones." That would have been his doting father, Carmine "The Snake," who pushed drugs, exterminated rivals, and ruthlessly killed anyone who got in his way. Carmine, who was convicted and given a double-life sentence for his crimes.

The "magic of the diaphanous veil" that protected "Papa" and the family, even against the "evil ones." He was referring to The Snake's ability to run his operations from prison and to avoid both the death penalty and deportation even as more charges were brought against him.

The "magical incantations" Micelli uttered to create the "spherical globe" around those most dear to him. That was his way of saying that he had decided to stay on the legit side of the family's businesses. As if what Frankie and Ribeye had done to me was legit.

He paused for a long time. I didn't say anything. I was exhausted and light-headed. And every movement of the boat made me aware of my festering arm.

Micelli looked at the huge gold wedding band on his thick finger and twisted it, turning it around and around. He then pushed the bag of money off the table and onto my lap. "Take it. If I kept, it would lead me to where the magic ceases."

I let the bag of cash slip off my lap and onto the floor. Why give me anything? Was this simply another way to frame me, to give him a reason to call Frankie and Ribeye back in to kill me?

Micelli went over to a locked cabinet and opened it, revealing the rest of the loot. "That's what is rightfully LaCIE's. It's the repayment of the loan my company made to G.G. – repayment in full. I keep what I'm owed, not a penny more. Do you want to see the accounting? I keep very precise records. You get the rest, the $513,113. Well, actually, the number came to $513,112.17 – I keep very precise records, but I've rounded this up to the nearest dollar. So take it."

I didn't reach for the bag that lay on the floor of the galley.

"Come on," Micelli said, trying to encourage me, "take it. It's so appropriate, and it keeps me and my business completely above-board. And as long as all I collect is principal, interest, and expenses – all documented charges that meet the letter of the law – I'm still wrapped in the magic; LaCIE protects me. Nothing that's done with or to the Camellia Industries property can touch me. No chemical spill can be traced to me. No toxic dumping is caused by me. No environmental cleanup bill can be laid at my feet. So, you take the rest of the money. I don't want it. You're the original escrow agent."

"You don't want it, so you just give it to me?"

Micelli bent over and put his mouth close to my ear. His voice had a terrifying coldness. "You won't go to the police, because you can't. What are you going to say? That you were kidnapped by some men who took several million dollars in cash that you just happened to have hidden in your house, money that you never declared to the IRS on a cash disclosure form. Form eight-three-double-zero, as I recall. And you're going to claim that you were released by these men along with half a million dollars that you still haven't declared? If you go to the police, do you think they'll let you keep the money? No, you won't do anything like that. You'll take the money. And you'll go home. And you'll say nothing."

He pulled the brim of the Saints cap down over his eyes and put on a pair of dark glasses as he moved toward the galley hatch. "And me? I'll be just a former creditor of Camellia Industries, looking for another loan to make."

CHAPTER 47

THE BOAT RIDE BACK COULD be described in one word – sullen.

I was in an untenable spot. Taylor had not told me about the transaction with Carmine "The Snake's" son, and I hadn't spotted it when I looked at the corporate books. Micelli was right; I couldn't go to the police about Micelli or Frankie or Ribeye without implicating myself in money laundering or worse – Sheriff Isiah Brown would have a field day. I had to figure out how to get far away, as fast as possible.

Frankie and Ribeye were sullen. When they found out that Micelli was giving me the remaining half million rather than sharing it with them, they said nothing, but their faces scowled with disapproval. They cast each other knowing glances, eyebrows raised.

The weather turned sullen. The humidity became palpable. The hot summer sky became gray and muggy. The gray turned to black, and the azure of the Gulf's deep water evolved into an acrid brew.

Micelli, on the upper deck, was steering the boat through the increasing chop. The wind came in ever-escalating gusts, a warm, damp breath that did nothing to relieve the heat. The sea roiled and the precipitation propelled down at an angle, splatting angrily wherever it hit.

The waves grew, building in bulk. The formerly gentle swells became mountain ranges. The big engines under the deck growled and vibrated as the vessel lumbered up the steep side of one wave after another, moving through the molasses of the sea. As the prow of the boat topped a wave, it teetered like a seesaw. The molasses turned to ice, and the vessel slid in a stomach-churning toboggan ride into the trough. The prow would crash into the inky water below, shake itself clear, and then the climb upward would begin again. Wave after wave after wave.

By the time we got back to the dock our clothes were soaked, and Frankie and Ribeye's mood was as foul as the weather.

Twilight was fading as they pulled the car out from its hiding place and made me lie down on the rear seat. My left arm was now a monster on my shoulder, a ghoul of liquid fire slowly and painfully gnawing at my nerve endings.

Ribeye opened up the back door again and angrily threw the damp plastic bag of cash that Micelli had given me onto the floor.

We drove for several hours. The twilight was long gone and it was black outside. I couldn't see a thing except the precipitation streaming down the windows, crystalline in the glow of Frankie's cigarette.

Eventually, the rain ceased. We were out of the storm. Ribeye, who was driving, turned the windshield wipers off. After a few more miles, he slowed and turned onto a gravel road. I could feel it under the wheels. Another ten minutes. Then the car came to an abrupt halt.

Ribeye shifted in his seat and turned around to look at me. Before he could see my face, I had closed my eyes, pretending to be asleep.

Frankie and Ribeye got out. I could hear them a short distance away.

"Thought I was going to fucking explode."

"Goddam, at your age you ought to know better than to think you could drink all that beer and drive hours in that rain without taking a leak."

"What about you, you old fart? From the sound of you over there, are you planning to fill up the damn bayou?"

"You're full of shit."

"Well, at least I'm not full of piss anymore."

They both laughed.

I knew better than to sit up.

"Fucking Tony Micelli. That little douche bag will never be half...hell, never be an inch of what his old man was."

Ribeye's voice was closer to the car now, somewhere behind it, near the trunk. "Tony the Dickface is going to piss away everything."

Frankie's dangerous voice cut through the darkness. "Damn right about that. First Tony walks away from the most profitable shit, lets Paolo take it, and then Paolo tells us we've got to work for Tony the Dickface. Then, Dickface can't do anything without shitting in his pants about maybe spending a few turns in the Louisiana state prison up in Angola or in one of the federal pens. No discipline. The old man made sure everyone knew where the line was. Cross it and you simply disappeared. Forever. Dickface here can't stand to even draw the line. I'm too old to sit by and let him ruin something the old man built up, running it all from Angola. Built it all up even bigger than it was before he went in. And now this little shit, who plays at being some kind of legit loanshark, thinks he can just give back half a mil? The old man would have cut his pecker off, son or no son."

I could hear their footsteps on the gravel as they paced around the back of the car.

"Frankie, do you think that fucker is going to keep his mouth shut?"

"Shit no. What the fuck does Tony the Dickface know about anything?" Frankie was furious now. "Does he know how to run an organization? Does he know how to get something done? Does he know how to push the right buttons?"

A loud, hollow thump came from the trunk area. The car rocked where Frankie must have kicked it. "Fuck! The only goddam things he knows are how to steer that pussy palace on the water, figure interest rates, and give untraceable money away to some shithead with a law degree."

Sounds of footsteps again moving away from the car. Their voices were now indecipherable but still full of vitriol.

I tried to raise myself up to see where they were.

My arm blazed in pain as I inched my way up slowly until I could just see over the back seat. Through the rear window, lined with streaks of water and road film, I could make out the dark figures of Frankie and Ribeye, backlit by the moonlight.

I tried to get a better look and peeked my head up a bit more, but just then Ribeye turned around, flashlight in hand, and spotted me.

I tried slinking back down but it was too late. Ribeye yanked the door open. "You fucking spying bastard!"

CHAPTER 48

RIBEYE HAULED ME OUT OF the car and punched me hard in the gut. I went down, trying to catch my breath. He pulled me back up and hit my bad arm.

I wasn't going to give him the satisfaction of screaming, although I was in agony. I bit my upper lip until it bled, but I couldn't keep from groaning as I staggered.

Ribeye reached in the car to retrieve the plastic bag filled with cash, slung it over one shoulder, and kicked me forward. He pointed the way with his flashlight.

I limped ahead, walking through damp grass, ankle high, and onto the muddy construction yard.

Heavy equipment was all around. Bulldozers. Cherry-pickers. Back-hoes.

And lined up, directly in front of us, were three large dark-green trucks, each with a huge, cylindrical canister behind the cab.

Ribeye led me to the door of one of the trucks. I could see in his flashlight's beam the logo on the door – an oval wreath of leaves surrounding the word "InDispoCo." The cab was high off the ground. The wheels of the vehicle were as tall as my chest.

Ribeye slung the plastic bag containing the cash up onto the front seat and strong-armed me through the mud to the rear of the vehicle. Ribeye pointed to the great metal maw of the oversized garbage truck. A yawning, rusty mouth with a tongue of soggy trash.

"Get in!"

I looked around. I was sure that, if my arm hadn't been injured and hurting like hell, I could outrun him. But I couldn't. Not now. Not in the condition I was in. And where had Frankie gone?

"Get the fuck in there." Ribeye pulled out a gun and aimed it at my face, its barrel a few inches from my nose.

I grabbed the metal bar with my good hand and painfully hauled myself up and onto the edge of the metal cave.

Ribeye waved his gun. "All the way back, you turd!"

I took a step into the cavernous belly of the container and sank up to my calves in slimy garbage.

Ribeye scrambled up behind me, perched on the top rung of the side ladder, and hit the edge of the container twice with his gun. The steel siding reverberated with a deep, metallic ring. The engine howled as it came to life and the truck sprang forward.

The abrupt movement threw me onto my back, and I sank into the contents of the container. Old papers. Filthy wrappers. Leaking bags. Decaying scraps of foul-smelling food. Soured milk in oozing containers. Smelly, greasy, putrid things. The detritus of homes and businesses. The useless cast-offs of society.

I lay there in the damp mass, my nostrils assaulted by the stench, and thought, with a curious detachment, that a few hours earlier I had been listening to Micelli weave metaphors. Now I had become one. A cast-off of the legal profession among society's cast-offs. A person Taylor had treated as trash for years was now lying in it. My life, in downward spiral, literally ending in garbage.

The truck rumbled through the dark night. Ribeye was silhouetted, positioned on the ladder outside the mouth of the canister, gun in hand.

I somehow managed to separate myself from the physical torment of my arm. As long as I had the power of speech, I had the chance to persuade. To challenge. To instill doubt.

I yelled, above the truck's din. "What will Micelli say, Ribeye?"

He flashed his light in my face. "Shut the fuck up."

"If I don't show up again, Micelli will know something happened. And then where will you be?"

"Asshole. Think you're so damn clever? You're nothing. You're not fit to lick the shit off this truck. Frankie's got it all figured out."

"Micelli will know it had to be the two of you. If I'm not around, what will Frankie do? Pretend it was your idea?

Ribeye leaned in and kicked a pile of debris at my head. It splattered over me. "You put your faith in Dickface Tony? What does Dickface really think *you're* going to do? Take part of the money? Not tell anyone? It doesn't matter. Dickface is convinced that the money isn't a problem for him, unless he keeps it. Stupid prick. So, the fact that the money disappears won't matter to Dickface. And you? If you're never heard from again, what'll he think? Frankie's got that down too. You're a fucking failure, and what do fucking failures do when they get their hands on money – real money, more money than they could earn the rest of their lives? They go live their life far from prying eyes. So, you could be somewhere in South America, in the Venezuelan interior, or in a mountain village in Mexico, paying safe money to some drug lord. You could be in Indonesia or in Cam-fucking-bodia for all anyone knows."

I shifted my weight and tried to pull my legs under me so that I could get into a crouching position.

"Don't you try to get up. And don't make me shoot you in this truck. The bullets will go right through you and punch a hole in the steel. Shouldn't have that. No holes in the truck, no blood here. But, I'll fucking blow you away right now if I have to."

I knew I didn't have much time. I couldn't grapple with Ribeye. I didn't have the physical strength with my arm all sliced up, and I doubt I could have overpowered him even before that. I didn't have a weapon, and there was nothing in the trash I could use, although I had been trying to feel around with my legs and good hand for something as I tried to steady myself.

I didn't know how much longer we had to travel. Or where we were going. But I knew this time that there was not going to be any Tony Micelli offering me a chance to leave.

The truck shifted gears, and the road surface changed. It was now a harsher, bumpier ride. The truck slowed somewhat as it went around a curve and then gathered speed again.

Another abrupt slow down. The trash shifted as the truck made a sharp turn to the left.

Ribeye leaned out, holding on to the rungs, and peered around the side to see where we had turned.

This was my chance. I raised up out of my crouched position, took as much of a firm starting stance as I could amidst the garbage, and jumped head-first out of the back of the truck, into the night.

CHAPTER 49

ITWISTED AS I LEAPED, trying to rotate and fall on my right side to avoid landing on my sliced and savaged left arm.

My right shoulder, ribs, and hips hit the ground at the same moment. The momentum kept me rolling from pain to pain as each part of my aching body came in contact with the rough asphalt. I heard the rending of fabric as the coarse surface ripped at my shirt and pants. The jagged pricks of the gravelly asphalt tore at my exposed skin, agonizingly grating it.

Dark sky. Flat marsh. The road inches from my eyes. Then sky. Then marsh. Then road. Over and over, I rolled helplessly until my momentum finally slowed.

I could hear the popping sounds from Ribeye's gun fading and the harsh bellow of the truck diminishing. But, while these noises were decreasing, others were gaining in intensity. The screeching of tires. Above the stench from my clothes, I could smell burning rubber.

I had come to rest face down on the road.

I lifted my head.

Something ominously wide and dark was looming over me, perched on all fours. Huge glistening teeth, the color of silver.

I blinked my eyes and focused.

The chrome bumper of a car had halted inches away from my head, close enough to comb my hair.

The vehicle's headlights, dark until this moment, came on, lighting up the rear of the retreating truck, illuminating Ribeye hanging on, gun still firing.

The truck turned a corner and sped off into the night.

I lay on the asphalt. Through the headlight's glare I saw feet. Old tennis shoes under jeans. First two, then four. Then a pair of hiking boots.

A figure attached to the boots bent down.

"Schex?"

It was Weegie.

CHAPTER 50

SUNDAY

"WE ALMOST RAN OVER YOU," Weegie said worriedly, wiping the grime and garbage from my forehead and cheeks. She sat next to me in the back seat of Rad Doucet's large SUV, continuing to gently brush bits of food and trash out of my hair.

"Make a habit of traveling in garbage trucks?" asked Rad from the front seat, as he steered down the road. "Strange way to get around at night."

"Enough, Rad." Weegie was in control. "Get him to a hospital. Did you see his arm?"

It was an effort to speak, but I forced myself. "No hospital." My voice was barely a whisper. "Just get me cleaned up. But no hospital. Please, no hospital."

* * * *

I felt a sharp pain in my left arm. I opened my eyes. It was morning.

I was in a small living room, lying on a couch. My shirt was off and a man was attaching butterfly bandages to every few inches of my sliced arm. He was gently squeezing the skin together and closing up the lengthy cut.

Weegie was standing, handing the man the bandages. "You're awake I see. Joleese was an Army paramedic in Iraq and Afghanistan. He can fix you up for the time being."

"You need a tetanus shot," said Joleese. "Can't help you there. Best I can do is to close you up and douse you with antiseptic, but you're gonna scar pretty bad unless you get stitches in this arm soon."

I smelled something warm and delicious. Rad entered the room with a steaming bowl. "Gumbo. Chicken and okra."

Weegie handed me a spoon and held the bowl while Joleese continued to work on my left arm.

Rad pulled up a chair to the foot of the couch and flicked a piece of dried crud off of my ripped and bloodied slacks. "Leaping out of midnight haulers? Damn if it isn't true that I can now legitimately call you white trash."

Weegie ignored him. "We almost hit you, Schex. Rad had wanted to show me a tracking mission on the midnight dumpers. Can't use headlights when he does that. He's had that yard under watch for some time."

"Industrial Disposal Company Inc., one of our fine local establishments," proclaimed Rad. "InDispoCo's got a great symbol – a wreath of greenery – for a company that hauls garbage during the day and then makes late night, unscheduled secret trips. Chemicals. Toxic industrial waste. That wreath of greenery should be a noose."

"Could have kicked myself for not having the camera turned on the whole time rather than waiting for the location shot," muttered Joleese, as he finished up the bandaging.

If they had video evidence of illegal dumping at Camellia Industries, there was no hope for Taylor or Camellia Industries. Not that I cared at this point.

Rad proudly explained. "Always carry high-def gear on tracking nights. When a truck gets to where it shouldn't be, we turn the camera on and film the unpermitted dumping. Put the date and the time right on the video. Got it also in infrared. Late night, low-light poses no problem. Got several hard disks of stuff. More than a couple of terabytes. All encrypted and loaded into the cloud for backup protection. After Weegie and I saw you the other night at Poirrier's, I told her that even if you were going to represent Camellia Industries in the injunction hearing that's coming up, I'd whip your ass. Now, I don't have to worry about that, do I?"

I knew what he meant. Why bother to respond? There was no point.

"You see," Rad said, turning to Weegie, "Schex can't represent Camellia Industries because he's now a witness. I'm going to subpoena him for this upcoming hearing to testify why he was on an InDispoCo hauler, why he jumped out, and what he saw. He can't be both a lawyer and a witness in the same case."

Rad sat back with smug satisfaction. "The hearing, Schex, is in four days. This coming Thursday. By the way, we amended the suit late last Friday afternoon. Named four more companies and sought injunctions against them, along with Camellia Industries, for environmental racism, for putting their plants where they do nothing but harm the black community. Gonna be a busy week. March on Monday. Gonna shut 'em all down by Thursday."

A march? A shut down? I didn't inquire and didn't care. And it was because I was worse off than where I had been before G.G. knocked on my door. No clients. No money. And now Frankie and Ribeye were out to get me.

I was screwed.

CHAPTER 51

R AD HAD TOLD JOLEESE TO drive me anywhere I wanted to go. I could think of only one place.

I couldn't go home. Ribeye and Frankie would be looking for me.

I couldn't go to my neighbor, Washington Eby. I wouldn't endanger the old man and his wife, no matter how much I had imposed upon them in the past.

There was only one place to head where Frankie and Ribeye would be unlikely to look, one place they wouldn't dare approach because the cops could have it under surveillance.

That made the decision disgusting but obvious.

I had to go back to Taylor.

* * * *

"*He* kept all the money that was mine, and then gave *you* back only $513,113 in a plastic bag, and you lost that too?" Taylor was livid.

I had taken a shower at Taylor's and was now dressed in some of G.G.'s clothes. His oversized T-shirt fell loosely around my body and his maroon sweatpants were too short on the bottom and so wide at the waist that I had to use one of Taylor's scarves as a belt.

I told her the whole story about Frankie, Ribeye, and Micelli. There was no reason not to at this point. About the entire $4,452,737 in cash G.G. had left with me. About the more than half a million that Micelli had given me and that Frankie and Ribeye had taken. About being kidnapped and sliced up and found by Rad and Weegie.

Did she show any sympathy for my injuries? Not in the slightest.

We were sitting in her kitchen drinking coffee. She was dressed in a thin chiffon robe that caressed her curves.

"Well, we're all fucked now, aren't we? And you did it, Schex! Blew millions away. My millions!"

"You hadn't told me about anything over the $1.6 million, Taylor, and you didn't tell me about the loan Micelli had made to the company, so don't act as if you weren't trying to pull one over on me."

"You were going to use part of the money to pay Lolly to defend me. What am I to do now?"

"Give Lolly a mortgage on this home," I said, calmly. "It's worth a couple of mil."

"Oh sure," Taylor snapped. "That'll fix my problems. Now, I'll have nowhere to live and no money to live on. If you had given me the money when I first came to you, it would be safe. But no, you had to keep it and act like 'Mr. Lawyer' and look for legal crap. Now you can't save me and you can't save Camellia Industries and it's all going to hell. Are you satisfied that you've destroyed me? You want all the fucking cards on the table? OK. What about I call Sheriff Brown and tell him that you had G.G.'s money all along? That makes you, not me, the perfect suspect for G.G.'s murder. Not to mention Spider's murder. Don't you think someone might say that Spider knew of the money and was just trying to get it to me, the rightful owner? Wouldn't everyone think that was a sufficient motive for murder?"

I had known she could be mean and vindictive, but I had never thought she would go this far. "And if you said that, Taylor, who would believe you? Particularly when I told them that you met Spider at Trey's plant that night?"

"But Schex," said Taylor calmly, "no one saw me there with Spider. And the only ones who have been told are my lawyers. You of all people should know that the attorney-client privilege can't be waived without the client's consent. So you see, Schex, it's a standoff. You can't do anything."

She paused for effect. "But I can do something for you."

CHAPTER 52

"TONY MICELLI IS THE KEY, you know." Her chiffon robe swirled as she went to the refrigerator and brought out a bowl of grapes. She took several and offered some to me. I refused them. "Don't change the subject, Taylor. What is it you plan to do 'for' me, as if you haven't already done enough to me?"

"How do you think Carmine, Tony's father, remained in control of everything from his Angola cell?

"Now you're asking questions rather than answering them?"

"Just listen, Schex. How do you think Carmine stayed in this country? Avoided deportation? It was Catch."

"Catch?"

"Catch did it. Carmine hired him big time, a few years after he was sent to prison. That's why Catch moved to New Orleans. That's what set Catch up in the big money. Suit after suit, appeal after appeal. Catch kept Carmine here. Catch set up the trusts that assured Tony the money he used to start his business.

"So, you're the one who put G.G. in touch with Tony Micelli?"

"Sure. G.G. had struck out with the banks and all the other commercial lenders. I knew Tony was in the 'special' lending business, and G.G. at that point was in the borrowing business. Which is why, when I found out that G.G. was siphoning money from the bank, I came directly to you. After I found out the bank account had been cleaned out, and after I had it out with G.G. at the Cotillion, I realized he must have put it somewhere and given the money or the information about it to you. And…" Taylor smiled ruefully, "I was right!"

She continued on, triumphantly blaming everyone but herself. "Goddammit, Schex. Men are so stupid. G.G was stupid, thinking with his prick when he met that Millie Sue girl. Thinking he could outsmart Tony. And you've lost all the money. I had to get some payments to Tony if G.G. wouldn't. And G.G. had started thinking he could outsmart me. The bastard!"

"Taylor, if you feel that way about G.G. now, how could you ever have taken up with him?" I regretted asking the question the moment it was uttered. I was giving her an opportunity to open old wounds, and she took it.

"You think beauty is found on the surface, Schex? It is found in character. You had it originally, but Catch had more character. And more money. And was a better lover."

She went on and on, rubbing it in gleefully. How happy she had been with Catch. How Catch had thought he was indestructible until he dropped dead of a heart attack on the tennis court. How Catch had time for everything except for planning for her if something happened to him. How G.G. had comforted her after Catch's death. How G.G. always put her first.

"Like the minute he formed Camellia Industries, I got half. Half. Just like that. Process stuff no one wanted. Stuff that people would pay him to take off their hands. Make it into something that could be sold. A great idea. He got paid to take in the raw materials. He got paid for the finished product. He got paid on both ends of the deal. Nothing could be sweeter. All he needed was the start-up money. But no bank would lend it to him. And that's where I came up with Tony."

"Taylor, it doesn't make any sense. G.G. was some sweet guy who put you first and also the same bastard that you told me and half of the town you wanted dead?"

"Schex, don't tell me you don't understand how you can love and hate someone at the same time. I know better."

She walked around the counter and stood in front of me. "You, of all people, know that it can happen. You want evidence of how it works?"

She dropped her chiffon robe to the floor and stood there, naked.

Her breasts were firm, her nipples erect. Her stomach was still smooth, her waist still thin. The soft brown of her pubic hair stood in contrast to the whiteness of the skin of her crotch and thighs. She posed in front of me, legs spread apart, daring me to desire her.

I remembered those breasts in my hands. I remembered those nipples in my mouth. I remembered licking that stomach. I wanted it all again, and I hated myself for wanting it.

CHAPTER 53

I TURNED AWAY FROM TAYLOR AND walked out of the room. When she caught up with me in the living room, she had her robe back on. "Love and hate *can* exist at the same time, Schex. Damn confusing, isn't it?"

She sat down on the sofa and casually sipped coffee as if nothing had happened. "Now just listen to me. I suspected that G.G. had money in addition to the funds in the bank accounts, but I didn't know how much until today. More than four mil. There's only one way G.G. could get all that money."

"How?"

"Doesn't matter really now, does it? I think I know where it came from, but the important thing is, I need as much as I can get my hands on, and Tony has got to help you get back the half million those guys took from you."

"Are you out of your mind? Even if he would listen to me, which he won't, those two meat-fisted killers are undoubtedly looking for me. That's why I'm here."

"You still don't get it? Tony needs you alive *with* the money. Because with the cash in your hands, you're compromised. You can bet he was filming everything that took place on his boat. The video is probably already duplicated six times and tucked away for safekeeping. But if you don't have the money, and if you're alive, then you're the thing that he fears most – someone who can testify against him and put him behind bars."

"Wonderful. You've just given him a definitive reason to kill me, as if Ribeye and Frankie didn't have reason enough already."

"Tony won't know who you've talked to or what you may have planned, or who you might have told that you're going to see him. He won't do anything to you, even if he wanted to, which he won't."

"And the other two? They're going to sit by and watch?"

"You let me deal with Tony about that. Just go to Tony and tell him about what his men did to you and that they took the money. That's all it will take. Trust me."

I didn't trust her at all.

But what she said had given me an idea.

CHAPTER 54

I HAD THOUGHT I HAD SUNK as low as I could go when I retreated to Taylor's, but I proved I could submerge even lower. By deceiving Washington Eby into helping me.

That afternoon Washington and I bounced down the highway in his ancient unairconditioned truck. I had taken a couple of pain pills before we left, but my left arm still ached with each jolt. Rolling down the windows did nothing to alleviate the heat, and the wind blowing in only seemed to increase the denseness of the air. Sweat poured from my brow and armpits as well as down my back. My jeans and collared shirt, which I had persuaded Washington to retrieve from my house, were now limp and damp.

The interstate highway from Baton Rouge to New Orleans travels through the heart of a delta built up over centuries by the Mississippi River; flat alluvial land without a hill, mound or swale to disturb the terrain. The road runs in arrow-straight sections for miles, a narrow valley bordered by tall trees.

Washington had gladly agreed to take me down to the Crescent City when I shamelessly lied to him that my car was broken. Washington slowed at the three-mile bridge that spanned a vast swamp. Trees reaching up from thirty feet below, nestling against the edges of the concrete railings, were silent ushers on the entryway to the city. We came across the Bonne Carre Spillway, whose floodgates were opened whenever the Mississippi River got too high, and wheezed around the last curve, passing the few cypress trees that remained, their elegant, gnarled trunks rising out of stagnant olive pools. Decapitated cypress knees encircled them, a muddy remembrance of what had once been a forest.

We weren't headed downtown. The meeting was not to take place in the French Quarter. That was too public. Too crowded with tourists. Rather, we took the Carrollton Avenue exit and drove southwest down this wide boulevard lined with oak trees, to where the river made the sharp turn that gave the Crescent City its name.

From Carrollton to Tchoupitoulas Street, along warehouses that lined the Mississippi River levee, where the river level on the other side of the massive earthwork rose higher than the roofs. This was the high edge of the bowl that was New Orleans, the 'sliver by the river' that hadn't flooded when the 17th Street Canal levee failed in the aftermath of Hurricane Katrina.

Washington had not spoken during the drive. But now, a few blocks short of our destination, he pulled the truck onto a narrow side street and turned off the engine.

"You know, Durnella said I was crazy to drive to New Orleans. She hates this city. Before the storm, her people lived here and she wouldn't come visit them. Then Katrina flooded them out, and there's no one left to visit. So, she didn't want me to come at all."

"You know I'll pay for the gas and for your time."

"Don't want your money. Won't take it. Now, Durnella asked why you didn't just rent a car or get your own car fixed. I told her you must'uv had a good reason. That woman worries about you. But, you're a young guy still. Told her you were probably out cattin' around. Jokin', I was. But Durnella don't cotton to talk like that. It just set her off. She thinks you ought to settle down with some nice girl, but you always seem to be sittin' alone in that house. Then she took the reins of her own argument and rode off with it, talkin' about how it ain't right for a man to be alone in his life. Talked 'bout all them loose girls and how it's that stuff in the movies and on that Internet causin' all this. If they just wouldn't show it, she complained, them young girls would stay home and go to church and learn right livin'. Talked 'bout how if all them kids went to Sunday School each week, there wouldn't be no foolin' around. If they'd just listen to the Preacher. But no, all the kids know better. Don't have no respect for the Preacher or for the church. No wonder, she said, they don't have no respect for their bodies. Went on and on, she did. 'Course, I didn't say nothin'. Don't usually, you know. Don't pay to argue. Take my advice. If a woman starts gettin' up a head of steam, just back off and let her crank that valve wide open. Can't win, you know. Just let her condensate on her own. But, served me right for talking 'bout cattin' 'round."

"Washington, it's nothing like that."

The old man patted me on the shoulder. "Know that, Neighbor. I know. Didn't want to scare her. She gets the worries too easily and it's bad for her pressure, the doctor says."

The more he said, the worse I felt for deceiving him.

"Don't think 'bout apologizing," he said earnestly. "Neighbor, you got some serious trouble. I know that. I see a lot. More people been at your house in the last week than I seen in a year. But, you didn't come home last night. My old bladder can't hold more than a thimbleful without wanting to be emptied. So, I'm looking out the window every time I'm passing to the bathroom. Your car is in the driveway and you're not home? That's not like you, I'm thinking. You're not there this morning. Then you called right before lunch today. Get your clothes? Mighty strange request. Meet you outside of the neighborhood and fetch you to New Orleans? T'ain't a usual thing to ask for a man who's got a car. Something's gotta be wrong, I'm thinkin'. So I joked about it so Durnella's not upset. Wrong joke."

Washington shifted in his seat. "But when she finally quiets down I go into the backyard and then into your house. What a mess. No lawyer's goin' to leave his files and papers all over the floor like that. Insulation all over the hallway; crawl space door popped open. Something very unusual's goin' on. Would have straightened it up a bit if I had time, but I didn't. Doorbell rang. So I looked out the latch of your door and there's this little man on the front porch. Chinese or somethin'. I calls out and asks him what he's wantin'. I wasn't goin' to open that door for no one. Says he gotta see you. I says you weren't in and didn't know when you'd be back. He slipped somethin' under the door."

Washington reached into his shirt pocket and handed me a wrinkled piece of paper that had been folded several times. "Didn't read it. Figured it was none of my business. But that man said he had to see you and to give you this note. I said if I saw you I would, and now I have."

I took the note and held it in my hand, unopened.

"Before I left, Durnella made me take this." Washington held up the brown paper bag on the seat. "Sandwiches. Made three of them. One for you, one for me, and an extra to share. Put in a couple of apples too, and a few cookies."

"Neighbor, I can tell trouble when it's around. I've seen too much in my day. I learned early to watch, but to look like I wasn't lookin' and say and show nothin'. But all the time, though, I was watchin'. And I been watchin' you. Your house. The way you look. The way you act. Things aren't right. You don't have no clients to speak of, then all of a sudden it's like a bus station over there, with people comin' and goin' at all hours. You wouldn't leave that house for days at a time, and now you stay out all night. You never asked me for much of nothin', then you ask to borrow my bateau and motor, and then you ask me to drive you to New Orleans, and I can see you got somethin' wrong with that arm you're favoring, all bandaged and all. No, things ain't right."

Washington reached back down into the well behind the seat. "I watch and I prepare." He pulled his shotgun out and laid it across his lap.

I just stared at the gun. Washington, on whom I had imposed without compunction, who hadn't even graduated from grammar school, was wiser and more thoughtful than I would ever be. All he wanted to do was to protect me. He had seen right through my ruse and had driven me to New Orleans, knowing all along that there was some kind of danger involved, never asking questions, just being ready with the double-gauged shotgun. Washington was ready to act. I had become an automaton put in motion by Taylor.

I was ashamed of the way I had acted towards Washington and the way I had mistreated and misjudged him. All I could muster was a quiet "Thanks." It was hardly adequate.

"Don't thank me, Neighbor. At least, not yet. Haven't done a thing so far. Just wanted you to know I'm ready if that's what's needed. But I don't think it should be. Now that we've come this far, what's to say there's a need to go any farther? Why don't we just turn around and head home?"

Go back to Baton Rouge? It made eminent sense. Why risk my life, and Washington's, on a venture that seemed so full of potential peril?

And yet, I was here. My standards had shrunk. First, I had dreams of the entire four million. Then a portion of it. Then I lost it. But I had a new plan. For the first time in years, I felt alive. I was in pain, and my sliced left arm was throbbing constantly, but I was animated by all the possibilities. I was fully awake, as if the last five years had been a bad dream. I was fully present. It was the fear of danger, and the excitement of it, that made me feel as if I had come out of a long hibernation.

"Washington, that's a fine offer, but I've got to finish this up, so please, just drive on and drop me off where I need to be."

"Are you sure you're not makin' a mistake, Neighbor? Tell you what, at least read this note before you go. The Chinaman said it was important."

I opened the wrinkled scrap of paper and smoothed it out. Spidery handwriting, in pencil:

MUST see you TODAY. <u>PLEASE.</u>
I will come by later. Mr. Trey fired me.
I know about meetings late at night at plant. I know many things.
I DID NOT tell the Sheriff or Mr. Trey. I need a lawyer."

It was signed "Kuo Htay."

CHAPTER 55

S O, TREY FIRED KIRK/KUO, just as he said he would. And Kirk/Kuo saw late-night meetings, probably including the one Spider had with Taylor on the night he died.

That meant that I had to talk with Kirk/Kuo to find out what he knew. Of course, Kirk/Kuo's not telling the sheriff about Taylor – if Taylor was whom he had seen – only increased the suspicion that would fall on me. And why didn't he want to talk to the sheriff? What else was he hiding?

I realized that by waiting until now to hand me the note, Washington was trying to give me another reason to return to Baton Rouge. But I merely folded the paper and stuck it in my pocket. "Washington, I've got to finish what I've started."

He shook his head unhappily as he cranked the ignition, "Not for me to run your life." He turned the truck at the next corner and headed back toward Tchoupitoulas Street. "I'll tell you, though, making a decision just to show you can make one don't seem to me to be very high on a list of good reasons."

To our right, behind decaying wood buildings and rusted metal warehouses, the levee loomed, dark and earthy.

"Now, I'm sure you're thinking that you can do what you want 'cause it won't affect no one but you. But, Neighbor, don't you understand? No one ever does anything that don't affect someone else, somehow, someway."

As we neared our destination, sickly trees lined both sides of the street. At last we saw a sign hanging perpendicular to the brick building two blocks ahead.

"TORCAMENTO'S."

"Washington, drive past it the first time and cruise around the area a bit, OK?"

"Now, Neighbor, that's a start. This city ain't safe at all any more."

The truck meandered slowly up and down the adjacent blocks. I did not see Ribeye, Frankie, or their car.

The unique pattern of New Orleans neighborhoods sometimes makes it difficult to determine what was ordinary and what extraordinary, for New Orleans is a checkerboard of housing types, races, and nationalities.

On one block, small kids on tricycles dashed up and down the street, their parents drinking beer and watching from metal chairs on open porches. On the next block, aimless-looking teenagers lounged against cars, throwing surly glances at the truck as it drove by. Another street over, a mother pushed an expensive baby carriage in front of columned homes hidden behind cast iron fences. Another corner – shotgun houses, narrow one-room-wide wooden buildings with sagging rooflines. A man in an undershirt bar-b-queing in a front yard that was only slightly larger than his grill.

If Ribeye and Frankie were waiting, they were well hidden.

We passed by the restaurant a third time. The gold letters spelling out "TORCAMENTO'S" stood out boldly against the sign's dark blue background. The building was distinct. Unlike the yellowed paint of the wooden homes and offices and the reddened rust of the sheet-metal buildings, the white brick restaurant with its fire-engine red door had none of the greenish tinge of mold and mildew that clung to anything porous in this damp city of verdant undergrowth. Even the cracked sidewalk in front of the restaurant was a chalky ivory, contrasting with the adjacent brownish grey concrete squares in front of the other buildings. Torcamento's spoke of upkeep, of frequent bleach-washes, of pride, and of success.

Washington finally stopped on a nearby side street.

I hopped out. "Don't park here. It will just raise suspicions."

"Look Neighbor, I know how to disappear when I need to. Spent a lifetime doin' that. I'll be back in an hour. If you're not here, I'm coming in that restaurant for you."

"That won't be necessary."

"I told you. I watch plenty. If it was just foolishness that you were down here for, you'd have laughed at my gun. You would have said something. But no, you just looked at that gun with big eyes liked you wish you had thought of it. So, I was right. This is all connected somehow. I don't know how, and I don't know why, but I do know trouble. That's what you've been in, and that's what you're now in. I told you. Every decision affects someone else. I'm not going home without you. Couldn't live with myself if I did."

He grinned slowly. "Sure couldn't live with Durnella if I did either. If you're not out of that restaurant within the hour, I'm coming inside. With my gun."

CHAPTER 56

WOODEN BARRELS CONTAINING EMPTY OYSTER shells crowded the sidewalk outside Torcamento's red door. Inside, the restaurant was dim, long, and narrow. Every surface was lined with tiles. White squares separated by black ceramic diamonds tessellated the floor, climbed up the wall, and gleamed from the ceiling. Old wooden tables, thick coats of dark black paint covering their marred surfaces, crowded against one another. The tile-topped bar ran along the left side of the room.

I looked around cautiously. There were only two people in the restaurant, the bartender and a customer, neither of whom was Ribeye or Frankie.

The bartender looked up at me. He had a broad chest and a narrow waist. He stood behind the bar, a small blunt oyster knife in his hand. His ears were tiny, or maybe they only looked that way because of his massive, muscled neck. Dressed in a white apron, he was expertly popping open oysters and placing them on a platter.

I recognized the customer sitting at the bar with his back to the door. It was Hubbard Estes, whom I hadn't seen since he had laid me off as Old Parish Mortgage was shutting down. Still wearing a button-down white shirt. Still dressed in black suspenders holding up dark pants over highly polished shoes. His attire never changed. His hair, or what was left of it fringing his head, was now completely grey, but he was unmistakable.

And, as always, Hubbard was eating. Seated on a tall stool, with one foot resting on the metal rail that ran along the base of the bar, he was downing the freshly shucked oysters as quickly as they were put in front of him. He ate rapidly, but with a practiced neatness, and without a slurp or sound.

Only after he had finished the dozen on the platter before him did he acknowledge my presence. "Schex, you're here! Been expecting you."

I reluctantly walked over to shake his extended hand, but as I did the bartender moved to the front door and locked it.

"It's OK, Schex. Trust me."

I hadn't admired Hubbard, not when I worked for him and certainly not when he let me go. And, I never trusted him.

The bartender positioned himself between me and the back exit. He made sure that I saw the gun tucked into the pocket of his apron.

"Now Schex, cooperate with the man. It'll only take a minute."

The bartender expertly frisked me.

I had expected this. I wasn't wearing a wire. I wasn't carrying anything with me except what I intended to say.

Finished with his examination, the bartender returned to his station and poured two beers into cold steins.

"Satisfied?" I directed my comments to Hubbard.

"But Schex, I'm always satisfied. Come on. You came to see Tony. You have to go through the procedures."

Hubbard grabbed the beers and led me to a table, but I deliberately avoided the chair to which he had pointed, the one whose rear faced the back door of the restaurant. No way I wanted my back to anything. I wanted to be in a position to see both the front and back door.

Once we were seated, the bartender brought over a tray of another two dozen shucked oysters and put them in front of Hubbard.

Hubbard attacked the bivalves with fastidious speed. He spoke between bites, never with his mouth full. "All these arrangements!" Hubbard said. "Lots of mystery. I'll tell you, it piqued Tony's interest. You go fishing with him yesterday. You want to see him again this afternoon. Something big is afoot, 'cause Frankie and Ribeye were sent out on urgent errands. Too bad they won't be back until tonight."

So far, things were going according to plan. While Taylor said she would handle it, I had told Taylor exactly what to say when she made the call, and Tony had believed her enough to send those two away while I was here.

"Come on," Hubbard urged, pointing to the frosty stein, "drink up. It's hot as hell out there."

I ignored his invitation. "I didn't know you worked for Micelli."

"Work for Tony? No. I'm just…well, you can call my role that of a consultant."

"What do you consult about nowadays, Hubbard? Running businesses into the ground?"

Hubbard paused to scoop down another couple of oysters. "Don't let old times at Old Parish sour you, Schex. That was unfortunate. Sure, a bunch of folks lost their homes when their subprime loans reset at higher interest rates, and sure we had to lay off a bunch of folks at the office, but I'm proud to say that our investors came out whole."

"I'm sure that was a big comfort to the homeowners and all the other former Old Parish employees. I feel better now knowing how well the investors did."

"Don't get so high and mighty with me, Schex. You know how business works. Lending is where the future is. It's the most service-oriented of service industries. People want money, and they're willing to pay you money for money. They pay points up front. They pay processing fees. Closing fees. Rollover fees. Rework fees. They pay interest, and then they pay principal. The trick is to stay on top of it so that you don't ever have to foreclose on the collateral securing the loan. They used to say that the three C's of lending were Collateral, Character, and Cash Flow. But that's wrong. It's all character, character, character. Lend to the right people, in the right way, and they'll pay you back. Lend to the wrong people, no matter what the cash flow or collateral, and you'll always come out on the short end. Old Parish investors had a good business model. I help Tony make sure his business plan is not just good but extraordinarily great."

Hubbard sprinkled more Tabasco sauce on the oysters. "You sure you don't want that beer? Mind if I have it, then? Good."

He reached over, grabbed my untouched stein, and took a swig before turning back to the oysters. "Character is crucial in any credit decision. Now G.G., he was a character all right. Wrong kind, or so some thought. But Tony said it would all work out. And, thanks to you, it has – 100% return of principal, plus all interest, plus all expenses. All precisely proper and legal. That's why I'm such a valuable consultant, Schex. Every dollar is accounted for. Taxes are paid. Audit trails are kept."

I had never thought much of Hubbard previously, and I thought even less of him now. I unwrapped the top part of the bandages that encircled my left arm so that Hubbard could see the sliced skin held together by the butterfly patches. "I'm glad you have such gentle business associates."

Hubbard looked genuinely pained at the sight of my scarred flesh. "These are things I don't know about and don't want to know about. Sometimes people are angry with Tony, and angry people sometimes carry guns. This," he said, gesturing in the direction of the bartender, "is no different than having a guard at the front door of the bank or a metal detector at the courthouse. It's a matter of protection. Nothing more. Besides, what I do is perfectly legal. "

Hubbard ate the remaining oyster. There was no napkin in sight, and Hubbard had no need of one. His hands and face were immaculate.

There was a single firm knock on the rear door behind the table.

Hubbard Estes moved the platter aside. "Tony is ready for you."

CHAPTER 57

THE REAR DOOR LED TO the interior courtyard of Torcamento's. Thick stuccoed walls, ten feet in height, surrounded the brick patio. Tall banana trees leaned against the walls, their wide leaves rustling, moved by the overhead fan that swirled at the end of its metal tether. The balcony above and the second-story eaves shielded the courtyard from the blistering sun. Large ferns grew in pots alongside the wall, and small ones pushed their way between the cracks in the brick.

Tony Micelli, dressed in pastels, was sitting at a black cast-iron table on which rested a plate with the remains of a half-eaten fried oyster po-boy. "Did you decide that your dreams were bigger than your grasp?"

I held out my sliced arm. "My reality is more than enough."

"That," he said, with apparent affability, "is an indictment of your dreams."

There he went again, with his curious mix of legal terms and metaphors. But I could play that game too. "You act is if dreams were the only things that could indict. Look, you did me a favor yesterday, and I'm here to return that favor."

I pulled up a chair next to his. I described precisely, without adjectives or emotion, what happened after he left me at the dock with Frankie and Ribeye and what the two of them had said about him. I explained how they took the cash from me. I told him about the InDispoCo truck and how I leapt out and about Ribeye shooting at me.

The story first piqued his curiosity and then his anger.

Micelli's complexion had gotten progressively more florid as I spoke. The fat folds of skin on his neck turned red. His nose, across which crept a maze of spidery veins, became fiery. Only his eyes, those dark slits, were cool.

"And…what…else? Tell…me…" Micelli said, speaking so softly and slowly that it was hard to hear him. It was as if he was building a dike around his emotions.

"That's it. I got away. I'm here." No need to mention Rad or Weegie.

Micelli raised his bulk out of the chair, went to the edge of the patio, and fingered one of the thick stalks of the large banana plants that towered over him. He pulled on one of the broad, flat leaves and began to crush it between his fingers.

Then, suddenly, he grasped the entire stalk with both hands. Although it was as thick as a column, Micelli wrestled it, ripping it up from the ground. Soil and leaves scattered onto the patio as he wrenched it from the earth. Cockroaches and spiders, awakened from their afternoon slumber in the dirt, frantically sought a dark spot in which to hide. Worms, the color of burnt sienna, slithered around, trying to dig themselves back into the damp humus from which they had been ejected.

As Micelli swung the stalk high above his head, the tips of the tall leaves hit the fan, sending it careening elliptically from the end of its metal pole.

Micelli flung the plant into the wall, where it clung for a moment and then slipped down, leaving a chlorophyll trail on the stucco as it settled into an odd resting position, half propped against the wall, half crushing the ferns in the pots.

Micelli came back to the table and wiped his hand on the checkered napkin.

We sat there silently for a few minutes.

When Micelli finally spoke, he wasn't looking at me but rather was watching the spiders, worms, and roaches as they crept and burrowed away. "You know, I was good to those men. I thought I had instilled trust in them. Trust. They wanted independent companies? Fine, I gave them layer upon layer of corporate entities, each more removed from me. I trusted them to run those companies properly. They wanted security? I trusted them to achieve it on their own. Maybe it was because I wanted to be independent of them as well, to separate myself from what they represented, to insulate myself."

He pulled a few crumbs off the edge of what was left of his po-boy and tossed it into the garden, watching the scurrying bugs pause and turn in search of the food. "Maybe I was wrong. Maybe the old ways are better, at least sometimes. My father did not believe in trust. Fear and greed were his motivators, not trust. First and foremost was fear. But greed had to be a part of it.

"'People have to believe they will be far worse without you than with you.' That's what my father always said. 'If they're both afraid of you and afraid of having to do without you, then you have their loyalty.' His words. That's how he thought. Greed was the motivator. Fear was the control. My father got loyalty. He got it from everyone."

On the worn patio bricks, the roaches and ants scavenged the crumbs that Micelli continued to toss their way.

"At least I got half the formula right. Greed. Frankie and Ribeye have gotten greedy. But they're not going to drag me down with them. No. There was a reason the old ways didn't work. Somehow, you always get caught. Well, not me. Not now. Not ever. Some threats work only if you're willing to follow them through to the final conclusion. A threat is only effective if everyone knows that it is real. But, reality catches up with you. It will catch up with them. With them, but not me."

He continued to scatter scraps of bread. The insects hungrily grasped at the food that fell around them. "Avarice alone should be enough of a motivator. Greed can be insatiable, even without fear."

He finally stopped feeding the vermin and turned to me. "And you, Schex. What motivates you? You could have gone directly to the police. You could have run away. And yet you're here. Why? Only one reason. You want me to give you back the money Frankie and Ribeye took, right?"

"I want more than the money."

"More?"

I had played it perfectly so far. This is what I had come for. "Of course I want the money. You clearly don't want to have those two getting it and thinking they can pull one over on you. That destroys the neat little island of protection you think you have erected. Plus, you've got the cops nosing around already. G.G.'s dead. Spider's dead. And you're linked to G.G. and Taylor – and probably Spider as well – if people look hard enough. Yesterday on the boat you spoke of the magic of the law. Well, you need a better shield than Frankie and Ribeye. They're only going to drag you down with them. Whatever control you thought you had over them isn't working. And I didn't know about Hubbard until I walked in here, but that's a laugh. You depend on Hubbard Estes to provide a patina of legality on what you do? He can't protect you from Frankie and Ribeye, and Hubbard will run your business into the ground. You want to do lending right? You want to stay clean? You want to stay out of trouble? There's one way."

"Which is?" Tony Micelli wasn't happy. He was suspicious as hell.

"Hire me."

CHAPTER 58

"HIRE YOU? THE SCOWL ON Micelli's face was erased as he broke into a chuckle. "I love it! You're now suddenly both self-righteous and hypocritical. Those are great traits for a lawyer."

"Yesterday," I explained, "you said you were happy to have me 'representing' your investments. Well then, go all the way. Hire me directly and let me protect your business."

There. I had put my new plan in motion. My old one, taking the money and running, had evaporated thanks to Frankie and Ribeye. My new plan aligned with both my current situation and Micelli's needs.

A lawyer doesn't take on the morality of his client. The law does not require a lawyer to be a shining knight, running to the rescue and righting wrongs. The law does not require a lawyer to strive for omniscient justice.

I was going to be the minimum that the law required in order to get my way. I was going to get back the money that Frankie and Ribeye had taken from me by being an amoral technician, by doing the client's bidding as long as it was not flatly illegal.

Micelli wanted to stay on the legal side of the line, if only barely, and that was all right with me. He had plenty of money. I wasn't going to represent Taylor, and with Rad planning to subpoena me, I couldn't represent Camellia Industries. But with Micelli as my client, I'd be climbing back up the ladder, back towards the money. It might not be the ladder of respect, but I didn't care.

The smile remained on Micelli's face, but the humor was gone from his voice. "You're awfully presumptuous to think you could protect me, Schex, when you didn't even bother to read the corporate papers thoroughly enough to find out about my loan to Camellia Industries. Now, I agreed to meet with you, without Frankie and Ribeye, as a personal favor to Taylor."

Of course. Taylor told him exactly what I instructed her to say.

"But then Taylor and I have known each other a long time. Maybe too long. Oh, she used to talk about you. Did you know that?"

No, but it didn't surprise me.

"She said that you were three things. Straight. Bright. And boring. Not right for a wild woman like Taylor. And after what she did to you, why you would want to do anything for her is beyond me, but that's your business. You want the money? That's OK. She called me about you, so clearly she thinks the money is hers. I don't care. You were the escrow agent. You can have it back. What you do with it from that point on is your own business."

"That's a good start," I said, leaving an opening for him to ask me what I was going to do if he hired me to represent him. But all Micelli did was stand up, a signal that our meeting was over.

He pointed to the door that led from the patio back into the bar. As I gingerly got out of the chair, careful not to use my painful left arm, he spoke with a sly tone. "You want to work for me? Prove that the legal skills you once had are back. Prove that you won't miss the obvious. Prove that you can find the truth. Then, and only then will I consider your offer."

So, he did want to talk about hiring me. "And exactly how," I asked, "do you want me to prove that?"

"Easy enough. Find out how Camellia Industries got its permits in the first place. Find out why DEH allowed Camellia Industries to operate in the face of all the complaints against it. Find out about old college days and the boy."

Why was Micelli playing games with me? He was the one who had said on the boat that I was the lawyer for his 'investments,' and now I had to solve puzzles? "Finding out those things," I said, "won't prove anything about my legal abilities. I'm a lawyer, not a detective, and you clearly know everything, so why don't you just tell me?"

"Tell you? I can't confide in you, Schex. You're not my lawyer. Not yet, at any rate. Come the day you work for me, we'll have a nice, long, confidential chat. Until then, I'm just a dispenser of clues."

"What about the money?"

"I meant what I said. You can reasonably expect that the money will be returned in due time. Don't you realize that money itself is just a metaphor? You want little pieces of green paper? OK, you'll have them. But they're just that. Paper. You want to transform them into something else? Electronic bits in a wire transfer? A line of ink on a cashier's check? An entry in a column? They're all metaphors, don't you see, until they become something tangible. A table. A chair. A sandwich. Until then, you're living with a pocketful of metaphors."

"I don't need metaphors. I need the cash," I said firmly.

"Impatience is a bad trait for an attorney, Schex. Stick to hypocrisy."

I turned to leave. I had come all this way and had gotten nothing, only vague promises wrapped in verbiage, plus a scavenger hunt through the past.

"By the way," he added, "one more piece of information to ponder. You might ask Taylor how well, in the biblical sense, she 'knew' Carter Herrington. Or his randy nephew, Trey."

CHAPTER 59

LTHOUGH MICELLI HADN'T HIRED ME on the spot, at least a portion of my plan was underway. Micelli had indicated that I might get the money back in due time. That meant he was going to deal with Frankie and Ribeye.

Washington and I sat in his backyard, resting in metal lawn chairs under the shade of trees Washington had planted years ago, watching the sky form a neon canopy as the sun set. Large bees flew noisily from flower to flower in Durnella's garden. Luther ran around snapping at them.

Just an hour earlier we had returned to Baton Rouge. We drove around my block several times to check it out. The neighbors' cars we recognized. No strange people were around. Even so, we took no chances. Washington and I went through the back gate of his yard to my rear door. We didn't bother to try to clean my house. We just lowered the shades to keep prying eyes out. I threw a razor and a couple of days' worth of clothes into a paper bag and locked the house up as best I could.

The late afternoon odors surrounded us – the moist smell of freshly cut grass, the sweetness of the green figs that hung in the tree above, and the distinctive scent of tomatoes ripening on the staked plants that Durnella carefully tended.

Intertwined with this bouquet of aromas was the menthol salve Durnella had applied gently under the freshly wrapped bandages on my arm and neck. It mingled with the effervescence of the beer in my nostrils.

From where we reclined, we could see my driveway and the back and south side of my house, but we were hidden from the view of anyone driving by in front of my place. I was waiting to see if Kirk/Kuo showed up after sending that urgent note. Or Frankie and Ribeye. Or anyone else.

The shadows lengthened as the sun went down. Washington put his feet up on the table that was placed between the chairs. Luther came and put his head under the elderly man's hands, and Washington absent-mindedly scratched the dog behind his ears. The chairs and table, although old and well used, were immaculately kept and looked freshly painted. Just like Washington's house.

"Neighbor, you can sit here all night waitin' for that Chinaman to come, but just sittin' don't necessarily make you any wiser."

Kirk/Kuo was Vietnamese, not Chinese, but I knew that Washington spoke the truth.

"You don't have to say nothin', you understand," he said, "but if you want to talk, that's OK. Listenin's a thing I can do."

Washington's chair creaked again, and the cicadas in the grass answered.

"You know, Neighbor, listenin's an art of sorts. Listen too hard and people get suspicious. 'Why's that fellow so peculiar?' they say. They can't put their finger on it. They think maybe it has to do with the way someone looks at 'em, but I don't think that's the reason. I've spent a lot of time listenin' and watchin'. A hard listener's lookin' for somethin' that may not be there. Lookin' for an openin', rather than for a meanin'. Maybe that's why people don't like lawyers as a rule. Lawyers tend to be hard listeners. On the other hand, listen too soft and you get all the words but none of the sense. There's an art to that too. Got to be lots of men who listen to their wives too soft, hearin' the words but missin' entirely what's goin' on. Seen that lots of time. Wife says somethin', you answer, and you got no idea what the question really was about. Did that sometimes when I was young; Durnella sure cured me of that. That woman can't stand no soft listenin'. She's right, of course."

"The art of good listenin's in the balance," he continued. "Got to hear the words and the feelin'. Got to catch the meanin' and the sense. You're full of worries and troubles, that's clear. And yet you haven't spoken about what's really botherin' you."

We sat there in the dark. Downtown had long since emptied out. Traffic had ceased. Luther strolled over and curled up at Washington's feet.

Overhead in the night sky, wisps of low-lying clouds softly glowed, reflecting the millions of yellow halogen lights of the chemical plants that were just north of the state capitol building.

All the questions Micelli said I had to answer swirled around. G.G. and Taylor, G.G. and Camellia Industries, Herrington and DEH permitting, Carter and Taylor, Trey and Taylor.

But how would Taylor's sleeping with Catch, G.G., Herrington, Trey and who-knows-who-else add up to permits for the plant or the money in the suitcase? When I told Taylor what had happened on the boat, she said that she knew where "all" the money must have come from. All? The more than four million that G.G. had left with me? How could she know that? And if it didn't come from Camellia Industries' accounts, what was its source?

The only other thing that Micelli had said was to "find out about old college days and the boy." Old college days, I realized, might be the string that could lead to unraveling of all these interlocking relationships.

I reached out for the empty beer can and tapped it on the table's edge.

"I'm not asleep. Don't need no alarm clock," Washington responded. "Got anythin' you want to talk about at this point?"

"Yes," I said. "A question."

Washington waited patiently. "Whenever you're ready, Neighbor, ask away."

"Can I borrow your truck?"

CHAPTER 60

T HE MAIN LSU LIBRARY, A 1960s structure sheathed in metal and glass, squatted as a heavy anchor to a courtyard filled with elegant archways, graceful buildings, and red-tiled roofs.

As originally envisioned, the campus was to consist of hacienda-influenced architecture reflecting Louisiana's Spanish heritage. But, over the years, it had grown into a pastiche of architectural styles.

I parked the truck and went directly to the library, passing a scattering of late-night summer students. Frankie and Ribeye had taken my laptop and tablet computer, and I needed a place to do a little quick research.

Quick but useless was what it turned out to be. A few short minutes of Googling revealed that, although what I wanted had been digitized, it was all contained behind paywalls requiring a credit card. My credit cards had been maxed out long ago, but what I needed could be gotten for free another way, which was why I was here.

The pimply student at the front desk, astonished that anyone would want what I was looking for, handed me a card with a map of the library and showed me where to go.

Down to the first basement. Past the long rows of metal bookshelves jammed with old journals. Past the high stacks of thick books that hadn't been opened in years. Past the water fountain on the wall, slowly leaking a dribble of water onto the vinyl tile and into the drain on the floor. Past empty desks over which fluorescent fixtures cast too bright a light.

All the way back to the rear stacks, near the concrete wall. That's where I found the dusty remnants of hours of work by students trying to provide themselves with instant history. Years and years of purple-bound Gumbos, the old LSU yearbooks. If there was something about 'old college days' that involved G.G. and Herrington, this would be the place to start.

The volumes took up four shelves. Thin ones from the 1920s. Slightly thicker ones in the 30s. From the 50s on the volumes bulged, inflated first with postwar success, then the baby boom years, then the 60s Vietnam era, which had seemed to pass by the campus in a haze of booze and football that drove out most political thoughts, and on into the heady 80s.

The books from the 60s were what I wanted. I pulled down the 1960 Gumbo. Black-and-white photos, crisp and sharp. Freshmen, heads shaved from mandatory ROTC, lounging in pressed shirts and narrow ties. Girls in wide skirts, holding books and purses, beamed from balconies and stairways and walked through what were then large, open parade grounds.

Team sports. A two-page spread for each of the season's games, with action photographs, scores, and play-by-play highlights lovingly detailed.

Fraternity houses, many now worn and faded, were all new and full of promise in these photos. Homecoming night on fraternity row. All the frat houses were decorated with paper-mâché players and figures.

More pages venerating the power of LSU's Greek system. Only the privileged were invited in to share its secrets, to endure its hazings, and to become campus royalty. The rest of the students were clearly peons. If they weren't playing a sport or in a fraternity, they were relegated to small pictures bulldozed to the back of the yearbook.

Clubs? Jammed four or five to a page with merely a listing of the members under each photograph. Boys in sports coats and ties. Girls in dresses hemmed demurely below the knees.

But fraternities and sororities? They got the biggest spreads after the football, baseball, and basketball teams. Pictures of the brothers and sisters. Pictures of each house. Prom night; white formal coats and black satin bowties escorting silk and satin encased filigree. Pictures of the pledge class. Pictures of the Greek rituals – 'South Sea Night' with large logs bound together with thick ropes in front of each fraternity house as walkways, entryways, sets too garish to be used in a stage production but which had a magical quality on one special campus evening.

It was all there. Acclaim and recognition that was so sought after at the moment, yet so ephemeral, except as encased in these paper time capsules.

I flipped to the back of the yearbook. The editors had carefully indexed the name of each student and the pages on which their corresponding pictures appeared. No Carter H. Herrington, IV listed in the index of the 1960 volume. No Gaynell G. Guidry either.

I started on the 1961 Gumbo and marveled at what it didn't show. An island of white faces in photographs. No pictures of the hundreds of students from India and Pakistan who had come to the Agricultural and Engineering schools, who had been treated as "Negroes" because of their skin color. Although one black student had been grudgingly admitted to LSU as early as 1953 as the result of a lawsuit, blacks were invisible and unwelcome in 1961.

Nothing of Herrington or Guidry in that index either.

I worked my way through the rest of 1962, '63, and '64. Nothing there I needed. Worked my way through 1970. Nothing. Started working backward from 1980. Finally, the indices from the 1973 Gumbo contained plenty about Carter Herrington, IV.

I looked at each page where his picture appeared. 1973 apparently was the year of Herrington's graduation. Here he was. President of the Student Government Association. Participant in intramural sports. Active on the Greek Council. Involved in fraternity life.

The 1972 Gumbo. Herrington as a junior. Student Government Speaker Pro Tem. ROTC Outstanding Young Officer. Fraternity officer. No Gaynell G. Guidry in the index, however.

The 1971 Gumbo. Herrington, a sophomore clearly on the move. Herrington, the joiner of clubs. The Language Club. The Spring Social committee. The Pre-Law Society. Herrington was in each one, often in the back row, but unmistakable in these small photographs.

And Herrington as a second-year fraternity man. No longer a pledge but a true member of the inner sanctum. In one picture, there he was, threatening an incoming pledge class with a huge paddle, and in the next he was surrounded by the admiring pledgees, his arms around two of them, the paddle broken in half at their feet.

I closed the book and put it on the table and yawned. I was tired and losing focus.

I started to pick up the 1970 Gumbo, but then I remembered I hadn't looked up G.G.'s name in the index of the 1971 volume. I ran my finger down the page to keep my eyes from skipping lines. I found "Gaynell G. Guidry" in the index and flipped to the one page where he was listed – 241.

Page 241 was part of a two-page spread of a single fraternity. On the left, page 240 was titled "A Year in the Life of a Pledge" – a picture of potential pledgees getting a tour of the fraternity house. A section labeled "Rites of Passage" – photos of fraternity members examining the pledge class, and one of the brothers and pledges gathered around a table piled high with cookies and a large punch bowl, the House Mother looking on with approving eyes from the end of the table, ladle in hand.

Page 241 was captioned "The Privilege of Passage." There were the two pictures of Herrington I had just seen before I put the book down. Herrington, with the paddle raised above his head. Herrington, with the broken paddle and the unbroken pledge class. I read the captions of both photographs.

I bent down close to the page. There was Guidry's name on the photo with the broken paddle. I hadn't recognized G.G. the first time I had looked at the picture, but there he was. Skinny. With tousled hair and wrinkled shirt and tie askew, with Herrington's arm around him and the broken paddle at their feet.

But what did I really know after having seen this picture? I guess anyone old enough could have told me that Herrington and G.G. were in college together, but why was it such a big deal that Micelli went out of his way to mention "old college days"?

I looked again through the indices in the yearbooks from 1965 through 1980. I hadn't been mistaken. I hadn't missed Guidry's name. He wasn't in any of the yearbooks other than 1971. Perhaps he didn't graduate. Was Guidry the "boy" that Micelli had mentioned when he spoke about "old college days"?

I couldn't figure it out.

I took out my cellphone and snapped a picture of the page. As a precaution, I took the book over to the photocopy machine and made several pictures of page 241 and tucked them under my shirt.

Now what?

I looked at my watch. It was after two in the morning. I called my house and checked the electronic answering machine. Maybe Kirk/Kuo had left a message after I had left Washington's to come here.

Beep. A click as a phone hung up as the message started to record.

Beep. Another bit of dead air.

Beep. A loud voice thick with anger. "Gonna get you, fucker. No second chances. The next thing you jump off of…if your shitty little heart is beating at all when you jump again, it won't be when you land." Click.

Nothing more. No mistaking Frankie's voice. There was no going home tonight.

Despite the hour, I quickly dialed Washington. The old man picked up the phone after two rings. "Hello," he said warily.

"Washington, it's me. Schex. You keep that shotgun loaded and close by. And don't go wandering over to my house. Understand?"

"Neighbor, what kind of trouble are you really in?"

"You just keep your and Durnella's door locked. I'll be in touch. And don't worry about your truck. I'll get it back to you."

CHAPTER 61

MONDAY

"OFFER THAT BOY SOME CREAM, W.T. You want him to ruin his stomach and burn his tongue like you, drinking that stuff black?"

I sat in Durnella and Washington Eby's kitchen. It was old but immaculate, the woodwork neatly painted, the linoleum floor freshly scrubbed. The curved edges of the appliances revealed their lineage; late 1950s or early 60s, but they were spotless. A pile of clean laundry was in a basket on the counter, and the ironing board and iron had been in use, as evidenced by a neat stack of crisply pressed clothes on a nearby chair.

"You want cream, Neighbor?"

"'Course he wants cream," Durnella said.

I really didn't, but it would do no good to disagree with Durnella.

Durnella sat down at the table and gave a motherly appraisal of my wrinkled clothes, unshaven face, unbrushed and matted hair, and soiled and sweaty bandages on my arm. "Slept in the truck, didn't you."

"Now Durnella, you and I have talked 'bout this before. Not appropriate to ask questions. What the boy done did is his own business."

Durnella ignored him. "Don't understand it. You got a nice house and a nice car, and you borrow W.T.'s truck. You're a professional man, Attorney Schexnaydre, and you sneak out at night. You, a single man, havin' to sneak out? Come the Judgment Day we're all gonna have to answer. Don't you want to get your life right and get back to church? Too much fast livin's not the way to get right in His sight."

"Woman. Please leave that boy alone. What he's been doin' or what he's got to do is none of our business."

"W.T., you can go on all you want, but it don't change things. What's right is right. And I can tell by lookin' at this boy that things are mighty wrong."

Washington gave me a look of resignation that told me he was not going to try to derail her.

"The devil works in mysterious ways," Durnella continued. "He tempts you mightily. He makes you think that what's goin' to give you lasting pain is pleasure. And the devil makes men look at women in a way that's the devil's own doin'. Those single women can be full of foolishness. They can lead you astray. You look at them and you don't see the devil in the temptation. You go dancin' with them and you don't feel the devil in your arms. You chase them and catch them and don't see the devil in your hands. The devil – he makes you ignore the signs. But those signs are there. Glory is just around the corner if you just raise your eyes up and look. The Lord can lift you up. He can. I've seen it and I know. What you need is to be raised up to glory and stop your foolishness."

I didn't dare interrupt her. Let her misconstrue what was going on. There was no harm. I raised the coffee cup to my lips, but the papers under my shirt crinkled audibly.

Durnella gave me a stare with her head tilted back, arms folded across her bosom. "Come on, now, that's not the starch in your shirt. Fact is, it doesn't appear that shirt has ever been starched. 'Course, that don't matter, when a person needs starch in their backbone more than in their clothes."

She put an arm out, palm up, demanding what was inside my shirt.

I looked across the table to Washington, who was deliberately avoiding me and gazing out the window.

"Don't go lookin' for W.T. to give you a way out, boy. He's seen the Lord too, or so he's told me, and he knows that I got the power of the Lord behind me. The Lord can help you stop sinnin' if you turn to the Lord."

I reached inside my shirt and handed her the photocopies of page 241 of the Gumbo, the one with the picture of Herrington and Guidry.

Durnella examined the pages and a look of puzzlement came to her face. Then consternation. Then anger. She turned to Washington, waving the papers in the air. "Old pictures. That's what this is. Some kind of pictures from some book, but not the kind I thought."

She handed the papers back to me and started in on her husband.

"W.T., you and me have been married too long for you to go misleadin' me like you've done. Here I've been thinkin' for some time this boy's been out sinnin' and you've done nothin' to say contrariwise. That's what I thought he was doin' in New Orleans! Thought for sure those pages were salacious things, the devil's things, things a man hides away, and I was all set to start some serious preachin'. Just knew for sure his papers must have been those kinds of pictures. And I was gonna save this boy's soul. I was just gettin' up a wind, and you knew where I was headed."

But she wasn't finished. She turned to me, taking my hands in hers. "You knew too. 'Course, you couldn't say nothin', I see that. Deny what I was talkin' about and I'd have thought you were just evadin' me and runnin' straight into the wicked clutches of the devil."

She patted my hands and then gave Washington a not-so-gentle slap on the arm. "But W.T., you've let me run on here and don't stop me? But this isn't about sinnin', now, is it?"

"Durnella…" I stopped. Calling Washington by his first name seemed entirely appropriate, but for some reason I couldn't call this lady, who was old enough to be my grandmother, by her first name.

I started again with the proper degree of respect. "Miz' Durnella, there was nothing Washington here was doing other than trying to protect me. And to protect you."

"Protect me? W.T., what's this boy talkin' about?"

"Miz' Durnella, you've got to trust me on this. It has to do with the fact that I can't be sure it's safe for me to use my car or to stay in my house at night right now. It has to do with some business outside of Baton Rouge. You don't want to know more, and I can't tell you more, even if you ask."

Durnella took a washrag and started to wipe down the kitchen table, cleaning off the damp rings left by the coffee cups, and spoke slowly as she worked. "You think I sit in my kitchen and tend my garden and don't know there's something unusual going on? You think I didn't know W.T. took his shotgun with him to New Orleans? You think I didn't worry myself sick about that until he came home? You think I didn't see the truck missin' from the driveway last night and know that W.T. must have known that it wasn't stolen, or the police would be here taking down his statement?"

She folded the washrag carefully, placed it on the edge of the table, put her hands in her lap, and faced me. "You think I sleep so soundly I didn't hear that phone ring last night? Knew it was you. Knew it must have been about the truck. But I thought all along it was bad sinnin' you was doin', and that W.T. was somehow tryin' to protect me from that, knowing my blood pressure would just shoot way up."

She looked pointedly at Washington. "As if it hadn't already, what with all this commotion goin' on."

She stood up and went over to the stove and poured herself another cup of coffee. "Why would you not want to use your car? Why would you not want to sleep in your house? Why would W.T. be oiling his shotgun before dawn this mornin'?"

Washington looked at his wife in amazement.

I started to speak, but she wagged a finger at me and said, "Now, you hush up, you hear. Don't say nothin'. If it was somethin' you could tell me, it would be somethin' you could have told W.T., and if you told him, I'd have sure known about it. But W.T. has said nothin' to me."

She looked at her husband again. "Nothin'!"

She leaned against the counter. "So, you don't tell W.T. nothin', and yet he could see you were in some type of trouble, and he was tryin' to help." The irritation was gone from her voice.

She affectionately rubbed Washington's bald head, and he squirmed with pleasure in his chair at her touch. "That's the kind of man I married. Sixty-odd years ago. If someone needs help, W.T. can't say no."

Washington craned upward to give her a kiss, "Woman, you amaze me every day."

She pushed him away playfully. "Get on with you, W.T. You and I are too old to go and start sparkin'."

Washington had a glint in his eye. "I don't know 'bout that."

"Too late in life and too early in the mornin' is what I say."

She took a seat at the table again and became serious. "Now, what I want to know is, Attorney Schexnaydre, do you really need to involve W.T. in whatever it is you're doin'? 'Cause we'll help you as neighbors all we can, but I don't like the idea of W.T. takin' his shotgun out. I don't like this all-night stuff, whatever the reason is for borrowin' the truck. And if W.T. ever came home in the condition you're in," she said, pointing to my bandaged arm, "I'd just..."

She stopped as her voice cracked. She reached into her bathrobe pocket, grabbed a wadded piece of tissue and held it to her nose a second while she composed herself.

Washington stood up, went behind her chair, and started massaging her shoulders.

Durnella put her tissue down and held on to one of Washington's hands while staring directly at me. "Look, if you need someone to be big and strong and young, I'll go call my grandnephew. He's a strapper. Had army experience. But don't involve W.T. Please don't."

"Woman, no need to involve Joleese or anyone else. Nothin's goin' on here that I can't take care of. I take care of you, don't I? Not gonna let nothin' happen to you or me."

I tried not to change expressions when I heard them mention Joleese. There couldn't be more than one person in the area by that name, and since he worked for Rad, there was no way I wanted Joleese involved.

"Miz' Durnella, you're right. Washington shouldn't be involved in anything. No more nighttime dealings. And I won't need his truck anymore."

I had figured out what to do next. I had to talk to Taylor. I could ask Lolly to set up a meeting at George & Beebo's Bar and Grill. I could walk there.

I looked at my watch. It was going on nine in the morning. Even with Frankie and Ribeye out there looking for me, I didn't think they would try anything in broad daylight on a workday. "I'm going to take my leave, Miz' Durnella, and go back home and clean up. I think it's safe there right now, at least before nightfall. And by then, I'll have other arrangements made."

I hadn't figured out yet what those arrangements would be.

Durnella's entire body looked grateful. The tension went out of her face. Her shoulders relaxed under Washington's massaging hands.

"Woman, you were gonna take a mornin' bath after you washed the greens. Well, the greens are washed. Why don't you do the same for yourself? I'll just go take Luther out for a walk. We'll be back by the time you're out and dressed."

Washington closed the kitchen door as we walked onto the back porch. Only after the door shut did he reach around the corner and pull his shotgun out of the closet. "Let's go check out your house together."

CHAPTER 62

WASHINGTON AND I CAREFULLY INSPECTED the perimeter of my house and the locks. We examined the driveway and ligustrum hedge and the street. Nothing unusual. We searched the interior of my home. The mess was untouched. No one was there.

I called Lolly's office. She wasn't around but I spoke to Beau and told him to give my message to Taylor. He didn't ask why, and I didn't tell him.

I didn't plan to be in my house for long. Just time for a quick shower and to grab my cell phone charger and another few days' worth of clothes in case I couldn't come back again for a while.

I let the showerhead water cascade down my back, being careful not to get the bandages on my arm wet. I soaped up, rinsed off and grabbed a towel. "Washington," I called out, "I'm done. Thanks for staying."

No response.

"Washington?"

No answer. That was troublesome.

I wrapped the towel around my waist and pressed my ear against the bathroom door. No sound. That was even more disturbing. I had thought we were safe here in my house, with cars passing by every few minutes, with the sun shining brightly. Maybe this was another instance of my having deceived myself.

I opened the door cautiously. No one was in the bedroom.

As I moved into the hallway I saw, through the windows on the front door, shadows on the porch.

With my pulse quickening, and my brain frantically trying to figure out what I was going to do at this point, dressed only a towel, I pressed my back against the wall and started to inch back to the bedroom.

The front door partially opened. I froze.

Washington stuck his head inside and, seeing me holding the towel in place, couldn't suppress a grin. "You got a visitor, and I've got to get back to Durnella. I'm sure you can handle this on your own."

He held the door open and Millie Sue came inside. She was squeezed into a tight skirt and wore a tank top that seemed to have been shrink-wrapped on her torso. She flaunted pink high heels.

As he took his leave, Washington said cheerfully, "Now, y'all have fun!"

CHAPTER 63

I PULLED MY TOWEL TIGHTER around me.

Millie Sue gave my body the kind of scrutiny I had given hers when she first appeared with Guidry. "I approve. You're in good shape, except for the nasty, nasty cut on your arm. You know, I tried to call *you* a couple of times last night. But there was only this silly answering machine. I didn't want to leave a message for *you* because I really had to see *you*."

Each time she pronounced the word 'you' she touched my chest with the long, red fingernail of her index finger.

"Yes I did. I had to see *you*. In person. I even came by late last night and knocked on the door, but there was no answer."

She came closer and I backed my way down the hall.

She kept moving toward me. Suddenly, she snatched my towel away.

"See, I told you I had to see *you*. *All* of you. And, you are," she said, as she gazed at my crotch, "*impressive*."

The last thing I needed was Millie Sue making advances. I went into my bedroom, closed the door, and quickly started getting dressed.

"You're so modest." She rapped impatiently on the door. "Are you decent yet...or do you want to stay indecent?"

She didn't wait for an answer and came on in. I was getting into my khaki trousers. I turned my back to her, yanked up the pants, and pulled up the zipper, but it got stuck in my underwear and I struggled to free it.

"Need some help? Something I can hold?"

"No!" I finished up and found her sitting provocatively on the edge of my bed.

She eyed the pillows on the floor and the sheets pulled free from a corner of the mattress. "A night of passion?" She rose and gently stroked my reddened neck where the wire had cut me. She examined the bandages on my arm. "Must have been some passion."

I wriggled away and grabbed a shirt. "It's not what you think. Get up and let's go into the conference room."

Millie Sue flung herself back on the bed, kicked off her shoes, and leaned against the headboard, letting her skirt ride up to her crotch, revealing her powder-pink thong. "Oh, I don't know. What I have to say is pretty private stuff. Maybe this is the best location for private stuff."

I went over, meaning to pull her off the bed, but she rose willingly into my arms.

I was not in the mood. Not with her. Ever.

I disengaged, slung her over my shoulder, and carried her into the conference room where I plopped her down on a chair.

She was not the slightest bit annoyed. "I rather enjoyed that. I like a man who's a little bit rough. Let's do that again!"

She could pull her wiles on G.G., but not me. I snapped at her. "What do you want?"

"Why, I want *you* to be my lawyer," she cooed, batting her eyelashes and ignoring my brusque tone. "You're the *only* lawyer I know, and if G.G. used you, you must be a *good* one. I bet you're real good. In *this* room, and," she said, pointing to the bedroom, "in *that* one."

"Out!" I pointed to the door.

She didn't move from the chair. "Pleeeease," she purred. "I signed all those papers the last time I was here, and G.G. said I was a real president of real companies. Well, G.G.'s gone. Promised me lots of money. Said he was going to give it to me, in cash. But he didn't. Scoots off on me and gets shot and ass-fixed or ass-fixiated or whatever you call it. Serves that fat bastard right, I guess, running out on me like that. I told him real clear; no money from him, no more fun from me. Being a paper president was fine, but money is so much finer."

Millie Sue had joined the ranks of those whose only grief over G.G.'s death was that they didn't get the riches they expected. I guess I was part of that group too.

"I want you to be my lawyer," Millie Sue said, resuming her seductive tone, "and tell me what all those companies do and how I can get paid for being a president."

"Didn't you understand? I'm not going to be your lawyer. Out! Now!"

"I know what you're thinking." She stood up, much too close to me, and opened the top four buttons of her blouse. She wasn't wearing a bra. "You're thinking that if I don't have a job, and if I need to hire you to tell me what to do and how to do it, I won't have any way to pay you."

She reached out and put my hand on her breast. "I can think of lots of ways to pay you."

I pulled my hand away. "Let me explain it to you very simply. First, I'm not going to be your lawyer. Second, I don't want to be your lawyer. Third, I can't be your lawyer. That's it. So go." I pushed her toward the front door.

She went out onto the porch, but as I got ready to close the door behind her, she said, "My shoes."

I retrieved her pink high heels from the bedroom, but when I handed them to her on the porch, she grabbed my crotch. "Are you sure that there's no way I can pay you to represent me?"

I jumped back. "Get out!"

"Are you some kind of faggot?" Gone was the purring and breathiness and seduction. "I'm not stupid. I'll get what I want when I want it! I got G.G., didn't I? Got to be a president, didn't I? I'll get those businesses or papers or whatever it is I signed, and I'll get someone to get me the money that's got to be there."

She ran down the steps barefoot toward her car, threw her high heels in the back seat, and, as she started her engine, rolled down her window and yelled at me through the opening. "No wonder G.G. was your client. You're just like him. Can't get it up!"

Her car raced backward out of the driveway, almost hitting a BMW that was pulling up at the curb in front of my house.

Millie Sue continued yelling, "You kick me out of your bedroom? You kick me out of your house? Well, screw you! Go try to get it up for someone else!"

As Millie Sue's car screeched down the street, the door of the BMW at the curb swung open.

Taylor emerged.

CHAPTER 64

TAYLOR STOOD IN THE YARD, hands on her hips, her face so red with anger that it almost matched her lipstick. "You and that tramp! First she's with G.G. and then with you! That's why you couldn't meet me at your house this morning! That's why you wanted to go to George and Beebo's! How could you stand to be with that slut? How could you do this to me?"

She came up the stairs, leaping two at a time, and started to pound on my chest with her fists. I pulled her back into the house, slammed the door shut, and grabbed both her wrists. "Stop this. I can't believe you, of all people, are going to make a scene in public at this point. That's all you need, to have the neighbors call the police."

She pulled away and started to hit me again. "You're a bastard, Schex. You turn away from me when I offer myself but you sleep with her? You fuck her and you want to meet me afterward? You're probably scheming with her to get my money. You're disgusting."

I simply backed away, ducked under her flailing arms, and grabbed her knees and flipped her face down onto the sofa. Then I sat on her back and pinned her arms.

"Are you going to stop?"

"No!" She tried to struggle out from under me, but I held her firmly. She twisted this way and that but couldn't get free. Finally she stopped trying.

"OK," she said, breathing hard after her exertions, "get off me."

"Finished? Truce?"

"Yes."

I moved off her back and let go of her arms. As she turned over she made a fist and hit me squarely in the jaw. It hurt.

"Now I'm finished," she announced.

We sat on my overstuffed fraying sofa, each of us in separate corners, like prizefighters between bouts. It was time to have it out with her. "Taylor, I'm going to give you one last chance to level with me. This is it. This is the last time."

"The last time for what? Meet you at George and Beebo's, Beau said. That didn't make any sense. Why not my house? Why not here? Something was up. That's why I came early. To find out what you were up to. And now I know."

"You don't know anything. Least of all about this. But you sure as hell know a lot that you haven't told me yet."

"There you go with your lawyer stuff. Evading questions by asking a question and changing the subject. Couldn't have been clearer." Taylor mimicked Millie Sue's voice, "'Go try to get it up for someone else' she said. Must have been a rough night for you, performance-wise."

"Now you're not merely jumping to conclusions, you're lunging at them."

"Am I? Well just answer my questions, Schex."

"You answer mine. You didn't last time."

"I told you all you asked."

"You told me what you wanted, Taylor, and avoided everything else."

"What did you learn from Tony?"

"What did you know about Tony that you haven't told me, Taylor?

"Answer me! Have you found the money?"

"No, you answer me! What about G.G. and Herrington?"

"What about the money, Schex?"

"What about you and Herrington?"

We both paused. This was not getting either of us anywhere.

CHAPTER 65

GEORGE AND BEEBO'S HAD FEW customers during the mid-morning hours. The bar and grill had survived the decline and then the gentrification of downtown. It survived changing tastes and changing fashions by changing nothing.

Beebo presided from a tall stool next to the cash register behind the bar. The only thing that had altered over the years was that Beebo kept getting bigger and bigger. Oversized and clothed in a tent of a dress, with a cigarette drooping from her bulbous lips and a beer in one hand, she was as much a fixture of the place as the scarred wooden tables, as the aluminum-topped bar, and as the faded photographs in dusty frames on the walls, pictures of former LSU football players caught in their moments of glory in long-forgotten games.

The dawn patrol – the fishermen stopping off before heading out across the Mississippi River bridge and into the nearby swamps and bayous, the cops coming off their all-night beats, the fireman from the nearby fire station – had started arriving before 5:00 a.m. and now were long gone. The lunch crowd wouldn't show up until noon or later and would hang around for hours.

It was almost 10:30 a.m., and Taylor and I sat at one of the back tables in the nearly empty restaurant, finishing breakfast. On my plate the remnants of *pain perdu* swam in a sea of molasses, the fried French bread turning soggy in the sticky liquid. On Taylor's plate, cottage cheese and dry toast.

"OK, Taylor," I said. "Let's start again. Uninterrupted truth. One question, one answer. No feints. No crawfishing sideways. Just a direct answer to a direct question. How about that?"

"One question, one answer. Fair enough. I'll go first."

She did it again. Jumping in. Trying to control things.

I let her speak.

"What about the more than half a million those guys took from you? What about my money?"

"That's two questions," I said, wiping away the molasses from the edges of my mouth. "Short answer. I didn't get it."

"You know that's not what I'm asking. Did you find out where it was? Did Tony agree to get it all back to you? When are you going to get it?"

"The deal was one question, one answer. My turn. What was going on between G.G. and Herrington?"

"Damn it, Schex," Taylor said, pushing away the table and causing the plates to tumble to the floor. "TELL ME ABOUT THE GODDAMN MONEY!"

Beebo, from her perch behind the cash register, merely took another puff of her cigarette.

I pulled Taylor out into the parking lot. "Are you planning to cause a scene everywhere? All you need is for cops to show up here and start questioning you about…about almost anything. In fact, given the way things are going, give me ten dollars."

"You are out of your mind!

"No. This is completely rational. We're going to go somewhere completely private, and I'm going to ask you a bunch of questions. And you're going to level with me once and for all. But, before we do that, you are going to hire me, for the princely sum of ten dollars, for the exclusive and limited purpose of advising you concerning your rights in and to Camellia Industries."

"Why the fuck should I do that?"

"Because then *whatever* you tell me connected with Camellia is protected by the attorney-client privilege. And the last thing you want to have happen is for Rad to call me to the stand with me unable to assert the privilege. So fork over the ten dollars."

CHAPTER 66

WE SAT IN TAYLOR'S BMW on top of the levee, under the I-10 bridge that soared over George & Beebo's. Taylor had turned the engine on and cranked up the air conditioning. Not even noon and it was already more than a sweltering ninety outside.

The bridge arched above us, its stalactites of support oozing into the syrup of the river. The vast Mississippi swirled in front of us, dark and brown, the color of café au lait. It flowed in thick currents around the concrete bridge pylons, looking as viscous as the molasses around my *pain perdu*. But, every so often, a speedboat of driftwood caught in the current swept by. Clumps of trees and branches, propelled downriver, crashed into the pylons, smashing to bits. Pieces were sucked under only to surface a hundred or more yards downstream.

"Let's try again, Taylor. Tell me about you and Herrington and G.G. What was really going on?"

"Permits. It was all about the permits."

"The permits to keep the Camellia Industries plant open?"

Taylor nodded. "The permits came because G.G. knew Cart. A favor for an old friend. Old friends sometimes feel that they can impose on one another, even after years of not seeing each other."

She certainly had imposed on me. And she had slept with Cart. I just reiterated "Old *friends*?"

"There are all kinds of friendship," she said finally. "Cart and G.G. had known each other at LSU, before G.G. had to drop out. Cart's family always had money. G.G. never had any. And yet G.G. always said that Cart would help him in any way he could. And he did."

I looked down the batture that ran on the river side of the levee. Today the river was a manacled creature, subdued by the man-made cage that ran hundreds of miles to the north and stretched southward almost to the Gulf of Mexico. The Mississippi River's levee withstood Katrina while the canal levees failed. This levee protected New Orleans from being completely washed into the Gulf of Mexico. This levee protected the homes and businesses along hundreds and hundreds of miles. And the river rushed by, oblivious to it all.

Taylor had built a levee around what she knew. And me? A levee around what I felt.

"Helping an old friend I understand, Taylor, but why would Herrington continue to help when all it caused was potential problems for him? I mean, everyone knows that Herrington wants to run for a higher office. Governor, they say. Why risk publicity opposing the environment? Or the black vote? What was in it for him?"

"I thought it was friendship, Schex. Just that. At least at first."

"At first? What was it at second?"

"I didn't know. I really didn't." She said it so earnestly that I almost believed her.

"I only realized what was going on when G.G. started planning to buy more land," she said.

Her answer revealed that she was retreating into her usual, evasive ways. "Either you lied to me then or you're lying to me now, Taylor, so stop it. When you first came to see me, you told me G.G. was taking Camellia Industries' money to run off with Millie Sue. Now you're telling me that you knew he was using the money to buy land, but the land was not going to be owned by Camellia Industries.

"Does it really matter, Schex?"

"How could you know that?

"He told me."

"I don't understand," I said.

"He told me when I confronted him about it."

"Where was that? When?"

"At the Camellia Industries plant. The night he died."

CHAPTER 67

I GRILLED HER. OVER AND over. Every fact repeated. I watched for the slightest inconsistency in her story or in her demeanor.

She told me how she had watched G.G. change over time, as he became more and more remote.

She went through being called by the bank about the overdrawn checks. No, she didn't know about the accounts at other financial institutions. She really thought G.G. dealt with only one bank.

Yes, she had told the bank teller that she wished G.G. was dead. She also told her hairdresser, the lady who did her nails, and three of her friends.

I made her tell me five times about how she and G.G. went to the Cotillion Ball last week, that same night G.G. had showed up at my house with the cash-filled suitcase. About how she confronted him at the Cotillion. Of him driving off after the fight and of her having to get a ride home…with Carter Herrington.

Only after we had gone through her story again and again, and I was as satisfied as I ever would be that she was being as frank as she was capable of being, did I question her about what happened after Carter Herrington had left her off at her house…after the Cotillion…on the night G.G. was killed.

"It was real late. I was trying to figure out how to royally screw over G.G., to kick him out of Camellia Industries. I had maybe three-quarters of a bottle of real good wine and I was in the living room, relaxing on the sofa in the dark. Heard his Mercedes drive up. The house lights weren't on. He must have thought I wasn't at home, because when I opened the door there he was, key in hand. I confronted him. Where was my money? My half of the bank accounts? My half of the corporation? But he wouldn't answer. He just jumped in his car and took off. So I grabbed my keys and went after him."

She told me about following him at high speed down the expressway and out of town, across the bridge, G.G. driving frantically and Taylor equally as reckless. Out into the countryside, onto the narrow roads of St. Bonaventure Parish, and into the Camellia Industries plant gates.

"G.G. had unlocked the gate, and I pulled in after him, before he had a chance to close it on me. I had it out with him, standing in the headlights of the two cars, him standing in front of his Mercedes, me in front of my BMW. Told him I knew all about the money. He swore to me that it would all work out, that he was going to invest it in more land. G.G. was making no sense. Thinking about not paying Tony? That was stupid. Taking up with Millie Sue? That was stupid, too. But taking money that was owed to Tony, staying around, and buying land? That was beyond stupid."

"So you threatened to go to Tony?"

"Damn right. And you know what he tried to do? Tried to convince me that I should wait because he was going to make not just millions, but tens of millions. Promised me, begged me, threatened me, and promised again. Said he'd give me my half if I wouldn't go to Tony."

"Buying land would bring him tens of millions?"

"That's what he said. The golf course would do it."

"Come on, Taylor. He took the money to buy land for a golf course? In the middle of St. Bonaventure Parish next to a plant that they're trying to shut down because it's supposed to be an environmental hazard?"

"I couldn't believe it either. A fucking golf course! But he went on and on about how he was going to head off Rad's group by developing the goddamnedest fanciest golf course and subdivision you'd ever seen. A big levee on one side, big enough to hide the plant, big enough to provide those in the subdivision a view of nothing but man-made hills covered with trees. Big lots and expensive houses that would line the greens. Was going to call that fucking levee a 'visual berm'! He said 'Nothing insulates you from an attack of the socialist-fascist-environmental-shit-head groups more than lily-white homeowners protecting their turf.' Said that he could make money selling the lots around the golf course and requiring golf memberships and maintenance fees from all the homeowners. Told me to hold on, that he couldn't tell me before what he was going to do because I wouldn't have let him do it. Well, at least that was right. If he had told me what he was planning, assuming that anything he was telling me at that point was true, I'd have pulled my half of the money out of the bank accounts in an instant."

Maybe G.G. had lied to her, but maybe he hadn't. Buying land was what G.G. had come to me for. I did some rough calculations in my head. If the land around the plant was bought, as G.G. had planned, for a low enough amount through the shell corporations, and if the lots were priced and marketed right – country living and a golf course within an easy drive of the city – then there might have been money to be made. G.G. may have really been on to something. No one could claim environmental racism against Camellia Industries if the things nearest the plant were fancy homes for rich white people. Assuming he could pull it off. Assuming people would buy the homes next to the facility. But then there was a golf course and fancy homes within a couple of miles of the nuclear power plant in St. Francisville a half hour north of Baton Rouge. Whatever might become of the crud dumped at Camellia Industries couldn't be a fraction as bad as what would happen if the nuclear power plant leaked, blew, or was hit by a plane.

"He was crazy, you know Schex, at the end. He didn't deny a thing about Millie Sue, but he said he and I could still be business partners. G.G. swore that we were good for each other, at least on the business side, and that if I'd just stick with him I'd get my half back and much more. 'Just don't tell Tony,' he begged. G.G. said he had to have a few more days but that he'd take care of Tony in his own way, and that Tony would get paid."

"And you believed him?"

"Hell no. Told him he could go fuck Millie Sue all he wanted. He could go fuck himself for all I cared. The only thing he couldn't do was fuck with Tony. Or me. Or my money."

CHAPTER 68

TAYLOR SWORE SHE DIDN'T KILL G.G. She admitted that, if she had known about the $2.8 million difference between the $1.6 mil from the bank and the $4.4 mil in the suitcase, she might have done something to him, but she swore on her mother's grave that she didn't know about the additional money. Not then. Not that night.

She swore on her mother *and* father's graves that she left G.G. alive at the Camellia Industries plant. That she had told him she'd give him a few days to get the money back, but that if she didn't have it in her hands by then, she was going to tell Tony everything.

We went over that evening again and again, and each time her story was consistent.

So I went back to the Herrington issue. How was it that Camellia Industries remained open? "What about the permits, Taylor? G.G. couldn't continue running the plant without permits. He couldn't build a subdivision without permits. Mere college friendship with Herrington wasn't going to solve those issues."

"It's the money, Schex. When *you* told me about the extra money, I knew right away what it was for."

"Then tell me. Was G.G. going to use the money to pay off Herrington, or was he paying off someone else?"

"You don't understand a thing, do you?"

"That's why I'm asking."

"As if when I tell you, then you'd understand? You might then know what I know, but would you understand?"

"No more games. Just tell me. Who was getting the money?"

"G.G."

"No. You know what I mean. Who was G.G. paying off?"

"You see, I tell you and you hear but you don't understand. G.G. wasn't paying off anyone."

"Dammit, Taylor, don't you use that tone with me. You told me that G.G. wasn't paying off anyone, but that the money was a payoff. I listen carefully, and now you're just going in circles."

"One more time, Schex. Don't you get it? G.G. wasn't *giving* money to anyone. He was *getting* money. He was the one getting paid off."

CHAPTER 69

UNTIL THAT MOMENT, I FELT I had gotten a roughly factual story from Taylor. With Taylor, you can never be absolutely sure whether a story is the entire truth or whether it just has enough confirmable facts to seem truthful.

Her statements until this point seemed to make some sense, but her last one threw me. "Someone was paying off G.G.? Taylor, why would you even think that the money was flowing *to* G.G. rather than G.G. paying off someone else? I mean, how else could he keep Camellia Industries in operation unless G.G. was getting money over, under, or around the table to someone?"

"Why is it you can't see, Schex, what's in front of your face? You never could, you know. You see what you want to see, not what's really there. You hear words but don't get their meaning."

Her comments made me think back to what Washington had said last night. What had the old man called it? Hard and soft listening? "I hear exactly what you say, Taylor, but I want you to explain why you're saying it. What makes you think someone was paying anything *to* G.G.?"

"Because of what I felt after I met Cart."

"Carter Herrington? What does he have to do with G.G. getting paid off?"

She had done it. She had set me off. I couldn't help myself. I peppered her with a stream of questions. "Your good buddy 'Cart' Herrington? How long had you been sleeping with him? Were you doing it while you were with G.G.? Did he know? Were you sleeping with Herrington while you were married to me and messing around with Catch?"

"You're missing the point," she said, and for the first time that morning a slight smile flickered across her face. She had played me, and she knew it.

"Just listen without interrupting me with foolish questions. Look, I've known Cart a long time, even before I met you. I first got acquainted with him when I was a freshman in college. We met and…well, it really doesn't matter how we met. Just say that for a while we were very good friends, and we've been friends ever since. So, what was I to do? That fucking environmental group was trying to shut down Camellia Industries plant, G.G. was dead, and you had not yet agreed to represent me. You wanted to see the corporate books first, remember? Although I agreed to get them to you, I didn't know if you'd do anything, or have time to do anything even if you agreed. And look at you. Here it is, three days before the hearing, and you still haven't done shit. Never got your $50,000 retainer, did you? Lost that to Tony and his buddies, didn't you. Well, I've paid you $10 today. Have you filed any papers with the court? No. Have you done any preparation for the hearing?"

I carefully avoided indicating that I was not planning to do a thing for Camellia Industries in court; all I had told her was that for ten dollars I would advise her about her rights concerning Camellia. If I mentioned this again, however, I would send her off on a tangent. I simply held up my bandaged hand and said, "Between being a 'guest' of Frankie and Ribeye and then going to New Orleans to see Micelli, I've been a little busy over the past weekend. But, of course, you're changing the subject again."

"No I'm not. You asked how I know about where all the extra $2.8 million, above and beyond what was in the accounts, came from, and I'm telling you."

"So, tell me."

"After you said you had to look at the corporate books, and after I said I'd get them to you, I knew I had to hedge my bets. I didn't know if you'd really agree to help, or if you could help – and it looks like, unless you get your ass in gear and prepare for the upcoming hearing in court, you won't be of any help – so I tried to get in to see Cart. His Department was a defendant as well. The injunction suit is as much an attack on the DEH permitting process as it is on Camellia Industries operations. I wanted to be sure Cart was going to protect me and Camellia all the way, to put the best of his attorneys on the case. I couldn't get an appointment to see him. Some bitch receptionist kept giving me shit excuses, but I know he likes to eat at The Gallery Steakhouse. That's where I went, hoping to find him, and I did."

"And you did this on the evening I was out at the St. Bonanventure gym? *Before* I got the boxes from Spider? *Before* we went to Poirrier's?"

"Yes."

"And you didn't tell me?"

"Why should I? You didn't ask. Besides, the very next day, in Lolly's office, I did tell Beau about the meeting. He questioned me for hours, you know."

"Don't change the subject again. What about the meeting with Herrington? What happened? And tell me in as much detail as you told Beau."

"If I did that, you still wouldn't know anything."

"What is that supposed to mean, Taylor?

"Well, let me tell you exactly what I told Beau, and then you tell me if you know anything more than you know now. You won't, of course, because you don't really listen."

"Just tell me, without all the asides."

"So I found him at The Gallery, with his usual corner table filled with the usual pols. He was working the room when I came in, shaking hands all around. You got to give it to Cart. He never passes up a chance to campaign, even if he's not officially running for something. Well, the minute he sees me, he's very polite. Tells me how sorry he was to have heard about G.G., about how I had his sympathies and all that. So, I thanked him and said 'I want you to continue to do for me what you were doing for G.G.'"

"Hell, it was like I had set his ass on fire. He hustled me out of the restaurant, furious. His face was all red, even his nose – he gets like that, you know, whenever he's angry or real excited, and it doesn't matter what causes the excitement, could be anger, or it could be passion, he just gets red all over – anyway, he was really, really angry."

I let pass her comment about Herrington getting red 'all over' from passion. He was just another entry on the scorecard of her lovers. Let her finish the story and then I could come back to it if I wanted. If I cared.

"We were out there, on the wide side porch of The Gallery. 'Demands' he says to me, real quiet like, so no one could hear him. 'I've had enough of demands,' he complained. 'G.G.'s dead. I'm not going to start getting demands from you.' I don't know what he's talking about, but I try to calm him down. So, I simply ask him, nice as can be, 'Cart, why get angry?' I told him, 'I haven't made any demands. If you were helping G.G. keep permits, help me. Just keep the permits up. Just make sure you've got your top lawyer sitting in that courtroom to fight the injunction. That's all I wanted to talk to you about. To make sure you put your best people on this, because Camellia Industries is all I have.'"

"And, when I said that, it was like turning off a boiling pot. He cooled down and looked almost relieved. He said he'd do what he could within the bounds of the law – those were his exact words, 'within the bounds of the law' – and then went back inside to his lunch, leaving me out there on the porch."

"Well?"

"Well what, Schex? That was the meeting. That's what I told Beau. Now I've told you. And I can see from your face that you still don't get it, do you."

"Oh, I get it all right. You haven't told me a damned thing. You said you suspected that G.G. was getting paid off by someone. Now you want me to believe that you suspected it was Herrington paying off G.G. because of what happened in the restaurant? Just because Herrington got angry when you asked him to do for you what he was doing for G.G.?

Just because Herrington calmed down when you said all you wanted was for him to make sure the Department had a good lawyer in court? Taylor, spare me! That's the flimsiest of theories on the limpest of facts."

"Schex, it makes perfect sense, but I didn't understand myself what had happened until I thought about it in light of your telling me about the extra money. I hadn't known about the extra $2.8 million, but when you told me about it, everything fit together. The $2.8 million couldn't have come from the business. I'd have known about it. No, it had to have come from somewhere else, from someone else. And that someone had to be Cart."

She was doing her usual. Working me up again. Taunting me while at the same time darting away from the truth. Like she did when we were married. You'd have thought I would have learned by now to deal with all that, but I felt myself slipping again back into the same pattern of her saying the incredible and my being incredulous.

"That doesn't make any sense at all," I said. I should have left it there, but I followed her down the path she had taken, trying to point out why it was a dead end. "Why would Carter Herrington pay anything to G.G.? It was G.G. who needed Herrington's DEH permits. Herrington didn't need anything from G.G. And you wonder why Herrington was angry with you? You know, Taylor, you make it easy for people to be angry with you. Herrington could have been angry that you – what with your name all over the news because of your arrest – that you were asking him for anything in a public place. Don't you see? He could be polite as long as he was consoling you on the loss of G.G., but the minute you asked him to do anything, it was like a demand. In fact, your life has been one long series of 'requests' that are really demands. And when someone doesn't immediately acquiesce to your 'request,' you blow up."

That did it. She started screaming at me. "Fuck it! Fuck it all, Schex! *My* money! *I NEED MY MONEY*! GO FUCKING GET IT FOR ME!" She unlocked the doors and pointed for me to exit.

I didn't budge from the passenger seat. "Now you claim righteous indignation? Righteous anything doesn't fit you, Taylor."

She took a deep breath and gritted her teeth. She adjusted the rear-view mirror. She started the car and drove back down the levee road.

By the time she pulled into the parking lot of George & Beebo's, she had regained her composure. "Schex, I don't care if you don't believe what I now know to be true, because it doesn't matter. It's the perfect truth, don't you see? Tony doesn't want the money. Cart can't ask for it back if he doesn't know I have it, and once I have it he still can't ask for it back without running the risk of some TV or newspaper reporter finding out about it…from me, if necessary, and he knows I'll do it if he tries to screw me on this. Cart wants to run for Governor or Senator so badly he can taste it. He can't afford to cross me. No publicity, no scandal. So, the money is mine."

She was waiting for me to respond, but I simply exited the car, leaving the door open, letting the humid heat overpower the BMW's air conditioning system.

"What?" she yelled as I walked away. "You're not going to get my money for me? After all I've done for you?"

After all she had done *for* me? It was all that she had done *to* me.

I came back to the driver's side of her BMW. She rolled down her window, and I said to her, "When you're finished with your fantasies and are ready to talk seriously, call me. I'll give you the full ten dollars' worth of advice you've paid for. But, I'll give you five dollars' worth right now. If you're so concerned about what's going to happen in court, you better get Carter Herrington's people there to make sure the plant can reopen."

CHAPTER 70

I SAT AT A BACK table in George & Beebo's for a couple of hours, working on some fried catfish and my fourth beer, trying to drive away the pain in my aching arm with calories and alcohol, and trying to figure out if anything that Taylor said could have made sense.

I had written down a series of numbers on the paper napkin. Round numbers would do for now. Didn't need to calculate down to the penny.

"$4.4 mil." The amount of cash in the suitcase G.G. had left me. Tony had kept all of it as a 'loan repayment' except for the roughly half a million that Frankie and Ribeye now had.

"$1.6 mil." The money G.G. had taken from the Camellia Industries bank account. The money Taylor had originally been looking for.

"$2.8 mil." The difference between the $4.4 million and the $1.6 million. The money that Taylor said she hadn't known anything about. Where did the $2.8 million come from?

And why did G.G. need the $4.4 million? Was it really for a golf course and a subdivision next to Camellia Industries? Or was it so that Camellia Industries could continue to operate? Or was some of the money going for each purpose? Was G.G. getting ready to leave Taylor for Millie Sue? Was G.G. going to build a high levee to hide the factory from the golf course and subdivision?

Was the $2.8 million really money that Herrington had given to G.G.? Paid to G.G.? Loaned to G.G.? If so, why? If it was a loan, why was it made without security and without getting an interest in the business, like Micelli obtained?

Something was missing. Or Taylor was wrong. Or Taylor was misleading me again. And why was Micelli spinning out clues as if unraveling them would save me?

On the other hand, G.G. had said, when he had first come to my office, that the neighbors wouldn't sell the property if they knew he was going to own it. And the entire reason G.G. had hired me was to form shell corporations to buy up the property. And the abstracts of title that Spider had brought for me to examine certainly were real enough.

So G.G. had planned all along to buy up property. A golf course might make sense in some distorted manner. Who would care or suspect how the mounds on the golf course were built? Who would question whether berms and sculptured fairways hid something ominous buried beneath? And land surrounding a golf course, with vistas of an apparent arcadia, could be sold at a huge premium. A golf course and club house itself might even be run profitably. But if the money was not for a golf course, then for what?

None of this shed any light on who would have wanted to kill G.G.

Taylor was the only one with a motive.

And none of this explained Spider's death.

And it didn't explain why G.G. had brought the suitcase full of bills to me in the first place.

I was still hungry, and I still had no answers. I went over to the cash register where Beebo sat on her stool, the thick skin of her upper arms falling loosely around her elbows, and ordered a plate of red beans and rice.

"With or without sausage, Dahlin'? We got some hot sausage in the back. George'll grill it up for you if you want. Also got boudin, if you want that instead."

"Hot sausage. And another beer."

"George!" Beebo yelled over her shoulder while pushing a bottle of Abita across the counter to me.

I went back to the table I had occupied all afternoon, still trying to puzzle it out. Did Taylor really follow G.G. down to the plant that night?

Why not wait to talk with him when he came back to the house, at another time? And yet, if it was not true, why did Taylor tell me this?

If she went to the plant, why would she leave without getting something more than G.G.'s promise?

On the other hand, if it did happen the way she said, it had its own weird logic. If G.G. thought Taylor was going to go to Tony, he'd have promised her anything.

And if Taylor didn't know that G.G. had all that cash, she might have believed she'd have to wait a few days before he could get his hands on any of the funds.

Maybe Taylor thought she had G.G. in a position where he couldn't do anything but pull money out of whatever accounts he had stashed it in to pay her off.

George came over to my table holding a large plate of red beans and rice topped by two huge links of sausage glistening with grease. In one movement he put the plate down and picked up the four empty beer bottles on the table.

G.G. and Taylor. G.G. and Spider. G.G. and Millie Sue. G.G. and Herrington.

Herrington and Taylor. Herrington and Trey. Trey and Taylor.

It was too confusing.

I drank the rest of the bottle and held it up for Beebo to see. She signaled me to come over to the bar.

"Got nowheres to go, Dahlin'?"

She was right. I didn't have anywhere to go. I had no intention of returning to Taylor's, and my own house was not safe with Frankie and Ribeye looking for me, leaving me messages on my machine.

"A beer, Beebo. All I need is another beer."

"You've been sittin' on your haunches all afternoon. George, come out here!"

George dutifully came out of the kitchen, the door swinging behind him.

"This boy's been sittin' here so long he don't even know what day it is."

George automatically nodded in agreement.

Beebo looked through the opening that separated the grill from the bar, and, spotting something that displeased her, commanded, "George! Go get that sausage back in the icebox. You want to let it go and spoil?"

Beebo rolled her eyes at all of George's perceived deficiencies as he slunk back through the swinging door, but she addressed me in a motherly tone. "Whatcha been doin' with your life? You come in here all scraped up and lathered like a horse that's been runnin' too long, and then you sit back in the corner and drink like you can't get to the bottom of the bottle fast enough. I've never seen you drinkin' like that. Now you've gone and forgot what's happenin' today?"

"Too much has happened already, Beebo."

"Whatever you say. But I didn't think I'd see the day that someone who lived downtown would forget about the march. Gonna have big crowds, I think."

She called toward the kitchen again, the motherly tone instantly evaporating. "George! You got those paper goods out? Plates? Napkins? And that canned beer iced down good?"

Beebo spun her girth slowly back around toward me. "That environmentalist march starts at five. Sun don't set until after eight tonight, and I know it's hot out there. By the time those crowds walk by here from LSU, they'll be hungry as all get out and six-pack thirsty. Me and George are gonna be ready. Make some good money tonight."

March? I vaguely recalled Rad mentioning a march when I was being patched up by Joleese.

Beebo yelled over her shoulder. "George! Don't let them red beans burn."

CHAPTER 71

MY OPTIONS WERE LIMITED. I couldn't stay at George & Beebo's all night. I couldn't even go to a cheap motel. The only money I now possessed was the ten dollars I had extracted from Taylor, and I still had that only because Beebo let me run up a tab. I promised her I'd settle up in the next few weeks.

There would be safety in a crowd. It would occupy another couple of hours, and then afterward I could decide where I might find a place to spend the rest of the evening.

By the time I finished two more beers and walked outside, the street was packed, with several hundred people stretching out in front of me on the last half mile of the march before they reached the capitol. From down the road that ran back to LSU were thousands more who would have to pass by George & Beebo's.

Some were carrying candles, shielding the flames to prevent them from blowing out. Others had cell phones with candle apps. Still others held flashlights. Only a sliver of orange illuminated the western horizon over the Mississippi River as night fell and the legato parade of lights, wielded by young and old alike, wended its way into downtown.

Students from Southern University, predominantly black. Students from LSU, mostly white. High school students bunched together, jostling each other and talking excitedly. Professors with beards. White haired couples. Middle-aged women walking arm-in-arm. Parents holding small children by the hand, pushing them in strollers, carrying them on their hips, or hoisting them onto their shoulders.

Hand-lettered signs. Soft drinks in large paper cups. Baby bottles held for tiny mouths to reach. Beer cans clutched, swigged, and discarded on the side of the road. Newspaper photographers kneeling to get interesting shots of the crowd. Television cameramen, toting their equipment, running ahead, setting up a shot, scanning the crowd, and then running forward once again. Policemen, standing next to their motorcycles at the corners, stopping what little traffic there was at this hour, letting the marchers continue without pause.

It was a cross between a vigil and Mardi Gras, between a political rally and a religious pilgrimage. But, despite the huge throng of marchers, almost no one stood on the sidewalks to watch. The side streets were eerily calm. It was a march of true believers, activists, and hangers-on with no one to view them but the media.

I caught snatches of conversation as I walked. Talk about the march. Talk by older marchers about grandchildren and restaurants. Talk about state politics. Talk about racism and the environment. Talk that maybe marching alone wasn't enough, that other, bolder actions might have to be taken.

I coasted along with the crowd, keeping pace. It took me a moment to realize that one of the marchers was speaking to me. He had been behind me but had jogged up and matched my stride. He was out of uniform, wearing cut-off blue jeans, a Southern University Jaguars baseball cap pulled down low over his forehead, and a "Say No to Environmental Racism" T-shirt. It was Sheriff Isaiah Brown from St. Bonaventure Parish.

"Attorney Schexnaydre. Where've you been? I've dropped by your house at least three times in the last few days and never found you at home. Mighty strange, I'm thinking. Attorney whose home is his office and he isn't there. Maybe he's trying to hide something. Maybe he's trying to hide himself. And why would that be?"

I didn't have to answer any of his questions. "Sheriff, I'm happy to see that you have so much extra time on your hands that you can take an evening off to march up here in Baton Rouge."

"Oh, you're good at trying to change the subject." Brown pulled a handkerchief out of his back pocket and wiped his brow. "Great evening for a walk, isn't it? That sun goes down but the coolness doesn't come. These crowds'll get hotter and more worked up."

Brown sidled up closer to me, speaking softly so others could not hear. "I *do* want to see that plant shut down. Got to protect my constituents. So, no, this is not official sheriff's business. Not tonight. Not yet. But that time will come soon enough. You and me are going to have a heart-to-heart, on the record, about Camellia Industries and all the folks involved, and exactly where you were and what you were doing when G.G. Guidry and Spider Louiviere were murdered. So, why don't you be home tomorrow around ten o'clock, 'cause that's when I'm going to come pay you a visit to look around and ask lots of questions. Officially, of course."

Brown took two steps in front of me and started to walk backwards, staring at me as he maneuvered, letting me know he was looking forward to interrogating me. Then he spun around and jogged on ahead like a broken field runner, disappearing into the crowd.

That was all I needed. Telling me he was coming on official business meant he would be arriving with a search warrant. Things were getting even more complicated.

CHAPTER 72

THE STATE CAPITOL WAS STRAIGHT ahead, a lighthouse of a building at the end of a broad boulevard. The marchers, who had been in a wide column, branched and eddied into the pathways that led through the memorial garden, walking around nine foot high azalea and camellia bushes and passing under the drooping giant oaks bearded with Spanish moss.

The flowing tributaries recombined where the garden abutted the parking area and flowed onto the wide steps of the capitol. The marchers cascaded over the steps and filled the parking lot. They crowded up against one another as more and more of them poured into the confined space.

Police guards kept the marchers back from the stand erected near the top of the steps, several stories above the parking lot. Klieg lights illuminated the microphone-laden podium. A multitude of loudspeakers hung from poles. Cameras sat atop tripods on the roofs of television trucks. Reporters were interviewing people in the crowd.

To the right of the stand, a band was setting up on high wooden risers. Trumpets. Saxophones. Trombones. Guitars. Amplifiers. Keyboards. Drums. Technicians were doing sound checks.

The band started playing the blues. A solid bass line. A strong beat. A song of love and loss. A wailing voice filled the air. The crowd clapped along in rhythm. Vendors with coolers hung from their necks squeezed their way through the throngs, hawking beer and soda.

The first number ended in cheers and applause. This was just the warm-up for the speeches. The crowd called for more. The band started up again. Slower. More soulful.

The dark of the evening brought with it additional humidity. There was not a trace of breeze in the air. A typical Louisiana summer night. A party atmosphere.

A third number. Rock and roll. The band cranked up the volume and launched into a song designed to ignite the crowd. But I wasn't watching the band. I was watching the podium. I had recognized Rad and Joleese up there. Weegie too. They were talking to each other with increasing intensity. Gesticulating arms. Emphatic hand movements. They retreated out of my line of sight.

The band rocked on.

There was a disturbance on the podium as the band wrapped up its song.

Rad reappeared and started to approach the phalanx of microphones, but a half-dozen State Troopers surrounded him and blocked his way. Rad argued with the troopers but to no avail.

The crowd began to boo the troopers. They were indignant and upset. They had come to hear Rad, and he was being usurped.

The troopers confined Rad in one corner.

Carter Herrington appeared from the other side of the podium and strolled unimpeded to the microphones. The crowd recognized him. A hiss began. It spread across the steps. The hiss quickly turned to jeers.

"I know," said Herrington, his amplified voice booming above the discontent, "you didn't expect to find me at this gathering, and I wasn't invited, but, as head of the Department of Environmental Health, I felt that it was my duty, especially when you come to the steps of this great building where my office is located."

The derision did not stop. Slurs and taunts were hurled. Little children, not knowing why their parents were yelling, gleefully joined in.

Herrington was unperturbed. "It was my duty, because I came here to say something you're not expecting to hear."

The crowd did not want to listen to him. Curses ricocheted off the capitol's marble-clad walls. The protesting crowd surged forward against the police barricades.

Large television lights snapped on, illuminating the dais even more brightly. Reporters strained to get closer, holding microphones in their hands.

"You don't have to listen, but I'm going to say my piece anyway."

No letup in the noise from the crowd.

"You see this?" Herrington held up a sheaf of papers in his hand. "You see? These are pleadings my staff has prepared. Pleadings in the lawsuit filed by Mr. Doucet over here."

The tone of the milling thousands grew angrier. And louder.

"The lawsuit seeks an injunction to shut down plants along the river."

Strong voices called for Herrington to get off the podium.

"The lawsuit names DEH, my department, as a defendant."

The mood grew uglier the more he spoke.

"It names me as a defendant."

The steps of the capitol were suddenly alive with thousands shouting in protest and raising their fists angrily. There was danger in their movement.

"Naming me as a defendant was wrong. Naming my department as a defendant was wrong!"

The crowd began to surge forward, up the stairs, breaking the barriers apart and trampling them. The policemen on the steps looked warily at one another as they tried unsuccessfully to restore calm. Some began to undo the safety snaps on their holsters.

"IT WAS WRONG." Herrington was shouting now. The amplification was not enough, and he wanted to be heard. "WRONG TO NAME ME IN THE SUIT. AND DO YOU KNOW WHY IT WAS WRONG? IT WAS WRONG TO NAME ME BECAUSE I SHOULD BE *PLAINTIFF*. YES, I SHOULD BE A PLAINTIFF, AND NOT A DEFENDANT!"

There was a momentary pause in the chanting. A moment of disbelief.

"YOU HEARD ME. THAT'S RIGHT! I SHOULD BE A PLAINTIFF ON *YOUR* SIDE OF THE CASE."

The movement forward up the steps ceased. The clamor began to lessen as increasingly larger groups strained to comprehend the meaning of these strange remarks.

"ON YOUR SIDE. THAT'S RIGHT. I SHOULD HAVE BEEN ON YOUR SIDE."

Loud murmurs in the crowd. Was he saying what they thought he was saying?

"I SHOULD HAVE BEEN ON YOUR SIDE ALL ALONG. AND SO..."

The murmurs diminished to frantic whispering.

"AND SO..." Herrington repeated, not as strident as before, working the crowd as it began to quiet down.

"And so..." Herrington's voice dropped again.

The marchers ceased their movement. They listened expectantly.

"And so...as of noon today, I ordered my staff back to work. I signed an administrative order, at three this afternoon..."

Herrington hesitated dramatically, drew a breath, and allowed his voice to rise again to a crescendo. "At three this afternoon, I signed an order REVOKING ALL PERMITS FOR CAMELLIA INDUSTRIES TO OPERATE."

A moment of almost silence. Then, the crowd went wild again. But this time, there were cheers. The steps were filled with elation and hugging.

Herrington paused cannily to let the effect sink in.

Some of the television cameras quickly spun from facing the platform to panning the crowd, trying to capture the ecstasy of the scene.

But I could see that, up on the podium, Rad and Weegie were not joining in the frantic exaltation that was enveloping the others. The two of them were conferring off to the side.

The horde on the capitol grounds continued to celebrate. It took almost five minutes before some degree of order was restored.

Only then did Herrington resume. "You have a right to celebrate. You have a right to cheer." A speaker's practiced effect. The cheers came.

"But that's only the beginning. My staff has been here working hard on this suit, and we'll be filing papers with the court before the hearing this week. *These* papers." He waved another hand-load of papers for the crowd to see. "These papers ask the court to realign DEH as a plaintiff in this suit and, in light of my permit revocation, grant a permanent injunction to shut down Camellia Industries once and for all."

The applause and acclaim began anew.

Herrington stood there and beamed.

Weegie and Rad continued talking on the side of the platform.

"Now some of you may call people who work for the state 'bureaucrats.' And some of you may call us other names. But I call them all dedicated public servants. And they've been working here in the house that Huey built. Huey Long, our greatest governor. The greatest of populists. The greatest of road-builders and school-builders and charity-hospital-builders. A man whose tradition lives to this very day."

Continued applause, now louder than before.

"Remember what Huey Long did to the oil companies? He made them pay."

Murmurs of agreement.

"Remember what Huey Long did to the utilities when he served on the Public Service Commission? He made them pay."

The crowd was being moved again.

Herrington was in his element. "Remember what Huey Long did back then?"

Answering voices in the affirmative from the steps, voices from those too young to remember but who knew the Long legacy.

"Well, we're going to do it again. You and me. We're going to make those who soil our environment pay."

Loud applause.

"We're going to make those who pollute our rivers and streams pay."

Louder applause.

"We're going to shut 'em down and shut 'em up and make 'em pay for the cleanup."

Again the crowd went wild.

And, over the din, Herrington proclaimed, "They're all going to pay. Starting with CAMELLIA INDUSTRIES!"

Hands waved. Hats were thrown into the air. Children were hoisted up into the air on outstretched arms.

Herrington looked at the band and raised his hand like a conductor, just as Huey Long had conducted the LSU Marching Band during football games. The music cranked up. It made the crowd even more boisterous and frenzied.

Over the song, Herrington leaned into the microphone and yelled so that he was sure to be heard. "Y'ALL ENJOY THE MUSIC! I'M PLEASED TO BE PART OF THIS CELEBRATION."

And with that he waved broadly, stepped away from the podium, and plunged into the crowd to pump arms and politic.

CHAPTER 73

A S THE CROWD CELEBRATED, I kept asking myself why now? If what Taylor said was true – that Herrington had helped G.G. get and keep the permits – why switch positions?

In any event, Herrington's performance on the capitol steps was going to be the lead story on every late newscast tonight, the headline in every newspaper tomorrow, and would light up the social media universe. Herrington had given himself a perfect opening salvo should he declare early for the governor's race.

Herrington had disappeared from view. The camera lights that had been on him while he pressed flesh in the crowd had been shut off. Where had he gone? The State Troopers had retreated from the dais. That probably meant that Herrington was already inside the capitol.

Rad approached the microphones. He motioned for the band to stop.

The videographers in their jeans and tennis shoes pivoted, readjusting the equipment on their shoulders.

"Listen, people, listen."

A guitar chord. A long drum roll. A cymbal crash.

The crowd grew quiet. This was the start of the program they had originally come to hear.

"Listen to the words of a great man," Rad said earnestly. "Not the one you just heard from, not some head of some state agency, some politician trying to position himself to run for governor. Not the words of Livingston or Jefferson, whose comments on the Louisiana Purchase are carved into the walls of this building behind me. No, listen to the words of a really great man, Martin Luther King. He spoke words that still touch us today. I invoke his *memory*. You knew him. I invoke his *words*. You know them."

The crowd murmured its approval.

"You know his words. You know what he said."

The approval grew into a "yes yes" that spread across the steps.

"You know what he meant."

The crowd spoke back. Yes we do. Yes we know. Praise the Lord.

Rad's cadence became emphatic. "Martin Luther King said '*I have a dream.*'"

The crowd applauded and echoed back "I have a dream."

"He stood on the steps of the Lincoln Memorial, looking towards the Washington Monument and spoke of his dream."

The crowd amen'd back in agreement.

"Tonight, we all stand on the steps of the capitol of a state that fought against the union. A state whose history is bathed in blood. The blood of my family…and the families of many of you here tonight. Blood extracted by whips and chains. Blood extracted by slavery and sin. Blood that watered the furrows in the fields of plantations. Blood that flowed like the river…from the slave ships to the slave masters. A state whose laws treated my great-grandfather and great-grandmother as legal 'chattel.' Chattel! The word itself is as noxious as slavery. Chattel! Mere property to be bought and sold. Chattel to be reproduced and disposed of, to be traded and profited on, to be thought of as anything but human."

"Tonight we stand on the steps of the capitol of a state that dares to inscribe on its walls these words." Rad turned to look to his right, where a quotation carved in two-foot high letters was visible to all on the steps and in the parking lot.

"These are the words of Robert Livingston, in 1803, in the slave territory of Louisiana, when it was sold from France to the United States, when people were still bought and sold solely because of their skin color. This is what he wrote."

Rad read it slowly. "'The instruments which we have just signed will cause no tears to be shed. They prepare ages of happiness for innumerable generations of human creatures.'"

"No tears to be shed? I shed tears every night of my life. For, if Martin Luther King had a *dream*, I have a *nightmare*."

The crowd didn't expect to hear this. It listened intently.

"*I have a nightmare*. Mothers and fathers, you know that when your children have a nightmare, you comfort them and tell them all will be better. But I have a nightmare. Is there no one to comfort me?"

A few voices in the crowd called back. "I will." "We will."

But they knew there was more. They knew he was building up to something.

"*Yes, I have a nightmare*. It keeps me awake at night. It haunts my existence. It's a nightmare of living in a state where blood still flows, but this time from internal bleeding caused by chemical exposure. It's a nightmare of living in a state where the water in our rivers and bayous contains poisons that you can't taste, that you can't smell, that you can't spell and can't pronounce, but which cause the brim and the sacolet and muskrat and the beaver to sicken and die. Chemicals that cause those who exist to enjoy the outdoors to come to fear it. *I have a nightmare*."

The crowd responded. "A nightmare." "Yes, a nightmare."

"*I have a nightmare*. It's a nightmare of living in a time where people in positions of power, men and women we elect to represent us, are more concerned about those who give them money than about those who vote for them. Where the luster of the endless stream of coins that it takes to pay for advertising themselves and their elections blinds them to the needs of those whom they serve. *I have a nightmare!*"

"Nightmare" responded the marchers. "Nightmare."

"*I have a nightmare*. It's a nightmare of words meaning something other than what is said, words twisted and used. Did you hear that speech tonight from DEH Secretary Herrington? Did you? Well, what did you hear? You cheered him. You cheered him when he said he would shut down Camellia Industries. You cheered him when he said he would join the ongoing case – your lawsuit – as a plaintiff! But did you hear what he did *not* say? Did he say that he would shut down the other companies in the suit? Did he say he would shut down Big Mudcaster Enterprises or FlowPipe Chemi-Petrols? Did he say he would stop InDispoCo from hauling those poisons from plant to plant only to dump them on our lands or in our bayous? Did he say he would make those plants clean up the damage they've caused, or move to locations where they can't harm our air and water, where they can't harm our families? No! He didn't say a word about that, did he?"

The crowd gave Rad its rapt attention.

"Did he tell you he would change any policies at DEH that let plants operate up and down the rivers and bayous with 'permits' on 'permissible discharges.' No! '*Permissible* Discharges!' As if the state could give permission to anyone to dump poisons into the public waterways, into the very arteries and veins of our state, only to find their way into the arteries and veins of your body, of my body, of the bodies of our children! He said nothing of the sort. He used words to mask the fact that nothing will change. *Nothing*! His words were as poisonous as the chemicals that course down the rivers and float upward into our air. *I have a nightmare!*"

Rad's eloquence intoxicated the crowd. They hung on his every word. They stomped their feet and shouted their approval.

"Look at the plumes that rise from the industrial plants next to your homes. Observe the man-made clouds. Not clouds where angels gather, but clouds where demons dwell. *I have a nightmare.* I can't rest. And I won't rest until the state awakens to the realization that this lawsuit is only a start. The injunction we seek, which is broader than anything Secretary Herrington said he would agree to, is the opening through which we will pour the forces of righteousness! So I say to you here tonight, *wake up from this nightmare and change this state*! And I say to you watching on television, listening on radio, or being part of this gathering through Internet feeds and YouTube rebroadcasts, *open your eyes and rid our state of this nightmare! Wake up!* WAKE UP! **WAKE UP...SO THAT YOU CAN ONE DAY DREAM AGAIN!**"

The crowd screamed. They yelled. They applauded. They cheered.

Rad had more to say, and the people pushed closer up the steps just to be near him.

But I didn't have time to hear any more. I happened to look away from the capitol and toward downtown. Far in the back, the shoulders and head of a man towered above the throng.

Frankie!

I cradled my left arm with my right and walked briskly into the shadows.

CHAPTER 74

I WAS MEANING TO WALK the three blocks to the levee, cross it, and then get down into the batture, the side of the levee facing the river. The batture was unlit, and there would be plenty of places to duck out of sight once I got there. Landings for tugs and supply vessels. Shacks on the docks. Stands of hardwoods in the muddy water. Mounds of driftwood stuck on the batture until the water level rose again and sent the pile spinning off downstream in the fast current.

My arm was pounding with pain now that my attention was no longer distracted by listening to Rad's speech. I didn't think I could run. I was afraid that abrupt movements might cause the butterfly bandages to open.

So, by moving cautiously, I was able to dodge my way through the crowd past the cordoned off roads where traffic had been halted because of the march. I covered the next two blocks, where the fringes of the rally thinned and evaporated. At that point, the path was clear.

River Road was a hundred yards ahead, and beyond that, the levee.

I paused as I neared the edge of the asphalt, watching for traffic before crossing it. The street was empty except for a black sedan coming from my right. I'd cross after it passed and then I'd reach the levee.

But then the black sedan's headlights picked me up.

The car accelerated.

It crossed over the center lane, and veered directly for me, trying to force me to retreat to the capitol.

I started to turn back, but that way was no longer open. Fifty yards away, silhouetted against the capitol's klieg lights, was Frankie, his ponytail bouncing as he jogged toward me.

The sedan's engine gunned as it barreled down my way.

There was no other option.

I took off at a dead run across the road, trying to ignore the agony in my left arm as I felt the wounds open up and the warmth of pulsating blood soak the bandages.

The sedan driver hadn't anticipated that I could run as fast as I did.

The car swerved to counter my movement. It missed me by inches.

I didn't dare look back.

I heard the squeal of tires as the car spun around.

The rise of the levee was before me.

I began running straight up its sloping bank. Small tufts of dirt leapt upward around my feet. I heard the popping sound of a handgun. Three shots. All had missed.

I gained the crest of the levee and headed down the dark batture. I hadn't realized that this portion of the levee was covered with rip rap – sharp-edged chunks of suitcase-sized limestone boulders dumped on the shoreline to stabilize it and keep it from being washed away. I felt the rip rap beneath my feet before I could see it, but it was too late.

On the second step I caught the toe of my shoe where one boulder overlapped the other.

Down I went, head first.

I twisted to avoid landing on my face.

My right shoulder caught the next limestone slab as my feet flew through the air.

The momentum flipped me. I landed hard on my left arm. The pain was excruciating. The bandages shredded as I slid down the stone. The entire cut, from my elbow to my wrist, opened up.

I couldn't help it. I screamed in anguish.

From above me, a flashlight shone down.

"We got the bastard."

CHAPTER 75

"Told you we'd find this little shit if we just looked hard enough." Frankie kicked me in the gut with his steel-toed boot.

I doubled over, trying to catch my breath.

Frankie tapped my left arm with his foot. I closed my eyes and bit my lips, trying to avoid giving him the satisfaction of hearing me scream again. "That's right, fucker! Don't even think of yelling for help."

Frankie bent down next to my face and shone the flashlight on his open switchblade. "If you want to continue breathing, you'll do as I say. Do you understand?" For emphasis, his knife traced a line up and down my nose.

I nodded weakly.

Ribeye pulled my cell phone off my belt and stomped on it. I could hear it shatter.

They pulled me to my feet, led me to their car, wrapped my bleeding left arm in a filthy towel they had in the trunk, and shoved me in the front seat of the sedan. Ribeye took the wheel, with Frankie on the passenger side and me squashed between the two of them, perched precariously on the console.

Frankie was so big his head scraped the inside of the roof, and I had to turn partially sideways to avoid having Ribeye hit my left arm every time he turned the wheel.

Ribeye, feeling me move, slung his elbow up hard and caught me under the chin. My head snapped back from the force and I heard a cracking sound come from my jaw. From the torment that enveloped me, I couldn't tell whether he had broken something. My mouth filled with blood. I felt a hard object in the liquid and spit it out. The blood dribbled down my chin and onto my shirt while my tongue gingerly probed the extent of the damage.

Ribeye used his elbow on me again. He jabbed my left arm.

As an involuntary howl began to emerge, Frankie snapped a handkerchief over my bloodied mouth and held it tight, almost suffocating me. "Don't you fucking spit in my car! I'm going to make you lick that up off my floor, you little shit."

Ribeye steered the car down River Road.

"Come on, Frankie," Ribeye complained, "it ain't worth it. Let's just do it now."

Frankie gave me the handkerchief along with a warning look that clearly meant to keep it in place. He pulled his switchblade from his pocket and started to clean his fingernails where my blood had seeped under them. "Nothing I'd like better, you know that, but Paolo gave instructions. Besides, now you owe me twenty plus a set of monogrammed handkerchiefs."

"Yeah, I know, I know. But it doesn't make any fucking sense."

Ribeye turned the wheel, and I groaned as his right elbow brushed against my left arm. I felt nauseous.

"And you?" Ribeye continued, glancing over at me. I was still holding Frankie's handkerchief clasped across my face, "You swallow your shit and don't you let any more of that drip on Frankie's car. You hear?"

I nodded and forced myself to swallow the blood that continued to fill my mouth. I started to gag.

"Don't you fucking puke on me. Paolo or no Paolo, I'll use my own knife and cut your fucking balls off."

"The hell you will," said Frankie, glaring at Ribeye. "You gonna cross Paolo?"

Ribeye gritted his teeth. "No, of course I ain't."

"Good. Then let's do what he told us to do if we found this shitty shyster here tonight."

"I still don't see why Paolo wants us to do *that*."

"Ribeye, if you understood it all, you'd be in charge, not Paolo."

I closed my eyes and concentrated on not gagging as I felt the car round several more corners, slow down, and then stop.

I opened my eyes. Ribeye had driven to the back of the capitol. We were near the marbled *porte cochère*, the private entrance that the Governor and other high-ranking state officials used to enter the building from their chauffeur-driven vehicles. This area was closed off with bollards, guard gates, and stanchions. How the car had gotten through the security, I didn't know.

Ribeye had pulled into one of the reserved parking spaces.

Frankie dragged me out of the front seat. As I staggered to my feet, Frankie hit me again in the gut with his meaty fist. "That's for messing up my car."

I fell to the ground and threw up on the brick walkway.

"Don't you fucking get that on my shoes!" Ribeye kicked me in the ribs and I rolled heavily on the bricks, ripping my shirt.

"Get up!" Frankie commanded.

The sound of a dog barking came from far behind us.

"Come on!" Frankie said, hauling me to my feet by the back of my collar and holding me at arms' length to avoid the blood and vomit.

"In," Frankie ordered, pointing to the heavy metal double doors ahead of us as I moved unsteadily forward.

Frankie held a plastic card against an electronic sensor in the wall next to the door. When the light went green, he grabbed my right wrist and made me reach for the door handle and turn it. Ribeye held the door open for me with his shoulder.

They followed me inside.

CHAPTER 76

WE EXITED THE ELEVATOR NEAR the top floor and strode onto a plush red carpet and into a hall where thick molding traced the floors and ceiling. I could hear, far below us, the muffled sound of the band still rocking away on the steps below.

The hall opened to a red-carpeted waiting room crammed with overstuffed leather furniture. In the center was a highly polished bronze door. A brass nameplate proclaimed 'Carter H. Herrington, IV, Secretary of the Department of Environmental Health.'

Frankie knocked once.

Herrington was in his shirtsleeves, the white cuffs rolled up almost to his elbows. Under each of his arms were large perspiration stains from the heat of the night and the excitement of working up the crowd with his speech.

He was sipping liquor from a Waterford crystal highball glass. The smell was on his breath and in the air. "Thank you gentlemen," Herrington said to Frankie and Ribeye. "I really didn't expect this would happen tonight, but I'm pleased to see that the stars have aligned."

"There really ain't a lot of stars out tonight," responded Ribeye. "It's gettin' cloudy you see."

"Shut up!" whispered Frankie to his partner.

Herrington examined me from afar. "What have you two done to him?"

"He just tripped," said Frankie.

Herrington took another sip and had them spin me around as he examined my face, my left arm covered with the filthy towel, and my ripped clothes. "That was careless of you, Attorney Schexnaydre."

Through my pain, I was startled to realize that Herrington knew who I was. Through my misery and dread, the questions kept coming. Why did Paolo Micelli tell Frankie and Ribeye to bring me here? Why were Frankie and Ribeye doing Paolo's bidding rather than Tony Micelli's? And what connection did Paolo have with Carter Herrington?

"Put him over there, in the wooden chair, where he won't leak onto the furnishings. They're too expensive and a bitch to clean."

Ribeye and Frankie shoved me toward a corner of the room, steering me clear of the white leather sofa, armchairs and ottoman.

They pushed me down into a polished wooden chair with the state seal embossed in silver on the back upright. I raised my head to see Herrington still holding his highball glass in one hand. But in the other, he held a pistol.

"That will be all, gentlemen," he said to Ribeye and Frankie. "I appreciate your delivery. You have done very well."

"Mr. Herrington, do you need us to…" Frankie began.

Herrington interrupted him, smiling, but with a tone that showed no further response would be necessary. "Now, just go downstairs and I'll let you know when this is over. Shut the door behind you, please."

Frankie and Ribeye departed. Herrington reached for a cask-shaped bottle of bourbon with a tiny silver statue of a racehorse and rider on the cap. He topped off his own glass and poured a small amount into a second Waterford tumbler.

I could hear the elevator doors open and close.

Herrington, still holding the gun, pushed aside a small credenza under the windowsill, causing a cordless phone to fall off its base onto the floor in an off position. Herrington kicked it out of the way and put the second tumbler on the windowsill.

"Come," said Herrington affably, "have a drink. Enjoy the view."

"Why?"

"Because," said Herrington, pointing the gun at me, "I insist. Over here, if you please."

Nothing here pleased me. With Herrington holding a weapon, I could foresee no positive outcome.

I played for time. I worked my way out of the chair, trying carefully not to move my useless left arm, which was knotted with excruciating spasms beneath the towel that was now damp from my blood.

Herrington stood aside, pointing with his gun at the window.

The wooden frames had been scraped and repainted numerous times. A latch separated the two large panes so the huge bottom section could be completely opened, a necessity because the capitol was built in the days before central air conditioning. Now, central air ran throughout the capitol, but the windows still worked.

Herrington pushed and the bottom portion swung upward.

I could feel the warm night air and could clearly see the foot-wide concrete ledge that ran around the rim of the building outside the window. It was thickly coated with a gooey paste of yellow, green, and brown bird droppings. Directly outside the window loomed the back of the head of one of the vast concrete pelicans whose busts marched around the top of the capitol. Its beak protruded outward at this level and the remainder of its body extended down another floor and a half below the ledge.

Far below, past the guano-crowned concrete bird, were the capitol's steps, the parking lot, and the illuminated memorial garden. The band and the remaining marchers, now dancing and swaying to the music, looked like figurines from this height.

Herrington let the window stay open. The strong air conditioning formed a draft as it rushed past me to escape through the window and into the evening.

"Wouldn't this be a good time for you to take a drink?" Herrington urged.

I didn't move.

"That," he said, waving the gun again, "was only a rhetorical question. Drink it."

I picked up the glass. I was unsteady from the beating I taken.

"Blanton's Special Reserve Single Barrel Bourbon," Herrington said. "*Drink.*"

I leaned against the windowsill and slowly drained the ounce or so that was in the tumbler. The liquid burned my cut lips and I tried to keep it away from the tooth that Ribeye had cracked.

"It's very nice, don't you think? That's all you get of that, though. Let's have you finish up on something less expensive."

Without taking his gun off me, Herrington went back to the cabinet and pulled out a bottle of cheap bourbon. He filled my glass to the top.

Stay calm, I told myself. Stay sober. Buy time. Be polite. Don't anger the man with the gun. "Thanks, but I think I've had my fill."

"I'll do the thinking. Now, Attorney Schexnaydre...may I call you Hypolite? Or do you prefer 'Schex'? Taylor always said everyone calls you that."

"You've got the gun," I said as softly as I could, trying not to irritate him. What else had Taylor told him about me? How often had they been together? Why had she...? No time for that. I cordoned off those thoughts. Could not afford to do anything but concentrate on Herrington. "You can call me anything you please."

"Speak up! Drink up!" He backed up, holding the gun steadily at my head. "No need to stand on formalities, is there Schex?"

I picked up the tumbler, searching for a non-confrontational way to extend the conversation. "If there are no formalities, then why not offer me the good bourbon? After all, pouring the less expensive stuff is not very hospitable to someone you've 'invited' up to your office, escorted by Paolo's thugs." Get him talking about Paolo. That might buy some time.

"Come now, Schex, you didn't receive an invitation. You came alone. Sneaked in. That's what you did. Barged right through my door all by your lonesome. Imagine my astonishment at finding you here. Can't imagine how someone could have been so careless as to have left a door open downstairs. Some guard will be fired over this. In fact, they'll probably be able to figure out which door it was that you used." He chuckled. "Undoubtedly, the one with your fingerprints on the handle. The one that was opened with a stolen passcard."

So that was why Frankie and Ribeye had made me turn the knob downstairs.

Herrington had already finished his second drink and had poured himself a third.

"Sorry, Schex," he said, taking a sip, "the good stuff is what I get. You know, I can't imagine why it was that you wanted to see me so badly. I was completely taken aback. You come in and surprised me as I was…as I am…" he took another big sip from his glass, "…as I am working as hard as I can for the people of this great state, toiling long hours into the night. Doing my job to protect my constituents. Thank you, Jesus, they'll say. And they'll remember that at election time, 'cause I'll remind them. Thanks be that Carter-Herrington-the-Fourth had the presence of mind to act as he did. I'm here late on a Monday night, and you burst in and demanded things. The audacity! I offered you a drink. You accepted. Your DNA is in the liquid. Your fingerprints are on the tumbler. But would you see reason? No. You got violent. You got upset. You were involved with that monstrous Camellia Industries, poisoning our state. You were involved with the treacherous Taylor Cameron, a woman who fucks first and kills later."

So now he hated Taylor too? No! Can't afford to speculate about anything. Not now. Keep focused on one thing at a time. For as much time as I had left.

"What else was I to do, Schex, when you started to assault me? No sir. There'll be no love lost for you. And there'll only be accolades for me. I can see the headlines now. Secretary Herrington fends off killer! Taylor fries. Spider Louiviere's murderer, a fallen lawyer, is stopped. It all ends so neatly, and after that, who could successfully challenge me for governor? No one. No one at all."

That's why Frankie and Ribeye had brought me here? For Herrington to kill me?

I wasn't going to wait to be slaughtered. Despite the pain, despite my physical exhaustion, I forced myself to stand up straight and put down the glass.

I searched for a mode of escape, for a weapon, for some way to create a delay.

As if I could, with only one good hand.

Herrington, holding his gun, was across the room, and he stood between me and the door. He tsk'd his disapproval at my movements. "You really don't want to stray from that spot."

I slumped back and rested my rear on the sill. Conserve my strength, I told myself.

"Hey! Don't drip blood on my floor or on the windowsill!"

I looked down at the towel wrapped around my left arm. It was now crimson. That was good. My blood would leave a mark.

Herrington leveled his gun at me. "Hell, another goddamn mess to clean up. Take another drink. NOW!"

I didn't pick up the glass.

"I'm not kidding. Do it! This is a Walther P99QA Double action. Semi-automatic. Light pull. You have no idea what I am capable of."

There was no time left.

"What about the boy, Herrington? Even if you kill me, that won't solve your problem," I bluffed, "because I've taken precautions."

Herrington clenched his teeth. His face turned florid.

Tony Micelli had really been on to something. I had no idea what "the boy" meant, but Herrington obviously did.

Herrington put down his glass and gripped the pistol with both hands. Approaching me, he aimed at my forehead.

CHAPTER 77

THE BAND'S BLUES MUSIC WAFTED through the open window, echoing up from the capitol steps twenty-four floors below. There was utter hatred in Herrington's face and a deadly weapon in his grasp.

I quickly tried to figure the angles. Could I knock the gun away with my one good hand? Unlikely. Herrington had carefully stayed at least an arm's length away, and I couldn't be sure I was steady enough to jump him. He'd shoot the moment I stirred.

Could I yell for help? Who would hear me? Although the window was open, the band below was playing so loudly it would drown out any noise I could possibly make.

No one other than Frankie, Ribeye, and Herrington knew I was here. No rescuers would arrive.

And even if Herrington didn't shoot me here, he clearly had something in mind. Something that he had carefully planned. Undoubtedly with the help of Paolo Micelli. Which meant that Tony Micelli was headed for disaster too.

We both stood motionless for several moments. I didn't dare move a muscle.

Herrington seemed to loathe my very existence.

Then, as if in slow motion, he backed away, the gun still leveled at my head. He turned one of the leather chairs around, sank into it, and rested his hand on his thigh, the pistol now pointing squarely at my chest.

Without taking his eyes off me, he reached back and grabbed his glass and took a gulp.

"The boy. The boy. Fucking G.G. and the fucking boy."

He put down the glass and, without loosening his grip on the pistol, pulled his cell phone off the clip on his belt and hit a speed-dial number. "Come on back up. I'm going to need your assistance. You're gonna like this."

Back went the phone into its clip and up came the tumbler of bourbon. "You have just made two guys very happy. Plan B is what they wanted all along. I won't get headlines for fending you off, but at least the press will have the satisfaction of knowing that Spider Louiviere's killer died a horrible death in a tragic car accident."

He had called Frankie and Ribeye. Once they arrived, I would have no chance at all.

So, I did the only thing I could do.

I tried to stand up straight, chin high, but my knees buckled.

I collapsed to the floor in front of the credenza.

I fell on my left side and I screamed in agony as my injured arm hit the floor and the blood poured out.

I had pretended that my knees buckled.

But the screaming and blood were all too real.

CHAPTER 78

HERRINGTON DIDN'T MOVE OFF HIS chair to help me.
"Get up. Now you've done it. Ruined my carpet! God, I had hoped to avoid this. I love this furniture. But it can't be helped."
He got up and started knocking over lamps and turning over tables.

I had landed exactly the way I had planned. My body was between the cordless phone and Herrington so that he couldn't see it. I grabbed the receiver with my one good hand, stuck it in my waistband, and headed towards the open window, keeping my back to the room.

"JUST FUCKING WAIT." Herrington shouted. "We'll get to that soon enough. But first, we need to find out exactly what you know and whether you were really taking any precautions. Because once we figure that out…"

I didn't stop. I worked my way up onto the windowsill, my back still to Herrington.

"Oh God! You're an idiot," Herrington said, seeing where I was headed, "and I'm a bigger one."

I scrambled out the window, trying to ignore the flames of torment that consumed my left arm, and clambered onto the narrow ledge. Moving to the right, I pushed my body flush against the marble exterior of the building, trying not to look down. Blood from my left arm smeared the marble behind me and dripped onto the thin ribbon of concrete beneath my feet.

Herrington grabbed at my leg.

I yelled loudly, although there was no one to hear me except Herrington, because the music below was blaring. I shook free and inched further down the ledge, away from the open window, my feet sliding dangerously on the bird guano that coated the narrow concrete perimeter. I crawfished sideways along the ledge as quickly as I could.

"YOU WERE BLUFFING! YOU LITTLE SHIT! YOU WERE BLUFFING!"

Herrington was now leaning out the window, gun in hand, yelling at me and trying to make himself heard above the music billowing up from the steps far below.

The first of the concrete pelican busts loomed before me, lit brightly from below by the ring of huge halogen lights positioned on the eighteenth floor ramparts, illuminating not only the top of the capitol but also the pelicans on the twenty-fourth floor.

I managed my way around the pelican and continued my tiny sideways steps, each one taking me farther from Herrington's window.

"IF YOU HAD TAKEN 'PRECAUTIONS,' AS YOU SAID, YOU WOULDN'T BE OUT HERE." Herrington was screaming at me, knowing no one below could hear him.

The bust of the second pelican was before me. I straddled that one, trying to shield my eyes from the glare of the eighteenth floor lights, got to the ledge on the other side, and kept moving away. But I made sure Herrington heard what I had to say. "I know about the payments you made to G.G. as well."

Another bluff. Let's see how close Taylor was to the truth.

"THE FUCKING PAYMENTS! G.G. WOULDN'T STOP, WOULD HE? PERMITS WERE NOT ENOUGH! HE WANTED ALL THAT MONEY TOO? AND THEN TAYLOR WANTED IT? AND THEN SPIDER? WELL THEY ALL GOT WHAT THEY DESERVED, DIDN'T THEY? I MADE SURE G.G. GOT IT. AND SPIDER GOT IT. AND NOW YOU'LL GET THE SAME!"

Perfect! That gave me exactly what I wanted.

I got too confident.

I lost my focus.

My foot slipped on the guano.

"HA!" Herrington was triumphant. "KILL YOURSELF! SAVE ME THE TROUBLE."

I struggled to regain my balance.

Only by the barest did I steady myself, but I found I couldn't move further down the ledge. The soles of my shoes were slippery from the bird droppings.

It was all I could do to stay exactly as I was, forcing my body against the wall, and praying that my shoes stayed on the thread of concrete.

Herrington perched his ass on the windowsill and squinted, trying to see me fifteen yards away, the bright lights on the concrete pelicans making the shadows where I hid even harder to penetrate.

Herrington leaned out the window, holding onto the wooden frame with one hand.

"This is going to be fucking easier than I thought, Schex." He had ceased yelling. He had calmed down. "It's just a matter of time! I'm going to enjoy watching you weaken and then fall. I can sit here all night, if necessary."

"Too late, Herrington." I slowly extended my right hand from the shadow into the glare of the lights.

Herrington leaned out further to get a good look to see what I was holding.

"FUCK IT ALL. **FUCK YOU!**"

He had seen the cordless phone. The green light was on. I had managed to pull it out of my waistband and dial my own number right after Herrington had grabbed at my leg and before he had stuck his torso out the window. My screaming in pain as I lay on the floor after my knees 'buckled' hid the dial tones. The answering machine at my house was recording everything.

"DIE NOW, YOU BASTARD!! LEAP!!!!"

A spurt of light from the barrel of Herrington's gun.

The marble a few feet to the left of my cheek shattered.

I tried to move another few millimeters. It was too slippery.

Another shot. Above my head. Splinters of marble showered down.

I looked back.

Herrington wasn't deliberately missing. He just couldn't get a good aim from this angle. The bourbon he had consumed wasn't helping either.

Herrington crawled out onto the ledge.

A third shot. This was closer.

If it had not lodged in the concrete head of the huge pelican bust between me and Herrington, the bullet would have hit my groin.

He was now yelling again. "YOU THINK I CAN'T GET AND CONTROL RECORDS OF CALLS MADE FROM MY OWN PHONE! BEFORE YOUR BODY IS COLD WE'RE GOING TO KNOW WHERE YOU CALLED AND THAT WILL BE AS DEAD AN ISSUE AS G.G. AND SPIDER…AND YOU!"

He climbed out near the head of the first pelican too so that he could get a direct hit.

I felt it before I heard it.

A sharp shove in my left shoulder. My injured left side.

It was someone pushing me with a blunt club.

I held on to the wall.

Someone hitting me with a bat.

Someone ramming me with huge pole.

Someone ripping open the skin and pulling out my muscles.

The agony from the bullet coursed from my shoulder to my gut, and yet I also felt strangely detached, as if this unbearable misery was being experienced by someone else.

I rested my cheek against the cold stone and used all my remaining strength to stay on my feet.

The recoil from the pistol had thrown Herrington off balance.

He started to lose his footing on the ledge.

Herrington moved his feet too quickly, trying to catch himself. His shoes slid over the pigeon droppings and off the ledge.

Herrington reached out for the windowsill with his left hand, his stomach now resting on the parapet, his feet dangling in the air inches from the pelican. His right hand still held the gun.

Our eyes met.

Herrington tried to bring the handgun up again to shoot, but his body slid further off the ledge. Only his chest was on it now.

Herrington fired again.

The shot hit the wall inches from my stomach, pelting me with white marble gravel.

Herrington lost his grip on the windowsill. He let the pistol drop. It fell in and out of the shadows of the building as it plummeted down, a dark shape growing smaller and reflecting odd rays of light.

His body slid off the ledge. He tried to grab onto the sill with his right hand, but could not.

Herrington frantically kicked his feet, searching for the head of the concrete pelican. He tried to get his legs around it as he fell from the ledge onto the crown of the bust.

He rested there a minute, the pelican clutched between his thighs, riding the large sculptured creature and gazing at me with unbounded malevolence.

The look on his face turned to utter panic as he began to slip downward.

He flung his arms around the bird, embracing it, clinging to its huge head and neck like a terrified baby cleaving to its mother. But, he couldn't hold on. Couldn't get a grip. He dug his fingers into the concrete, looking for a non-existent handhold, tearing the flesh off the pads of his palms.

The last I saw of Herrington? It was his fingers slipping off the pelican's head and neck. They left five narrow trails of blood on either side of the concrete creature.

CHAPTER 79

THE NEXT TWO WEEKS WERE a blurred continuum of painkillers, sedatives, sleeping pills, phone calls, and visitors.

I don't remember how I got off the ledge. I learned that it must have been Frankie who had pulled me in and summoned an ambulance. It was his voice on the 911 call. I couldn't figure out why Frankie would have helped me. By the time the capitol police and the state police and ambulance arrived, Frankie and Ribeye had disappeared and still haven't been located.

The hospital? I have no memory of the emergency room or of either of my two operations. All I recall were the washed out pastel green walls of my room and the nurses who disturbed my fitful sleep, prodding and poking me for this test or that medication.

Next? Endless questioning. The Baton Rouge police. Sheriff Isaiah Brown of the St. Bonaventure sheriff's office. The State Police. EPA investigators. DEH investigators.

The State Police played my answering machine recording over and over. They parsed each of Herrington's statements. It convinced them that G.G. had been blackmailing Herrington, which gave Herrington a motive to murder G.G.

In light of Herrington mentioning phone records, the cops went back and reviewed every call to and from all of Herrington's many numbers. The two lines at his house. His cell phone. His multiple office lines. The phones at each of the businesses in which he had an interest – one of which turned out to be Wholesale Flesh and Fur.

They also subpoenaed all the phone records of Taylor and Spider. Spider's cell phone was never found, but they were able to retrieve a record of the calls he made the night he was murdered. The last call was to Herrington.

When the police asked me why that might be, I reminded them about what Spider had told me after he gave me the Camellia Industries' boxes in the parking lot of Poirrier's. Spider had been upset to learn that I was not going to be Taylor's criminal lawyer. Spider said he would get the money to hire a top-notch criminal lawyer. Who would he approach? The man he knew G.G. had a close relationship with, a rich man with a bundle of assets – Herrington. But Spider didn't know about G.G.'s blackmail, so when Spider went to Herrington for a loan to help Taylor, Herrington probably assumed that this was more blackmail, and that's why Herrington killed him.

What really happened no one will ever know. But I'm sticking with my theory on that one. I'm figuring that Herrington was as concerned about additional blackmail from Spider as he apparently was when Taylor came to him for help. But, of course, I couldn't tell the police anything about what Taylor had told me without violating the attorney-client privilege I had with her.

I told the police about the loan Tony Micelli had made to Camellia. No reason to hide that. No privilege protected that information. The cops questioned Micelli extensively, but his financial paperwork was in impeccable order. How G.G. used the blackmail funds didn't affect the legitimacy of Micelli's loan or of G.G.'s repayment of it. Herrington had apparently dipped into his campaign funds and siphoned money out of other business interests in which he had held a secret interest to avoid reporting those on his annual state ethics forms.

What about the missing $513,113 that Frankie and Ribeye had taken from me? There was no need to mention any of that. Besides, what could I say that wouldn't incriminate me?

CHAPTER 80

LOLLY CAME BY THE HOSPITAL to tell me that the charges against Taylor had been dismissed. The authorities were convinced Herrington had murdered both G.G. and Spider. They closed their investigation. Lolly also told me about Camellia Industries being permanently shut down by the courts. The DEH was being reorganized. The EPA was examining Rad's videos and the records of all the plants serviced by InDispoCo. And Lolly thanked me. She still held the mortgage on Taylor's home, the mortgage Taylor had given her when there was no cash for Lolly's fee. Lolly had given Taylor another week before starting foreclosure proceedings.

Even got a visit from Sheriff Isaiah Brown. He had located Kirk/Kuo and had found out why Trey's former employee had been trying to see me. After Kirk/Kuo was fired, he wanted some legal advice on getting his job back – he had six young kids, a sickly wife, two elderly parents, and was his family's sole breadwinner. He desperately wanted to be rehired, and he knew that Herrington was a silent partner of Wholesale Flesh and Fur and the real brains behind the operation. The "late night meetings" Kirk/Kuo had referred to in his note to me were meetings between Herrington and Trey at the plant. Kirk/Kuo didn't trust Trey and hadn't trusted the sheriff initially, because he wasn't sure whether the sheriff was allied with Herrington. Sheriff Brown, however, was not allied with anyone.

The sheriff came to the same conclusion that I did. Kirk/Kuo had locked the freezer. Herrington had either murdered Spider or arranged for his murder. When the sheriff confronted Trey about Herrington's silent ownership, Trey admitted it, as well as the fact that his uncle had a key to the facility. Of course, Trey had been too thickheaded to suspect his uncle of any wrongdoing – Trey owed his entire career to Herrington. And now that his uncle was gone, Trey would own Wholesale Flesh and Fur outright. He would find another waste disposal company and continue operating.

I received lots of get-well cards, including from Weegie, Rad and Joleese, the President of the local Bar Association, and even from the Governor. Also got a card from Hubbard Estes with a hand-written note inside.

Taylor hadn't come to the hospital. She hadn't sent a card, and she hadn't called.

CHAPTER 81

AFTER THE DOCTORS RELEASED ME, Washington spent a week at my house nursing me along, and Durnella took over my kitchen. "Put meat on those bones," she'd say, forcing me to take another helping of crawfish etouffee, turtle soup, fried shrimp, and oyster pie, as well as the French bread that she baked every morning. As she heaped each meal on my plate, she'd lecture, "If you don't eat, you'll never get on the healin' side."

Beebo had called and sent George over with gumbo and jambalaya. Ice chests full of food. Enough for a month. Of course, that got Durnella furious and she sent it all to the orphanage. She said that she didn't rightly know how I was going to get well if all I ever had was "plate lunches from a bar!"

Ten days later I was finally on my own. I wasn't fully recovered, and my left arm was still in a sling, but everything had quieted down.

I was surprised, therefore, when early one morning there was a knock at my front door.

It was Tony Micelli.

We went into the conference room and he placed an expandable briefcase on the table. "It's all here," he said. "I didn't even deduct costs. As you know, I play for the long term. Always want to have complete legality and traceability. At least from my end. So, sign the receipt."

I looked inside the briefcase; it was filled with neatly wrapped stacks of money with some loose change on top. Micelli handed me a document on which was written: "*Received, the sum of Five Hundred Thousand One Hundred Thirteen and 17/100 ($513,113.17) Dollars.*" A place for a date and a signature.

"Do you want to count it?" he asked.

"No." I knew that either it was exactly that amount, in which case counting would be superfluous, or it was something less, in which case I was not in any position to complain.

I signed and dated the receipt. Micelli carefully folded it into an envelope that he stuck in the inside pocket of his sports coat.

"See. Accountable. Traceable. I'm in the clear. The question is, what are you going to do? Did you get the message Hubbard enclosed in the card he sent?

"I'll give it due consideration."

"A lawyer's answer. I like that. Not a rejection. Not an acceptance. It leaves the door open and therefore creates possibilities. You want to ask me anything? Anything at all before I go?

"I do have a couple of questions," I admitted. "But you know, since I'm not your lawyer at this time…"

"I know. No privilege. That's OK. Let's see where your questions lead. I owe you that much, if not more."

"All right. Frankie and Ribeye?"

"I figured you'd ask about them. I found out that they were also working for my cousin, Paolo. In fact, I got a message to them right after they left you off at Herrington's. Good thing I did, wasn't it? Let's just say that Paolo and I have an understanding about our spheres of influence. Anything else you want to know?

He wasn't going to tell me more about Frankie and Ribeye. The fact that he told me he called them after they left me at Herrington's meant that he was responsible for Frankie pulling me off the ledge. Tony's telling me that he and Paolo had an "understanding" meant that I was safe from Frankie, Ribeye, and Paolo's retribution. It also probably meant that Frankie and Ribeye were working somewhere else for Paolo, no doubt far out of state.

There was only one more thing I had to know. "What about the boy? What was all that about? What was the truth about 'the boy' that Herrington was so afraid of?"

"What a fascinating question! You ask about the 'truth,' as if we can discern 'truth,' as if we can we can independently evaluate, quantify, and then freeze it as an omniscient fact. Sometimes, however, it is the choice that counts, not the truth."

"Which means what?"

"Which means that *if* you ever become my lawyer, you'll get my version of the truth. Until such time as that, however, let me take you on a literary excursion. Let me ask you to imagine an organization. A hypothetical one, of course."

"Of course," I agreed. There was no rushing Micelli.

"An organization that, like all entities, existed even though you couldn't find it on paper, couldn't locate it in a building, couldn't penetrate its invisible skin. This hypothetical organization was linked by honor and kinship. That was what held it together and nothing more. And when honor was lost, well, kinship was nothing. Are you following?"

"I'm listening."

"This hypothetical organization was, for the purposes of this story, an ancient guild. A guild of wizards. There was a chief wizard, whose magic and power were beyond reach of all others. And there were subwizards and their assistants, as well as the assistants' apprentices. And even below that, there was a boy, an apprentice to an apprentice.

"This guild had a number of rituals, and it sometimes put honor to the test. If that test was not passed, those who failed could not continue in the organization. The chief wizard could not only transform base metals into gold, he also could transform those who displeased him back into base materials. This transformation back was always witnessed by other apprentices, who needed to understand the meaning of honor.

"So, imagine a lowly boy – an apprentice's apprentice – trying to escape before the transformation was complete, frantically wandering in the dark of night, only to emerge into the path of outsiders.

"The guild members could not afford to be seen by outsiders. But they watched.

"Now, the apprentice's apprentice believed he had escaped transformation, but he was wrong. Imagine the impact – and I stress the word impact here – the impact the sudden appearance of such a boy on outsiders. Imagine if, at that very moment, those outsiders transformed the boy and furthered the guild's plan, all without the knowledge of the outsiders. These outsiders – call them a pair of young outsiders, one rather sophomoric – who had emerged from their own citadel on a hazy errand. They were the ones who had made such an impact. They might be of use to the guild without even knowing it. And if the two outsiders later had a falling out among themselves over this impact, that itself could accrue to the guild's benefit."

I nodded for him to go on, but Micelli's story was over.

"That's it. Think seriously, very seriously, about the initial request you made at the end of our visit in New Orleans and the counter-offer contained in Hubbard's card."

CHAPTER 82

AFTER MICELLI LEFT, I PUT his briefcase under my desk, went back to the kitchen, and grabbed a beer. I popped it open and strolled out to the front porch.

I sat on the mildewed wooden swing and thought about what he had said.

The gist was clear enough. I was on to Micelli's metaphors and elliptical references.

The boy, the apprentice's apprentice, was someone in Micelli's father's organization. He had done something wrong, even if was just a "test of honor" as Micelli had said. He was to be scared, or bullied, or killed. They were in some rural area where outsiders would seldom stray. But the boy had run. Had run through the swamps or maybe the cane fields. Had run as if he were being chased by demons, which, considering the reputation of Micelli's father, Carmine "The Snake," was undoubtedly true.

The young outsiders were Herrington and Guidry. They were outside their citadel – Micelli was referring, perhaps facetiously, to LSU. Micelli, the former English major and current loan shark, was talking about a citadel of learning.

Herrington and Guidry were on a "hazy" errand. Guidry was undergoing fraternity hazing imposed by Herrington, the sophomore. A hazing where the brothers, in the middle of the night, would roust a pledge out of bed. One of them would drive the pledge south on the River Road and leave him, in his underwear, to make his way back to campus. Herrington must have been driving his pledge – Guidry – to the rural drop-off point when the "apprentice's apprentice" ran out into the road.

286

Herrington must have hit and killed the boy with the car. That was the "transformation" upon "impact." Now Herrington and Guidry had to get rid of the body. Somehow they did it. And all the time they were being watched by The Snake and his men.

So, The Snake had something on both of them, and Guidry had something on Herrington.

Tony Micelli knew all about this, but he apparently had never asked Herrington for anything.

Did Paolo know this and have ties to Herrington? No doubt. That must have been why Frankie and Ribeye delivered me to Herrington. Which meant that Herrington had either done Paolo a big favor previously or was about to grant him an even bigger favor when Herrington got to be governor.

Whatever the ultimate facts were, Tony Micelli had trusted me enough to tell me a metaphorical story, giving me sufficient information so that I could figure out what really happened.

But how has that helped me?

CHAPTER 83

INOW HAVE WHAT I believe to be the truth about G.G. and Herrington. I also have the $513,113.17 from Micelli, but how can I explain it? How can I use it safely?

The police don't know about it. Taylor thinks it disappeared with Frankie and Ribeye.

Sure, I could spend it, a bit at a time. Given how I've lived the last few years, and assuming I wanted to live in the same degree of squalor and anonymity, I could make it last a decade or more. But it's hard to live the way you used to when you've suddenly come into a lot of cash.

Maybe I could leave town and start a new life. Maybe I could join EarthResponsible. It might be good to have a cause I could learn to believe in.

Perhaps I could complete the negotiations with Hubbard and move to New Orleans and work for Tony Micelli. Within his own limits, Micelli's a man of his word, even if he sticks to just this edge of legitimacy.

I have some tough choices. And I want to be sure that, legally, my use of the funds I now have cannot be questioned in any way.

That's why I'm sitting in your office today, counselor. That's why I'm paying you, in cash, the $9,750 non-refundable retainer you have demanded.

I need your advice.

Remember, we have an attorney-client privilege.

[The End]

About the Author

A NATIONALLY-KNOWN SPEAKER and humorist as well as a full-time appellate attorney, Michael H. Rubin has had a varied career. He has also been a professional jazz pianist in the New Orleans French Quarter, a radio and television announcer, and an adjunct law professor. His debut novel, "The Cottoncrest Curse," received the Book-of-the-Year Gold Award at the annual meeting of the American Library Association in 2015 and was named the top thriller/suspense novel published by a university or independent press. Rubin is the winner of the Burton Award, given at the Library of Congress, for outstanding writing, and is a member of the Author's Guild, the International Thriller Writers, the Mystery Writers of America, and the International Association of Crime Writers.

CPSIA information can be obtained
at www.ICGtesting.com
Printed in the USA
LVOW11s0401140917
548684LV00001B/65/P